Neighbor George

Neighbor George

including the short story
Bolinas Venus

Victoria Nelson

Design/Layout by Maïa Gaffney-Hyde
Set in Caslon and Gopher

ISBN : 9781913689308

Strange Attractor Press
BM SAP, London,
WC1N 3XX, UK
www.strangeattractor.co.uk

Distributed by The MIT Press, Cambridge, Massachusetts.
And London, England.
Printed and bound in Estonia by Tallinna Raamatutrükikoda.

Neighbor George

Each man is in his spectre's power
Until the arrival of that hour
When his humanity awake
And toss the spectre into the lake.

– William Blake

1

It was the summer of 1979. I had just graduated
from college and was housesitting for my aunt and
uncle while they were in Europe. Their white frame
Craftsman sat between two other identical bungalows
under a cluster of bay laurels in the little town of
Bolinas, in West Marin County, on the northern
California coast just above the Golden Gate Bridge.

Bolinas was not your usual coastal village. Cut
off from civilization by the looming bulk of Mount
Tamalpais, it had a land's end aura that drew the
desperate fringe: aged hippie burnouts, street people,
loonies who knew they wouldn't be arrested for
lying down in the middle of the road or screaming
about God's conspiracy with the CIA. People who
lacked either the sense of drama or the energy to hurl
themselves off the Golden Gate came from all over
to kill themselves along this foggy stretch of coast.

Drunks drove off the mountain. Ancient bohos gassed themselves in their VW vans. Drifters overdosed on reds in sleeping bags on the beach. Now a patina of commuting professionals had spread itself across, but failed to penetrate, the community's entrenched bohemian scruffiness.

There was also the Industry to contend with. My friends back at school warned me of what I hadn't been aware of, spending summers out here as a child – that if I ever stumbled onto a marijuana field up on Bolinas mesa, especially near harvest time, I should throw up my hands at once, close my eyes, and walk backward as fast as possible. Except for the ocean, the mountain, and the black labs in the backs of pickup trucks, in a way it was just like being back in Berkeley.

Two retired schoolteachers lived in the second house in our little compound. The third house, the one on the other side, had been empty for as long as I could remember.

"It's the first of the month, Dovey," Al Finch said to me early one Saturday morning over the chicken wire fence separating his yard from my aunt and uncle's. (Al's real name wasn't Finch, by the way, and mine isn't Dovey.)

Al liked to dangle these little remarks and wait for a response. When he saw I couldn't think of anything to say, he jerked his thumb toward the third house in our culvert. "Comp'ny."

I glanced over hopefully. The front yard was overgrown, the blinds were drawn. The squat frame house looked as deserted and depressing as always.

"Jaguar Jim at the realty says a guy from out of state is renting it."

I looked again. The rusty latches on the sagging garage doors were fused with age.

"He must be invisible. And have an invisible car."

"Well, he *hasn't* gotten here yet," Al said impatiently. He turned back to his zucchini in the ragtag garden plot that bordered our two properties, giving me a clear view of the widely separated platinum hairs sprouting from his pink dome. They looked sewn in, like the Orlon tresses of the dolls I played with as a girl. "Now you won't be all by yourself."

Mr. and Mrs. Finch – Al and Sally – worried about me, I knew. Sally said it was because I didn't know any young people my own age in Bolinas, but I knew what she really meant was the Tragedy. The first time Sally saw me that summer, after a decade away from Bolinas, she looked at my bitten fingernails and said, "What's the matter, honey?" And even though it had never occurred to me that not having fingernails meant something was the matter, I didn't mind her bringing it up. I didn't think she was being nosy at all; it made me feel looked after. Like my mother before her, my aunt was much too well bred to bring up anything like that during the years I was under her care, when I spent my summers with her and my uncle across the bay. The sisters shared what you might call a light touch when it came to child rearing.

I can't say I noticed the lack of attention at the time. If something too big happens to you when you are very young, it freezes you at that moment in time, just like those bodies of people who get trapped in

Alpine glaciers: when the ice melts they haven't aged a minute while all their townspeople have grown old. Early on I froze, and because I froze I felt nothing.

"Goddamn deer," Al was saying, kicking at the dirt. "They've gone and trampled everything. Looks like a tank came through."

Sam nosed my knee with his head and I saw that his fur had gotten matted again. Since Al and Sally never seemed to get around to it, I brushed their unkempt black cat when they weren't looking. That was the thing about Al and Sally. They seemed very caring – I had vague memories from childhood of Al fixing my broken wagon when my parents and I had been over for a visit – but up close I wasn't sure how truly interested they were in their own lives or anyone else's.

"Another thing," Al said. "Hear anything last night out in the grove?"

I shook my head.

"Hell of a commotion. Sam came streaking in like nothing you ever saw. Thought it might be a bobcat. I checked this morning. No scat or anything. And now the damn deer."

I said nothing because that thick stand of eucalyptus trees behind these three houses had always terrified me for no good reason. I had steered clear of it ever since I could remember.

"So long," I said to Al and climbed into my uncle's 1964 Bel Air, a perfectly preserved two-tone beige and brown steamboat with pushbutton automatic transmission. "Like a Waring blender," I had once commented to my uncle, who took offense because he thought I was laughing at his car.

Al, who was down on his knees, grunted. To the Bel Air I said, "Puree!" punched the Drive button, and lurched off to town for a pastry at the Blue Heron before work.

I parked at the end of Wharf Road near the beach, bought my cranberry muffin at the converted Victorian bakery and sat down on the front steps to eat it. Across the way in the empty lot next to Smiley's some of the street guys lay snoozing on the hoods of their big old American cars.

"I never see you here in town."

Grey-haired, blue-jeaned, down-vested Sally Finch stood over me. Was this an accusation? It was true I didn't frequent Wharf Road. Though I didn't like to admit it, I preferred Stinson Beach down the road because the people there weren't quite as weird and I did so want to be normal, it was my great goal in life.

As I opened my mouth to answer, Sally was already hailing a woman across the street. "That's Sheila Robbins," she said to me. "Did you know she and Rob are having a poetry conference here next week? You ought to get in on this."

Sally was always going on about the Bolinas poets and what a tight little circle they had. But since I couldn't tell who sitting next to me on the bakery steps was a poet, who was a carpenter, and who was a dope dealer, I would have had the same trouble starting up a conversation with a poet, if not more so for wanting to get to know him, as with anybody else. What's more, I knew from my friends in Berkeley that the golden age of Bolinas poetry was over and done with; it had petered out some time back, the same way, even farther back in the mists of time, the Sausalito bohemian scene had self-destructed. By the time people found out about it and started moving here, the real poets had left.

The woman crossed over to join us in the bakery yard. She wore a black loose-fitting Japanese tunic and dirty pink ballerina slippers. Her brown hair flecked with grey hung in a long braid. Sunbursts of tiny crow's feet rimmed the corners of her eyes. I noticed them right away because I was only twenty-two and already had my first crow's foot. This event was so significant I was always looking to see how many of them other women had, even while it seemed inconceivable to me that I would ever get any more.

Sally introduced me and Sheila smiled warmly. "Dovey wants to know about the Parliament of Poets," Sally went on, though this was news to me. "She has just graduated from the University of California at Berkeley with honors in literature."

As Sheila homed in, I sensed that responsibility for me was being handed on. "Oh, you *have* to come! We're having James Harrier."

I felt grateful for her interest, but I was not much of a poetry reader because unlike novels poems did not provide, page for page, the kind of long-term total escape from Planet Earth I craved. I had only vaguely heard of James Harrier and my lack of recognition must have registered.

"He's arguably our greatest living poet." The delicate tracery around Sheila's eyes twitched, weblike, as she made this proud assertion. As an earnest literature major I always wondered why people who

wrote criticism were so fond of saying "arguably."
Did they want to argue? Or did they just mean "I
am arguing that – "? And who was she talking about
when she said "our"? Hers and mine and Sally's? Or
hers and somebody else's?

That was not the sort of point Sally wasted her
time worrying about. "Dovey hasn't lived out here
since she was little," she said briskly. "She needs to
meet some interesting people."

"Everybody who's coming is interesting!"
Sheila declared.

I shifted uneasily from one foot to the other. It was
nice these two women wanted to help me, though I
had the uneasy feeling Sally had already briefed Sheila
about the Tragedy. Yes, I was lonely, desperately lonely
out here in Bolinas after all the bustle of school. For
a while I had tried to think of people I knew to invite
out to stay with me. Nick, my old boyfriend who was
still my friend, was in Montana. My roommate Betsy
was still working in the Peace Corps in Nicaragua.
Thinking I had so few resources to draw on made me
even lonelier.

All the same I wanted to be alone. Important things
were about to happen, I just knew it. As soon as I had
gotten to my aunt and uncle's house, I had felt deep,
mysterious stirrings. Something was approaching.
Outside, inside, not quite with me but very, very
close. And I had to be by myself to welcome it.

I bobbed my head at Sally and Sheila. "Sorry, I've
got to get to work."

Walking back to the car, I paused at the bulkhead
above the beach. Here under the eroding cliffs you

could look across the fast-moving water in the narrow channel to the sandspit tip of Stinson Beach a scant fifty feet away. Sally had told me that one of the Bolinas derelicts tried to take a shortcut to Stinson by swimming across the channel towing a garbage bag full of his possessions. The current had swept him and the bag out the channel mouth, where a surfer on the first line of waves had providentially snatched him from the rip and towed him back to shore.

The street person lost his stuff, but not his life. My mother hadn't been so lucky.

I drove back through town and turned right on Highway 1 into a scene of primeval stillness. A line of undulating hills marched one after the other down the coast to the Golden Gate. Ghostly veils of morning fog hung over the lagoon, creeping up the broad folds of Mount Tamalpais that rose steeply on the other side of the road. All this land surrounding Bolinas and Stinson Beach was part of a gigantic park called the Golden Gate National Recreation Area. Transient creatures of every kind – ducks, butterflies, and whales as well as hawks and humans – passed through the Golden Gate National Recreation Area on their way north or south. Few stayed. Many of the people only roosted a season or two.

From the earliest I could remember, I loved this West Marin landscape. Sometimes I could feel myself losing my boundaries and simply dissolving into it, drawing my soul's nourishment from this beautiful place like the motherless kid I was. Just now, for example, the strange sensation I was experiencing seemed to be seeping out through the pores of my skin into the outer world, then turning back on itself and breaking over me like a big wave.

> What wondrous love is this, o my heart, o my heart?
> What wondrous love is this, o my heart?

The Shaker hymn kept spinning circles inside me. Yes, *he* was coming. It was love at last, I knew it. The great love my own heart had always yearned for. Something out there loved me, or rather, I loved something out there as yet unmaterialized. What I yearned for was finally upon me. Here, now.

Just as I had this thought, a big shadow slid across the Bel Air's ample hood.

I craned my neck up. A bird with large black and white checkered wings – a hawk or vulture? – circled overhead. A split-second later it dropped like a stone into a clump of roadside sage about twenty feet ahead.

As I zipped past around the curve a great thrashing came from inside the bush, and without any warning my stomach turned over twice and I felt very uneasy.

2

"Gnawed."

Roy was steaming milk so loud I barely heard him.

"What was what?"

"The head. Gnawed off."

The owner of the Big Cup was a stocky, sandy-haired middle-aged ex-parole officer from Red Bluff whose face flushed when he laughed, which was most of the time.

"Heard about the missing hiker?" he'd asked as I put on a clean white apron behind the counter.

The missing hiker was the latest standing joke among the regulars. The week before, a member of a birding group from Davis had gone missing up on Bolinas mesa. Searchers had been brought in, an action that provoked much ironic comment among the locals. Out here in the dubious wilds of the Golden Gate Recreational Area – where the park trails, wide as freeways, doubled as fire roads and bristled with directional signs – getting lost took serious effort.

And when I'd answered, a little impatiently, "Like he's all you ever talk about," Roy had pointed smugly to a front page in the discarded newspaper basket next to the counter.

The headline gave me a jolt. "Human Head Found on Bolinas Beach." I scanned the article quickly. The day before somebody had come upon a man's battered head wedged among the kelp and anemones in a tidepool below the cliff trail. DNA matches were being sought with the missing hiker's family.

"It wasn't cleanly severed from the spinal cord," Roy went on, now that he had my attention. "It was mangled. And covered with bite marks." Possibly because of his former profession, my employer relished all the gory details of the human misfortunes so frequently enacted out here.

The guy who owned the garden shop next door was at the counter. "Thank you for sharing that."

Roy rang him up briskly. "You're welcome."

"It doesn't say that in the story," I pointed out.

"One of the sheriff's deputies stopped in early when I was opening up. They think it might have been a shark attack."

"On Bolinas *mesa*?"

"They think he might have gone for a swim at the beach. Palomarin, near the waterfall."

From the murder mysteries I devoured, I knew that was the kind of detail police investigators usually withheld from the public in order to determine the true culprit. But this was West Marin, where everybody knew everything.

"Don't ask for lettuce next time you go to the Point Reyes Station farmer's market, Dovey."

One of Roy's jokes was on the way. "Why not?"

"Somebody might try to sell you an extra head."

The laughter from the locals sitting within earshot was muted. Except for low-level drug-related encounters, serious crime was unknown out here. Violent death, when it happened, was either accidental or self-inflicted.

Memories of the Tragedy sent a few ripples lapping against the shore of my consciousness. I chose to ignore them. If the great white sharks were doing their thing out there – well, folks, just stay out of the water! A shark gobbling up the missing hiker was unfortunate, but at least his family knew what had become of him.

The rest of the morning I smiled at my customers as I served them coffee and poppyseed cake, but it rarely went beyond that. When we did talk, it was your basic small town greeting, ritualized as a Noh play and just about as personal. And these Stinson Beachers were clannish. It was their hip village, their post office, their fire department, their softball team, their complicated love lives. Until you joined up, one way or another, you didn't belong. And even though it felt less crazy than Bolinas, I didn't want to join up. Stinson was like some old boys' club. The truth was, I didn't fit in here any better than I did across the lagoon.

My shift ended at noon. As I walked out the front door, there was Chevy Jim sitting on the porch with his golden retriever Isaiah. Isaiah's tail flapped a couple of times, but Chevy Jim stayed pointedly engrossed in the paper. I was glad he was back at the cafe, even if not to the point of sitting inside or acknowledging me.

Before Chevy Jim decided to look up, I hurried across the highway toward the north end of the beach park. In my free time I was supposed to be studying Latin and German to get ready for graduate school back east in the fall. I hardly ever did, even though not doing it made me feel guilty. Instead I took long walks on the beach. Sometimes I lay in the dunes and slept, or I read a murder mystery I had bought in the little bookstore.

People were always telling me I was aloof. If aloof meant aloft, I could understand that. If I was anything, it was airborne. It wasn't just because of the Tragedy. I had always been this way, or at least I remembered already being like this even when I still had a family. In an emotional vacuum children's hearts drift skyward. By the time I was seven, my deepest wish was to fly like Peter Pan; I often pictured to myself how amazed people would be, far down below, when they saw me soaring high overhead! Even now I zoomed myself up to the top of Mount Tam, under Tomales Bay where the great whites bred, beyond the massive fogbank that loomed off the coast every night, and when this began to unsettle me too much I read murder mysteries or paperback romances and fell in love with the heroes. I was floating through the complicated universe inside me, scarcely ever touching down. And when you are buying coffee from a young woman with a universe inside her, it's hard to start up a conversation.

Now I was all wrapped up in the stubborn joy that kept rising. An unquenchable feeling that my life trapped inside the glacier was ending and my real life, my wonderful real life, was finally about to begin.

The surf crashed loud as I made my way through the tall pampas grass between the houses that fronted the beach. A recent storm had eaten the wide flat expanse into a narrow ribbon; what the ocean had thrown up overnight lay strewn along the sand. I waded through the gullies gouged by the storm surges. Pieces of lumber and dirty clots of foam streaked the high water mark. There was gravel everywhere, jellyfish the size of dinner plates. A dead seal lay trapped in greenish-yellow tentacles of kelp.

What would a human head look like tangled up in those long bulbous ropes?

The thought made me beat a hasty retreat from the water's edge. I found a protected spot in the dunes and opened up the battered paperback I had brought with me, a Gothic romance I had picked up in the Free Box outside the Bolinas health food store. *The Secret of Rowena Manor* was well below the usual level of my escape reading and for that reason even more delightfully compelling. I was bitterly ashamed of these books and hid the copies under my aunt and uncle's bed even though there was no one else to see them.

If Catherine, the penniless young heroine, meets Randolph, the arrogant, darkly handsome lord of the castle, as she crosses the deserted moor one moonlit night, what did that have to do with me? Why should some part of me eagerly respond, saying yes, Catherine, Castle Rack and Ruin does hold a dreadful secret only you will discover, and Randolph, that cold, insulting, distant, demonic figure, will be revealed as your true love forever and forever?

What would Jacques Lacan have to say about a young woman who read this kind of stuff? Nothing very flattering, you could be sure. But here was the weird part: I was perfectly capable of applying the most sophisticated psychoanalytic theory to the lives of my friends and works of literature alike – was, in fact, for just this talent the constant object of my professors' praise and admiration – but when it came to applying them to myself, I drew a total blank. I had no idea at all what Lacan or anybody else would say about me; it was as if a protective wall reared up around my psyche at the very prospect. I am young and unformed, I told myself by way of reassurance; there's not that much in me to analyze yet.

My former roommate Betsy, who scorned romance novels, said flatly, "They're about abandoned girls who want their remote fathers." That's what I liked about Betsy; she never tiptoed around the Tragedy. But my father hadn't abandoned me, had he? Unless you counted death as abandonment, which hardly seemed fair. Was being dead the same as being "remote" – a kind of character flaw?

The fact was, during his lifetime people – women – tended to abandon my father, not the other way around. "You're the only female who never left me," I remember him telling me during one of his weeping fits those last years. I spent most of my time, I remembered guiltily, trying to extricate myself from his incessant hugging. That was after Dad's girlfriend Gina, his former graduate student, had just moved out.

Gina was a nice, polite person and they didn't fight the way he and my mother had. But by then my father was drinking even more than usual, and his rages, though unilateral, were more frequent.

No, if anything, I had felt more abandoned by my mother. She was the deserter in my eyes. (He had been neglectful, too, as the therapist had taken it upon herself to point out, but of course I knew that even as a child, and I had always excused my charming, charismatic father.)

Okay, the Tragedy.

Once upon a time long, long ago my parents owned a summer house in the village of Inverness, a few miles north of Bolinas on the Tomales Bay side of the Point Reyes peninsula. It was on one hot August afternoon when I was nine that my mother disappeared while I was playing at a friend's. Her towel and sunglasses turned up on the beach below our house, but my mother didn't, ever. The culprit? The famous Tomales Bay tidal bore, it was finally decided. Four years later my father smashed his car into a tree on Highway 1 just past Olema and he was gone, too.

Our Berkeley house was rented out, and since my father – much to my uncle's chagrin – had already sold the Inverness place, I began boarding at my private school until I went to college. Summers I spent with my aunt and uncle in Piedmont. For the last few years after his retirement my uncle had reopened the Bolinas house and they began returning here for the summer.

Other people tended to react more strongly to the Tragedy than I did. Working with the therapist I had been sent to for most of my adolescence, I tried very hard to "mourn." It seemed this process had to unfold in stages, a bit like a metastasizing cancer. But there was no good place to start. I knew if I moved an inch in that direction all was lost, and I was afraid of falling into the pit. I don't want to feel like a freak, I told her. I want to get on with my life. She nodded as I explained all this, then, curiously, nodded some more, but I got the impression, more from her thinly veiled impatience than from anything she said, that our time together had not been entirely productive.

Guilt, pointless guilt, was a bigger burden than my grief. Secretly I believed it was all my fault my parents were dead. I never told this to the therapist because it was so ridiculously obvious. When a major trauma occurs – so said all the psychology books I compulsively read – children always believe they have caused it. Infantile narcissism, I told myself each time the sick sensation intruded, which was fairly often. But saying that never made the feeling go away. Over time I learned just to endure it.

Around age fourteen I developed a habit of crossing my eyes to make the world all blurry. "Are you trying to see your mother?" Rebecca – as Dr. Moseley insisted I call her – once asked me, in a rare moment of perception. Maybe. I did remember my mother's eyes, full of love or pain, as they tracked my father across whatever room we were in, and I tried to copy the intensity of that gaze.

She had lived for him. It had been my deep wish to take up where she left off, for my father demanded absolute loyalty. But he was no longer here to be loyal to.

End of story, back to Rowena Manor.

I read and read all afternoon as the surf pounded hard behind me, out of sight.

3

The sun was setting when I steered the Bel Air gently around the curves of the lagoon road back to Bolinas.

Highway 1 follows the contour of the San Andreas fault, that earthquake-generating crack in the land where two great tectonic plates scrape against each other. The Stinson Beach side of the fault, along with most of the mainland United States, is located on the Continental plate, but the Point Reyes peninsula, including Bolinas, lies on the Pacific plate – and is moving, inch by inch, on a million-year crawl toward Alaska. Final proof, if you needed it, that Bolinas is situated in a realm apart, which was what I had always sensed about the little town to the north and sometimes, in a different way, about myself.

I was just passing the old Victorian farmhouse at the mouth of the bird sanctuary at Audubon Canyon when out of nowhere a very different thought, bright and bristling, lit down in my mind.

Had she taken her life?

Of course she had not. Everyone always said my mother had been a very life-affirming type of person. She was a painter. That was how she introduced herself, at any rate. She worked very hard on her canvases in that big light-filled upstairs room in our Berkeley house she called her studio, and she had had quite a few local solo shows, though no museum had ever bought her work. A frequent refrain of their arguments went something like this: Father rumbling, "Don't kid yourself, you're a faculty wife with a hobby I pay for," and Mother shouting back that someday she would leave him and fulfill her destiny.

Squinting in the fading light, I guided the Bel Air up the small private road that led to my aunt and uncle's. Their house, the Finches', and the third empty house all sat in a small cul-de-sac at the top of the hill. Down the road, at the corner I was now approaching, stood the weathered-shingle cabin where Old Lust lived.

Old Lust, Sally Finch had told me (like everybody else she called her neighbor by the Nickname and not by her real name, whatever that might be), was a potter or collagist or something, a neighbor of the fabled artist Jean Varda's from the great bohemian houseboat days of Sausalito. Now she lived in this hobbit hole somebody or other had bought her, along with her thirty-year-old daughter Young Lust and her daughter's baby girl, Perdita. Old Lust and her daughter fought a lot – even from my aunt's house you could hear the screaming some nights – but

Young Lust and her baby hardly ever seemed to be around. Mostly it was just Old Lust and her male visitors. Some mornings as I passed the corner on my way to Stinson Beach I would see a pickup truck or an old Dodge Dart parked in the hard-packed dirt in front of the house. Once I even saw a guy my own age coming out the front door at 6 a.m., tucking his shirt in his pants.

My foot was on the gas for that extra bit of V-8 to propel my uncle's chariot up the rest of the hill when the Bel Air's headlights captured something large and dark in the road directly in front of me.

I hit it hard. The big black thing smacked against the front fender, sailed an impossibly high arc over some bushes on the left side of the road, and landed out of sight with a sickening thud.

I slammed on the brakes, jumped out of the car and plunged through the roadside bushes into a small stand of Douglas firs. Searched the ground, tree by tree, in the gathering dusk. Nothing. Ran to the Bel Air, grabbed my uncle's big flashlight out of the glove compartment, went back, and shone it all around the base of the trees. Nothing.

Krkk, krkk!

Out of the tangle of branches high in a big pine above me came the high-pitched screeing of a creature in pain.

As I shone the flashlight up through dense clumps of needles, a fat brown short-haired dog dashed past me, barking furiously. There was a rustle. Then a *whoosh*. Something dark shot out of the tree like a crossbow and vanished into the ribbon of fading blue overhead.

I stared at the empty sky. Then walked back to the Bel Air. After an unhappy sniff of the tree trunk, the dog followed. I sat down in the driver's seat with the door open, head in my hands. What had I hit? A blurry image in my mind shifted between "man in dark clothing" and something else entirely, something my senses couldn't quite take in.

Across the road the cabin porch light winked on and the front door opened. A painted face peered out.

Now Old Lust was walking over to the car, her pale bony feet with their maroon toenails splaying out in the dirt. She bent over in the open passenger window and peered in at me, kohl-rimmed green eyes vivid against the paper-white skin of her face and her hennaed hair.

The voice was rich and dramatically vibrant. "Barkley."

"Pardon?" For a mad moment I thought the subject was philosophy – Samuel Johnson kicking the rock, that sort of thing. Was she questioning the reality of the material world?

"You must be careful coming around this corner. There are animals here, there are children." Old Lust was not addressing me as she said this but rather, it seemed, a throng of imaginary rednecks directly behind me. "You almost hit my dog."

"Not your dog," I said hoarsely. "A *person*. I think." Old Lust's skeptical glance flickered to the road and back to me. I felt myself flushing. It was impossible to describe what had happened.

I got out of my seat and paced a distracted circle through the trees again, shining the flashlight up and down as Old Lust stood by the car watching me. When I came back, I scanned the front end for signs of damage. A few tiny scratches on the fender, but hadn't they (I hoped) always been there?

The silence got awkward. Finally I said, "I'm Dovey. I'm staying up at my aunt and uncle's while they're away." Old Lust would know the car, of course.

I waited. Now, I wondered, would I find out her real name? But Old Lust must have felt she needed no introduction, for all she answered was, "A very special person will be living next to you."

"Al said it was someone from out of state."

"The poet James Harrier." Without another word, Old Lust walked back to her door, as slim and straight-backed as a proud girl in her twenties. She looked more like someone that age than I, who was one, did, I thought, feeling an absurd stab of envy that temporarily overrode what had just happened, or not happened. Not only was my new neighbor famous, I wouldn't even get to have him to myself because people like Old Lust with her secret sources of information knew about it ahead of time and were getting ready to stake their own claims. Already, you see, I was starting to fall in love with James Harrier.

Whispering "Grate," I punched low gear on the panel and pressed gingerly on the gas pedal. The stately Bel Air swayed up the hill on its enormous chassis.

By the time I pulled into my aunt and uncle's driveway, it was completely dark. The roar of the crickets was deafening when I shut off the engine.

Next door a rusty powder blue Volkswagen station wagon with Oregon plates sat in the driveway of the formerly empty house. In the front room the blinds were pulled up. All the lights were on.

A terrible thought struck me: What if the person I hit – if it *was* a person – was the poet James Harrier, taking an innocent stroll down the road from his new digs? Wasn't that how the poet and critic Randall Jarrell met his end, struck by a car as he walked beside a highway?

After a heartbeat, I walked over and knocked loudly on the front door. There was no answer. I waited and knocked again. Silence. Finally I turned and went back to my aunt and uncle's house.

I boiled a whole wheat macaroni and cheese package dinner on the stove and brought my plate into the living room. Sinking into my uncle's big Naugahyde chair in the living room, I had an unobstructed view of the brightly lit front room next door. It was empty – suggestively empty, it seemed to me, empty with the charged expectancy of a stage set before the show starts. Varnished orange wooden chairs, a sofa covered with dim fuzzy material somewhere between yellow and beige, streaked flowered wallpaper, the usual seventies summer house stuff. The windows were sealed tightly shut; you could almost smell the mildew inside. If I lived there, I thought, I would fling open all the windows and doors, cleanse it of the shut-in dampness of a foggy Bolinas summer.

I was still in a fit about what I had or hadn't struck with the car. Should I go out and search some more? Call the sheriff's office?

I picked up the phone. Put it down again.

The truth was, I dreaded police of any sort. In the weeks after my mother's disappearance they had been everywhere. My nine-year-old heart had clenched like a fist every time a California Highway Patrol or sheriff's car drove into our driveway and a uniformed officer got out. Against all reason, even now I still felt the same way about the men in khaki.

Ridiculous, I told myself, I hadn't hit anybody at all. I watched a horror movie, I think it was about giant flying spiders, that seemed to go on for hours. I must have dozed off because suddenly I was wide awake and my heart was thumping. I felt cold all over.

Down the road Old Lust's dog was barking.

Nothing was visible from the front except the empty living room next door, so I walked down the hall to the kitchen and looked out the back door.

The moon shone bright on the stretch of cleared ground that lay between the backs of the three houses in our cul-de-sac and that stand of eucalyptuses I found so upsetting. It was nothing special, this grove, yet after my mother's death I had shunned it. Doubtless I had drawn my fear of the place from my father. Once or twice, when I was little, we'd had picnics there. I didn't remember these occasions very clearly but one time, after my mother was gone, my father had exploded in fury when my uncle mentioned he was thinking of selling off that parcel. Family wisdom had it that my father associated the setting with happy times gone by.

In the moonlight a faint wind rippled the treetops like a sea of shaggy waves. Underneath them, deep in the grove, something was moving.

Then walked out of the trees.

A man with a bulky black garbage bag slung over his shoulder. He was heading across the clearing for the house next door. His face was hidden by some kind of puffy black-and-white checkered headgear that made him look like Yasser Arafat, but I noted with relief that he wasn't walking like an injured man.

Now his footsteps padded softly on the grass between the two houses. I tiptoed down the hall into the darkened living room and peeked out the front window. The man climbed the steps of the front porch next door. With the bulky bag still on his back, he took keys out of his pocket with his free hand and opened the door. He walked in carrying his burden. As soon as the door closed behind him, the living room went dark. A moment later, a light went on farther back in the house.

I sank down in my uncle's easy chair. My heart kept pounding even though there was nothing more to see.

The TV was still on. A quartet of fat middle-aged men in Western suits and bouffant sideburns smirked back at me from the TV screen. It was one of those horribly off-key Bible groups, singing:

Will you speak out, at last?
Will you speak out, at last?

About what? I thought angrily.

Come to Jesus today,
Let him show you the way.
Will you speak out against that great sin?

Looking at the glassy-eyed singers on the screen, I had the feeling they were staring right back at me. Out of nowhere the old guilty feeling washed over me in a sickly wave.

I punched the remote control button. The image swelled, brightened, contracted to a pinpoint, then disappeared with a sad little pop.

I went to bed in a daze.

4

Next morning I looked up from the breakfast dishes – and let out a yelp.

A large male head teetered rakishly over the lower half of the kitchen Dutch door. Impossibly, the lips began to move.

"Hi there!" The head lifted up as it uttered this greeting, and now I saw it belonged to a handsome black-haired man with a prominent nose and a black beard flecked with white who stood at the bottom of the kitchen steps. His big round eyes, brown shot through with gold, stared up at me out of a long, narrow face. They held a friendly, even childlike expression. Under each eye the faintest of moles was positioned like a teardrop.

"Didn't mean to startle you," he said. There had been no knock, just the head saying hello.

I waited for him to introduce himself, but he kept looking at me. "James?" I said hopefully.

"Who?"

"Are you James Harrier?"

"I'm George. Your neighbor."

"Are you a poet?"

"A poet!" He seemed extremely taken with the idea and repeated the word several times.

"You're not a poet?"

"No." He said it reluctantly. "No, I'm not."

"Oh," I said after a moment, swallowing my disappointment. Old Lust's excitement had been contagious. This morning my head had been full of fantasies about having a poet next door. In spite of his mysterious appearance last night from the grove, I pictured my neighbor as redheaded, Irish, bursting (but not too bursting, I cautioned myself, not a drunk) with the life force. A laughing, merry poet who was going to fall in love with me and make me happy.

"I'm Dovey," I said finally. "This is my aunt and uncle's house."

George nodded. "Al told me you were here for the summer."

It took me aback that he was already on such cozy terms with the Finches, as if he were the one who had always lived here and I were the newcomer.

He was also showing no inclination to leave. One sturdy jeaned leg was now planted a step higher on the back stairs. Though the morning was cold and foggy, he had rolled his shirt sleeves high on his muscular arms. Fine brown chest hair peeked out of his open denim workshirt, contrasting oddly with his thick black mane streaked with white. All the while he looked at me with the liveliest interest.

"I'm a student," I offered.

George seemed struck by this piece of information. His forehead actually wrinkled with interest. "Really? A student? What's your field?"

"Literature."

"What sort of literature?"

"Comparative." It sounded ridiculous when you said it – compared to what? – but George didn't seem to think so. "Wow, have you got your books here? I'd love to see them."

His enthusiasm seemed a little unfocused, but it unbent me. "Come on in."

Now I have to say that Bolinas protocol in those days promoted an open door policy, at least for fellow Bobo-ites; welcome your fellow humans into your abode went the credo. It was also very much part of my makeup to be obliging. Still, this was the first time I had let anyone besides Sally or Al in the house and hearing this stranger's heavy bootsteps behind me, his little exclamations of pleasure about this or that item that caught his eye, felt a little weird.

He stopped at my uncle's massive rolltop desk, where Cicero and the *Kleines Aufsatzbuch* sat untouched next to a black notebook I had bought on impulse.

George pointed at the notebook. "Do you write?" he asked. Then: "In that?"

I squirmed uncomfortably. It was as if he'd read my mind. One of my dreams, hardly more substantial than a pink fog in my mind, was to write something, someday. But except for my name printed in capital letters on the inside front cover, the notebook stayed empty. I had put no address in it; between my aunt and uncle's house and graduate school – which, though imminent, seemed as far away to me that summer as the next century – I had none. Not only hadn't I written in it, I hadn't once sat at the imposing desk. Secretly I thought it looked like a coffin. Once I sat down at it, I feared, the top would snap down on my hands and trap me like a rat, unless I screamed loud enough for the Finches to hear.

"It's for notes," I said finally. "For when I study."

George nodded, but he looked disappointed.

"I only brought a few books," I explained, reaching for the Kristeva and Lacan and the three-volume paperback of Musil's *The Man Without Qualities* I had been soldiering through intermittently, between the paperbacks. George didn't seem to hear me. He was looking intently at the titles in my uncle's somber built-in bookcases. Glossy hardback book club selections, musty Reader's Digest five-in-one condensed novels, a few old Ellery Queens I had already read in desperation, lots of paperbacks on ancient spacemen and the Bermuda Triangle.

My aunt and uncle believed implicitly in "chariots of the gods," spacemen building landing strips in ancient Peru and that sort of thing, and they had amassed quite a collection on the subject. After the first few conversations I learned not to talk to them about these matters, as my views tended to make my uncle excited. He was a retired insurance company president and felt his opinions should still carry the same weight they always had, especially in these new areas to which he now had the time to devote his full attention.

George looked at the shelves a long time, inspecting the books row by row. I waited for him to make a comment. Then, I reckoned like the little snob I was, I would really know what sort of person he was. But he said nothing. Finally he turned his attention back to me. To my shame, I was still holding my own books out for him like a friendly puppy.

"Let's see what you've got there," he said kindly, taking them from me and holding up each volume in turn. Apparently George was judging them for something other than content, for he carefully scrutinized the spines and bindings as well. Opening one of the Musil volumes at random, he read aloud: "'A murder may appear to us as a crime or as an heroic deed, and the hour of love as a feather that has fallen from an angel's wing or one from the wing of a goose.'"

"A feather fallen from an angel's wing!" George repeated, his voice full of wonder. He looked up at me, the moles quivering like exclamation points under his lively eyes. "May I borrow this one?"

I nodded, but as he slipped the book into the deep front pocket of his workshirt I felt an unexpected pang of loss. I did not bring up the fact that he had chosen volume 2. Fine points like this, I sensed, would be of minimal interest to someone like George and besides, I was already on volume 3.

"I'm writing a story," he announced.

"You are?" For all his interest, George did not strike me somehow as a literary person.

"Yep, all in longhand. In a special book I made."

As much as I wanted to like him – and already my imagination was working overtime again in that department – it didn't sound very promising. That was just how Marin County people engaged in the creative act, transcribing their feelings in custom-made journals with little seagulls embossed on the cover. As a Berkeley person I routinely turned up my nose at such efforts. But who was I to talk, with that empty notebook sitting on the rolltop desk right next to us?

At the very moment I had this thought George glanced back over at the desk. This time his gaze fell on the two photos on top. I didn't want him looking at them, but it was too late to steer him away. He didn't say, as I expected him to, "Who's this?" Instead he examined the two pictures in their silver frames, first separately, then side by side. "The man's the same," he said finally, "but it's two different women. The portrait is older than the candid shot," he went on, looking over at me. "Your father."

"Yes."

He held up the first one. "Your mother?"

"Yes."

"And this woman with him on the lawn – your stepmother, right?"

"Sort of."

George looked pleased with himself. "Know how I figured that out? Your mother has an older hairstyle in the portrait. That outfit your stepmother's wearing in the second picture? I'd put that about ten years ago. She's a lot younger, too."

"They're dead. My mother and father, I mean."

"Really?" George's voice was neutral, unusually so for someone first hearing this news. I was upset with myself for revealing it so fast but felt a private burst of gratitude at his restraint. The high drama of the Tragedy was so hateful to me.

"Not Gina, my father's girlfriend. She's married now. They live in Santa Barbara." When George said nothing, I offered, "I like that one of my father."

George looked back at the first picture. "A very big man and a very little woman."

I smiled wistfully. "Oh yes." My father had been the gaudy, plume-displaying rooster, my mother the wry quiet hen. As befitted his self-regard, my father had had a special theatrical way of talking – "Olympian," my mother once sarcastically described it to me. For as long as I could remember these learned asides had always been delivered to me by both parents with no concessions for my tender age. Their young daughter was precocious if solely for this reason, to keep up with their barbed, high-level badinage.

George said, "I think about my mother all the time."

I liked him for saying that. "Is she still living?"

"Not exactly." He laughed at my puzzled look and thumped his chest, giving me a beautiful smile. "But she's always with me!"

I thought about that. Was my mother alive in my heart, which was surely what he meant? I had to say no. Unlike my father, she was elusive, a dim memory dissolved in seawater. I remembered her best in smells. Cigarettes, turpentine, oil paint, Pond's face cream. Dad loomed over my life a hundred times bigger than she did.

"I guess it's my father that's still in my heart," I said finally, though the feeling I had toward these memories of him was not love exactly but a kind of cosmic awe. I was interested to hear more about George's mother, if he chose to offer it. Had she died when he was a child, like mine had, or when he was already grown up?

All George said was, "An attractive pair," and set the photos back in their precise positions on the desk. I appreciated his care, but the fact he had handled them at all made me uneasy. I didn't like strangers touching anything of my father's, especially the photos. It made me wish now for George to be out of the house.

Just as I was thinking this, he startled me by saying, "Must be off." Smiling, he patted the bulky Musil in his shirt pocket. "Thanks." Over his big shoulder he gave me a quick, direct look. Then he stepped lightly out of the room, very lightly for such a big man, and was gone.

I was left with the eerie sensation of my thoughts pushing George away – push, push, push, just like they pushed away everybody. I started scolding myself even before the kitchen door shut behind him. Here was a very nice, attractive guy presenting himself to me – that last little glance, I decided after the fact, had been thrilling – and I turned away from him just like I always did.

That was what had happened with Chevy Jim at the Big Cup. For a while, right after I started work there, Chevy Jim would stay on after everyone else had gone and chat with me about this or that. Then, abruptly, he stopped coming. He had given up on me, like they all did. I knew I didn't want to go out with him – it was hard to imagine "going out" with somebody old enough to be my father who didn't work, lived in his van and hadn't been on the other side of Mount Tam in more than a year – but I wasn't aware of giving him this message. In fact, I tried extra hard to be friendly and polite. But there is something in me that gets them every time and one day he quit showing up at the Big Cup during my hours. It must have been hard on Chevy Jim because the other breakfast place didn't open until nine; as an AA member and living in his van he would have had a long wait for his coffee every morning. Still, it hurt my feelings that he quit showing up, and after a while it even got twisted around in my head so that I believed that he had turned me down rather than the other way around.

This was something that the therapist kept bringing up – how hard I was on myself. "People who are so self-critical usually have something they haven't forgiven themselves for," she used to say, but I had no intention of revealing my silly feelings of guilt to her of all people.

Just then I glanced out the front window. Looking ceremonial in a purple caftan, Old Lust was advancing up the road bearing a steaming pot in her outstretched hands. Passing the Finches' house and then mine without so much as a sideways glance, she climbed the front steps of the third house and set down the pot. She knocked on the door and waited. Then she knocked again.

I felt a pinprick of curiosity. George had left my house only moments before and the station wagon still stood in the driveway. Where could he be? As I was thinking this, the phone rang. Still watching the window, I picked up the receiver.

It was Sally. "What's Old Lust doing?"

"She thinks he's James Harrier."

"What?"

"She thinks James Harrier is renting that house."

There was a brief silence while Sally mentally scanned her gossip database. "No, Harrier and his wife took the Bunting place up on the mesa," she pronounced. Then she hooted with laughter. "Old Lust's in a feeding frenzy because she thinks there's a celebrity next door! Wait'll I tell Al. And by the way, have *you* met our new neighbor?"

"Yes, he just came over." I looked over next door, where Old Lust, face severe and beautiful as a Cherokee's, had turned to go. The pot sat perched on the front porch like a votive offering.

"Well?" Even though I was well underway with my crush, the coy suggestion in her voice revolted me.

I forced myself to answer. "He seems all right."

"Be nice to him," said Sally sternly. "He won't bite." And she rang off. I set down the receiver. Immediately it rang again. "You'd better go fetch that pot or the raccoons will get it."

I walked over to George's front steps. The heavy ceramic pot was warm, but not too hot to pick up by its greasy handles, which I started to do.

What possessed me, then, to set the pot down, walk around to the locked garage door and press my eye up against one of its many large weathered cracks?

Fuzzy blackness met my eyes. Duct tape had been stuck over the gaps from the inside. Finally I located a small knothole a foot or so above the ground that hadn't been taped over. I crouched down and peered through it.

Dim light from a tiny window high on the back wall lit the garage's interior. A metal tool chest sat open on the oil-stained concrete floor. In the corner a narrow plywood box five or six feet long was mounted on two sawhorses. Its lid lay tilted against a cabinet, but I couldn't see inside it. What caught my eye, though, rested on a cable spool table close by my peephole. It was a huge album of some kind, a Gargantua's yearbook with wood covers on metal hinges.

But just as I hunkered down for a better look, someone cleared his throat a few inches from my ear.

5

George had come up beside me so quietly I hadn't heard a thing. His big head was so close his wiry beard brushed up against my arm.

It took a moment to recover. "God, you scared me," I stammered.

George just watched me with those big round eyes.

I tried to laugh, not very convincingly. "You must think I'm awful."

"Heck, no," he said finally. "It's human nature to be curious."

"Well, that's nice of you to say."

Awkwardly I got to my feet. George got up, too. We stood like that a moment. Then I pointed to the pot on his porch. "The woman down the road brought you that." It didn't seem right to say the Nickname and I didn't know what else to call her.

"Terrific," George nodded. He was still looking at me.

"Well, see you." I gave a little wave and beat a quick retreat. From my living room window I watched him pick up the pot and go in his front door. Waves of mortification washed over me. My summer romance was over before it began; of course he wouldn't want to have anything to do with me now.

The rest of the day I tried, with no success, not to read *The Secret of Rowena Manor*.

Early the next morning I found myself trapped inside a noisy dream. It seems I had this boyfriend who was very dashing and romantic and I was madly in love with him. My new boyfriend was actually an extraterrestrial of some sort. He paid for everything with his Mastercard and Betsy was just starting to warn me about this when a background disturbance gradually got too loud to ignore. It came from the bay laurels over the house and – as it always seems when you are caught in that special no-man's land of half-dreaming, half-waking – had been going on in some form or other all night. There had been leaves thrashing and branches cracking and above all there had been field mice in the trees, crying – had Sam the cat brought them up there? Flying mice stranded on fog-shrouded branches that were scraping against the roof?

Once you have started on the road to waking up, there is no turning back. Keeping my eyes shut, I rolled over and tried to go back to sleep, but it didn't work. The crying mice drew me, reluctantly, into consciousness. And just like in a fairytale, there I was, alone in the still center of my aunt and uncle's enormous bed, though I hadn't opened my eyes yet. I thought: Not mice–birds! It must have been the jays, those screeching California blue jays with their rodentlike cries. The woods were full of them.

A less exotic noise intruded now. Power sawing. At first I thought it was Al, except that the sound came from the right rather than the left, which meant it was coming from George's house.

I opened my eyes. A filmy screen softened the hard outlines of the room until I pinched away my father's fine linen handkerchief. I had slept with this piece of cloth over my face since I was twelve or thirteen; whenever roommates or intimates commented on it, I just said it came in very handy for keeping off bugs.

I got up and went into the living room. When I looked out the window, my heart sank. George's garage door now had a broad sheet of plywood tacked across it, along with new metal hinges and a shiny brass padlock.

He said he hadn't minded. But he had.

In the days that followed, the sounds of hammering and sawing continued. The old Volkswagen station wagon sat like a rusty paperweight in the driveway. The garage now stayed locked and closed even when George was working inside. Without ever glimpsing him, I was intensely aware of George's presence, his constant busy-ness.

With all the nightly commotion in the trees, now a regular pre-dawn experience, I found it hard to sleep. Sam the cat seemed to have stepped up his activities, too, though unfortunately his target was not those pesky jays who seemed to have lit down in our grove with such a vengeance. Every morning chewed-up tails, livers, and other body parts of field mice and moles littered the back yard.

The Friday night after the weekend George moved in I sat alone in my darkened living room. In my lap *The Secret of Rowena Manor* lay open. A difficult choice faced me: I could turn on the lamp and vanish happily through the great oaken doors of the old manor, or I could go to the poetry reading Sheila had called up that afternoon to tell me about. Rowena Manor seemed a lot more inviting, but it had been very nice of Sheila to remember me in the middle of all her organizing. And Sally would be sure to get after me if I didn't go.

I had just gotten to the most exciting part of the story and couldn't resist sneaking a peek. *Randolph shut the door firmly behind him, eyes glinting fiercely. Catherine's heart pounded with fear. His hand, she noted, rested firmly on the leather volume on the desk. Was he about to confess his unspeakable crime? And would this confession cost Catherine her life?*

Randolph was the young lord who was always arching his eyebrows quizzically, uttering low oaths, and storming off down the moor, the angel-devil the heroine was desperately in love with who might or might not have killed his heiress wife.

Grasping her arm so fiercely that she cried out, he clasped her urgently to his chest. (Two "fiercelys" in as many pages, the ever-vigilant critic in me could not help noting, but as this was Randolph's first open display of affection for the heroine and therefore the story's true climax – in all senses of the word – I read grimly on.) *Catherine could scarcely believe it was happening as he pressed his burning lips on hers in a kiss that blotted out all their losses and suffering. "Darling, darling Cathy," he muttered into her tangle of honeygold hair.*

I gave a sigh part happiness, part disappointment. In these old-fashioned romance novels you had to wade through several hundred pages of aggravating foreplay and paranoia to have your patience rewarded with one measly kiss, and then, before you knew it, the big scene was over. The great dark secret that was always played up in the beginning deflated in feeble spurts of unlikely explanation. In the remaining pages the real villain would be exposed while matrimonial arrangements were briskly attended to, leaving the Byronic hero well on his way down the road to happy domesticity.

Reluctantly I set the book down, cover side up and open to my place. Picking up the car keys from the kitchen counter, I walked out to the Bel Air. I would be late, very late, but at least, I told myself, I was making the effort.

Pulling out of the driveway, I saw that George's car was gone – the first time, to my knowledge, he had moved it. The window next door was dark, but after that first night it always was; George never seemed to use the front room.

I hated going out at night on those lonely country roads, but by the time I had made the short trip to town I felt reassured by all the cars parked along Wharf Road – nice cars, cars you didn't usually see down there. The usual crowd of wastrels was packed into Smiley's, swilling beer and playing pool. I parked near the end of the road next to the beach entrance and walked back to the Community Center.

A grey-haired woman I didn't recognize sat behind a card table at the entrance. "It's half over," she said as I put three dollars in the jar with a hand-lettered sign reading "Donations" and walked in. The hall was about three quarters full of people in rows of folding chairs facing the stage like a high school auditorium. A woman onstage was reading, but her voice was low and I couldn't hear her very well. At first I didn't see anyone I knew. Sally and Al would not be here, of course. For all Sally's talk of culture, they preferred staying home at night with their North Coast Chardonnay and satellite-dish *Masterpiece Theater*.

With a jerk of surprise I spotted a familiar dark head bobbing above the crowd. What was George doing here? It gave me a pang that he had found his way to this event completely on his own – more proof, I thought, that he was avoiding me. But beyond that, and even though he claimed he was writing a book, George just didn't seem sophisticated enough, somehow, for an event like this. Yet here he was displaying every sign of belonging, sitting right up in the front row next to the poets who were reading.

My skin prickled with jealousy. Somehow – despite his nonappearance after our first encounter – George had made me feel that I was the sole object of his attention. Now it seemed as if his keen interest were directed toward all sorts of people, not just me.

The crowd clapped, the poet left the stage, and now Sheila was at the microphone. "I feel celebratory about our next reader," she said. Since I couldn't see her face clearly from this distance, I had to imagine her web of wrinkles twitching. Sheila sounded nervous and I began to feel excited, too. "I feel celebratory about his work, his life, his being here . . ." She trailed off with a gulp and the audience laughed sympathetically. I tried to pick out from the backs of heads on either side of George's which one might be James Harrier's, but it was impossible to tell.

The man in the front row who got up was tall with the rugged features of a character actor. A lock of black hair fell rakishly over his forehead. He wore a dark blue jacket over pressed jeans and a crisp white shirt open at the front. When he opened his mouth to thank Sheila, the voice that came out was wonderfully mellow.

Just as James Harrier set a volume of his poems on the podium, a baby howled near the front. Everybody laughed. The baby howled louder. Its mother stood up, patting it frantically. James Harrier extended a propitiatory arm. "What is the baby's name?" Inaudible reply. "Samantha?" His rich voice made it sound like a benediction. "Samantha is welcome. Samantha is our blessing." Magically, the baby fell silent. A pleased murmur rippled through the audience. Cannily eyeing the crowd, James Harrier flipped through his book for a different reading selection. After a pause, he began. "Out of that first terrible birthing –"

Samantha let out a scream that shook the rafters. The audience laughed even harder. There was a brief moment of hopeful expectation that this was all, but the baby was only catching her breath before settling into relentless, rhythmic wails. This time James Harrier did not extend an arm. Instead he fastened a no-nonsense look on its mother, who humbly got out of her seat and carried the squalling infant up the aisle and past me through the outer door.

James Harrier flipped to a different page in his book and read us a poem about a hawthorn berry bush, then one about meeting someone in an airplane who might have been his great love, if he had been brave enough – there was something for Sheila and me and all the others to chew on, the unquenchable cynic in me noted – and finally a whole raft of poems he preceded with a long statement on the Apollonian versus the Dionysian that I must say, even though he was a riveting performer, sounded pretty old-fashioned to me. I remembered my cultural anthropology professor quipping that poets had minds better equipped to fashion images than to perform the simple task of *thinking*. Instead, he said, they spat up big half-digested ideas from their ethnic and philosophical reading in a kind of confused, runny Rorschach streak. But I forgave James Harrier for being maybe a little second rate. People were always calling me brilliant, for example, but I knew only too well that even though I read constantly my head was only stuffed with dreams, not real ideas. Maybe James Harrier was the same way – a link between us, I thought hopefully, with half a mind toward reviving my original crush since things had gone wrong with George.

He read a final poem and stepped down to heavy applause. As far as I was concerned, the reading was over. But there was more. Next in the lineup was a slight, balding man with glasses named William Grebe, whom Sheila introduced as "Bill" though she had not ventured to call James Harrier "Jim." I had read a poem by William Grebe in one of my English classes. Staring straight ahead, light refracting off his thick rimless glasses so his eyes were invisible, he delivered two or three collections of words so condensed I could only take in the third or fourth concentric ring of echoes. Then he walked offstage like a man underwater.

Sheila came back to the podium and read out a list of poetry-related activities that would be going on in Bolinas that week, workshops and readings and hiking excursions. For Bolinas it seemed awfully organized – "paramilitary," I could already hear some local saying. At the end she only said, "I want to advise our visitors, please be careful if you're out on the trails." She didn't mention the missing hiker or his no longer missing head.

Then it was over and the crowd got up from their seats. I hurried out in front, anxious to avoid George so he wouldn't think I was following him. Suddenly Sheila was at my side. "Wasn't Jimmy fabulous?" She handed me a piece of paper. "There's a party at my place now." It was a map of the mesa above town. A dotted line led to a big X showing Sheila's house. Before I could say anything, she was gone – and I was left with my old dilemma again. A party.

It was the usual case of ought versus want. I wanted to go home and get into bed and pull the covers over my head, but I knew I ought to go to the party and mingle and meet interesting people the way you were supposed to do if you were leading a normal life and not floating a hundred feet over terra firma.

As I headed toward my car, I was struck by how purposefully people leaving the Community Center were walking. Except among the street psychotics, purposeful walking was something you rarely saw in Bolinas.

An unfamiliar sweetish smell hung in the close air inside the Bel Air when I climbed into the driver's seat. My foot hit something in the darkness and I opened the door again for light. Wedged between the accelerator and brake pedals was an empty pint of Smirnoff's.

Someone groaned right behind me. I jerked around. A man lay stretched full length in the back seat. I squealed with fright and tried to leap out of the car. Instead my foot caught on the rim of the dash and I fell sprawling in the dirt.

I got up and brushed myself off, then peeked in the window. The man in the back seat hadn't moved. That meant, I managed to think, he wasn't after me. As a matter of fact, as I looked in through the window, he made an unintelligible grunt and rolled over wearily, as if to dismiss me. A large disheveled fellow with dead white skin and grey hair. Short-sleeved shirt hiked up to expose a large blubbery belly. This did not look at first glance like *genus* street person, a type that usually came skinny, weatherbeaten, and deeply suntanned.

He was too big for me to drag out of the car and the possibility was always present, as with other large sleeping animals, that he might turn ugly if disturbed. The street had emptied quickly; there was no one outside except the drunks in front of Smiley's.

It was obvious who I had to ask for help. I walked back to the Community Center and poked my head into the empty hall. A handful of people were still gathered down front. Someone stepped aside and there was George, talking intently to a white-haired man in a sailor's sweater and jeans. I caught his eye as I walked up.

"Hey, Dovey."

I listened in vain for any special joy in his voice. "George, can you help me? Some drunk passed out in my car."

He laughed. "Excuse me," he said to the others and followed me out of the hall.

It was nice feeling the rhythm of his body next to mine as we walked down the street. We said nothing to each other until we got to the car. I opened the door part way so the light would come on. Half curled in a fetal position, the unconscious man was loudly snoring.

"Who is it?"

"I don't know."

George glanced down the road. "If we just leave him out here, he might roll onto the pavement and get run over." He thought for a moment. "We'll put him in my car," he said. "I'll take him up to the party – did you know there's a party? We'll see if anybody there knows who he is."

This plan seemed a little unorthodox. "What if they don't?"

"Then I'll bring him back to my house," George said casually. "Let's go get my car and load him in."

We walked back down toward town. This time I had a hard time keeping up with George's long, energetic steps. Suddenly he said, "Well, what did you think?"

"Of what?"

"The reading."

"Interesting," I said politely. "I wasn't there for all of it."

We were passing Smiley's. The roar of voices, jukebox music, and cracking pool balls erupting from the open door drowned out George's next question.

"What was your favorite poem?" he repeated.

That stopped me. "Gee, I don't know. What was yours?"

"I liked them all," he said emphatically, making me wonder if he, like me, had really been listening. We reached the powder blue Volkswagen station wagon and I climbed in the passenger side. I looked around at the back. It was full of tools and scrap lumber. "How are you ever going to fit him in there?"

"No problem," George said airily. He turned on the ignition. The old station wagon shook as we sped up the street, making the little plastic bathing beauty hanging by the neck from the rear-view mirror jerk up and down. It seemed like a strange ornament for George, or anybody, to have in their car. Making a sharp U-turn, he pulled up smartly behind the Bel Air, jumped out, lowered his tailgate, and was making for the other vehicle before I had even gotten out on my side.

"Shouldn't leave your car unlocked at night," George remarked, opening the Bel Air's rear door. He leaned inside and began grappling with the sleeping drunk, who let out a few hiccups of protest.

I came up beside him, ready to help.

"Stand back," George ordered. "I've got him." Grasping the unconscious man firmly under the arms, he dragged him out of the Bel Air around to the back of his wagon. The heels of the man's filthy Nikes left two long skid marks in the dirt. George hoisted the top part of the body up onto the tailgate and then pushed the legs after it. But the man didn't quite fit in the Volkswagen station wagon's cramped back compartment; his knees dangled over the edge of the tailgate.

George stood back to give this problem his undivided attention as a steady stream of cars coming from the poetry reading passed us on the road. Nobody slowed down; passing out in public was not an uncommon occurrence in Bolinas. In the meantime George had settled on a course of action. Moving toward the legs, in one quick movement he jackknifed them smartly first to one side, then under – a perfect fit. Knees bent beneath his torso, head forward, the drunk looked deep in prayer or, possibly, engaged in the yoga pose called the Rabbit. With a quick look over at me to claim my admiration, George closed the back hatch.

"On to the party," he said. Then, after a pause – "Where was it again?"

By the casual way he said that, I could tell George had only overheard people talking about the party; no one had actually invited him. But suddenly the prospect had become a lot more appealing.

"I have a map," I volunteered.

"Super. I'll follow you."

We each got in our cars and started the engines at the same time. For a split-second the narrow double beams of the VW's headlights blazed in the rear-view mirror, blinding me.

I blinked in confusion, almost went off the road. Corrected my steering just in time. Gave George the thumbs up and off we went up the mesa.

6

Sheila's house was a Northern California custom fantasy, drab weathered redwood on the outside with a two-story living room, huge dirt-streaked picture windows and sleeping lofts on the inside. Many of my friends had spent freezing cold, unprivate childhoods among the wilted dichondra, Navajo rugs, and yarn-and-seashell murals in houses just like this. We all hated them.

When we reached the long dirt driveway lined with cars, George pulled up beside me and motioned that he was going to park up at the front door. I nodded and pulled the behemoth Bel Air onto the cement strip in front of the garage.

George had already rung the bell and was introducing himself to Sheila as I came up. He motioned casually to the doubled-up figure in the back. "We've got someone here that might belong to this group."

Sheila responded with a loud scream. It did look a lot like a corpse.

"Just drunk is all," George said as more people crowded in the doorway.

She placed a hand over her bare breastbone. "Who is it?"

"We thought you might be able to tell us."

Almost on tiptoe, Sheila approached the station wagon. Finally she said in a strained voice, "I can't see his face."

George raised the hatch and a curious disgusted noise ran through the group. "Peter *Chook*," someone said.

Sheila turned around anxiously. "Is that him? Is that who it is?" she said to me, though she could have been addressing anybody. "He wrote me a letter asking if he could come as an auditor, but he wasn't at orientation this afternoon. I had no idea what he looked like."

A tall slender man with a reddish beard came up. It was Rob, Sheila's husband, who ran the food co-op in town. He peered in the back. "They threw this guy out of Smiley's early this evening." A ripple of horrified admiration ran through the locals in the crowd.

Rob turned to his wife. "Did you book him a place to stay?"

Sheila made a noise. "Auditors are supposed to make their own arrangements."

In the light from the doorway the huddled form looked like an overnourished Inca mummy trapped in its thousand-year sleep. George lowered the hatch gently. "We'll see if he comes to before the party's over," he said as it clicked shut. "If he hasn't, I'll take him back to my place."

Sheila hesitated. "Won't it be too cold for him out here?"

"Not when he's this zonked."

That seemed to make up her mind. "Well, then, everybody come back inside."

We all marched after her into the house. I made for the big slate fireplace, where three oak logs were toasting. Sheila came up to me. "Who's that?" she whispered.

"My neighbor George."

"What a *nice* man. Come, Dovey, I want you to meet all our guests." She steered me away from the fire toward a group that had formed in the kitchen. As we came up, I heard a white-haired man in a turtleneck say, "Peter has totally gone off the deep end." It was George's neighbor in the front row.

"He should be in rehab," a woman in denim pronounced.

Sheila flushed. "He *has* published one well-received book of poetry." You could feel how nervous she was, hosting all these people and not wanting to come off looking provincial.

James Harrier stood in the middle of the room. His eyes were modestly lowered but even from that position he managed to radiate the unspoken assumption that everyone was looking at him. Next to him stood a small auburn-haired woman with a sad face who looked too well-dressed and too wounded, somehow, for this group. I knew instinctively she was his wife. Both were sipping wine from plastic glasses without talking to each other.

Sheila saw me looking. I tried, too late, to back away, but she grabbed me and dragged me over. The woman spotted us coming and melted into the crowd without a word.

"Dovey, have you met James Harrier?"

"How do you do?" James Harrier gravely shook my hand. "Where's Bill?" he asked Sheila.

Sheila's lips pursed. "He *said* he had a migraine." To me she said, "That's Bill Grebe. You remember, he read after Jimmy."

"Bill's the hermit type, you know. Doesn't care that much for social engagements," James Harrier was saying. "*Wonderful* poet." I could almost hear both of them thinking, "But not compared to James Harrier," when he changed the subject abruptly. "I flew down here this morning on a plane called the Smile of Spokane." He paused and I wondered why he only said "I." Had his wife flown down on another plane? I looked over at the woman, who now stood alone in the hallway. A residue of my childhood feelings began to cluster over her well-coiffed head like a small rain cloud. In a group my father had always been the center of attention, too. My mother played her sidekick role to the hilt, but underneath I don't think she was ever that happy about it.

I looked away, embarrassed at my own nosiness. What was it like, being a famous person or worse, married to someone famous, having everyone always watching, sizing you up?

Sheila was eager to pick up the dropped ball. "And if you were in a bad mood you'd take the Frown of Spokane." James Harrier's mouth smiled at her while his bright hunter's eyes roamed the gathering. Then someone beckoned to Sheila, and we were left alone.

"And you – Dovey? Are you an aspiring poet?" he asked politely.

"No."

"Do you live here?"

"Just for the summer." A more worldly response, I hoped, than "housesitting for my aunt and uncle."

"Ah, the summer . . ." His voice trailed away.

I wracked my brains for more to say, but the conversation, never having really started in the first place, was dying on the vine. He was attractive, but I couldn't help thinking with a certain satisfaction that George was better looking by a mile. Now that my crush had been transferred like a floating trust to my real neighbor, I found myself wishing James Harrier's wife would come back.

"Think I'll get another drink," the poet said. "Would you like one?"

I shook my head and he was gone.

Now, at last, for George. He did not seem to be anywhere in the room, though you would have thought he would gravitate eagerly to all these intelligent literary people gathered together in one place, chatting away and sipping wine. I walked to the front door and peeked out.

George sat perched on the railing deep in conversation with a very large man. I could not see behind them into the back of the Volkswagen station wagon and was still trying to when suddenly it dawned on me that this very large man was the former occupant of my car, now miraculously restored to life, talking, listening, gesticulating like a regular human being, even though in my imagination he was fixed forever as a lifeless lump in the back seat of the Bel Air.

Too engrossed to notice me, the ill-matched pair continued their discussion. I watched, fascinated. Peter Chook wore only a wrinkled short-sleeved shirt and jeans, but the freezing night air seemed to have no effect on him. I remembered those stories that the only *Titanic* passengers to survive the icy North Atlantic waters were alcoholics whose blood temperature had been raised by hours and hours at the ship's bar. Drink had its uses, it seemed.

But what, just now, had gotten George so worked up, nodding his head up and down in a frenzy of excited agreement? Craning forward, I heard Peter Chook say:

"There are ghost animals on this mesa."

His deep, rumbling baritone held the spurious authority of a movie trailer voiceover. "Listen. The Miwok hunters are getting closer. Sister Mountain Lion cries, 'Aiee!' She despairs, you see. She senses Death is near. But Coyote cries, 'Aiee, you'll never catch me!'" Peter Chook held up a huge admonitory hand. "Sssh! Listen."

He and George cocked their ears like a couple of collie pups. Silence. A car backfired in the distance – probably one of the marijuana farmers' security guards on evening patrol. Somewhere out in the bushes a cricket chirruped. Up here on the mesa they were not really as loud or as numerous as they were down in the hollow where my aunt and uncle's house sat.

"Hear that?" said Peter Chook. "Hear the ghost animals?"

"Yes," said George eagerly, and I felt embarrassed for him. "Yes, I hear them."

"Take my hand. Take it. We'll perform the men's hunting chant, the chant in praise of fellow animals we're about to kill. Take a deep breath. A deep breath. Now!"

He threw back his head and began a high-pitched ki-yiing. To George's credit, he did not join in but kept his head down, handsome face knitted in concentration.

Abruptly Peter Chook stopped chanting and dropped George's hand. In a different tone entirely he barked, "How about some booze?"

"Good idea," said George. "Let's go in."

I retreated back inside the door as George shepherded his charge into the living room. Heads turned, conversation flagged as the two of them bore down on the liquor table, all the while chatting away as if they were having the most interesting discussion imaginable. George took a little bottle of Calistoga mineral water and twisted off its cap in a single lightning-quick movement. Peter Chook hoisted a gallon jug of chablis and poured himself a generous tumblerful.

That George really takes the cake, I thought. Here was a man he'd just had to lift bodily out of one vehicle into another and now he was allowing, no, encouraging, him to keep on drinking. Out of all these intelligent people – me included – why had he zeroed in so intently on this pathetic creature?

Coming straight from school as I did, where all that went on was a little wine drinking, Ecstasy dropping, and dope smoking, I felt a squeamish fascination for drunks, especially the old drunks so plentiful in coastal Marin County. It was awful, the few times I ventured into a local bar, to get buttonholed by one of these zombies who made you sit there and listen as their slow, slurred speech washed over you in a greasy wave, buying you rounds of drinks you didn't want, maddeningly intent on making some vague but terribly important point, mood shifting in an eyebat from smarminess to unpredictable fury.

How did a person get to be a drunk? It was impossible to picture what any of these toads had looked like pre-curse and equally impossible to imagine any of them ever changing back to their original form. True, my father had been a very heavy drinker, but I never thought of him in the same category as those people in the West Marin bars. What my father did and what the rest of the world did was ruled by two entirely separate standards of judgment. By anybody's else measure, I suppose, he would have been considered authoritarian as well. Yet I had never had a problem doing exactly what he told me to even though other people, including and especially my own relatives, found me self-directed to a fault.

Watching Peter Chook with fascinated disgust, I couldn't get over the feeling he had somehow been illegally reinstated as a living human. And that Native American rap – it occurred to me to check, while his puffy white face was turned away from me, for Navajo jewelry. Nope, to his credit there was no flash of silver or turquoise around the neck or wrists. Though his thick greying hair fell across his forehead in a strange echo of James Harrier's, this was a singularly shabby and unornamented man.

Someone brushed against my shoulder and a cloud of patchouli enveloped me. It was Old Lust in a rose print sari. Standing near her, though not actually with her, was Young Lust, minus baby, in a long stained jersey dress. Mother and daughter must have patched up their differences for the big occasion.

"Hello," Old Lust said to me in a voice devoid of expression. "This is my daughter." Young Lust didn't seem to hear the introduction. She fiddled with her long blonde hair and like her mother gazed over my shoulder. Both were "homing in," as Sally would say.

I glanced over at their quarry. James Harrier was looking in our direction. Looking intently. Which of us was the object of his attention? Definitely not Old Lust and her majestic profile; this much was clear from the angle of his eyes. That left Young Lust and me. No, it was not the tan, blue-eyed, only slightly frayed-around-the-edges surfer girl daughter. And even though there is absolutely nothing the matter with the way I look and even though I was the youngest, I knew those predatory eyes were not after me.

I turned around discreetly. In the far corner of the living room stood a slender, dreamy-eyed, black-haired sixteen-year-old shifting restlessly from foot to foot. I remembered vaguely having seen her around town. Somebody's daughter. The girl looked like she wanted to run out of the room into the night, though not in exactly the way I myself wanted to run into the night. She looked like she might like having someone run after her.

I knew who wanted to.

Well pleased with my worldly deduction, I looked reflexively for James Harrier's wife. There she was in a far corner, smoking. Whether she had seen any of this I had no idea.

When I turned away to get another glass of wine, I ran straight into George with Peter Chook in tow. Peter looked directly at me with his awful bloodshot eyes and I dropped my head instinctively.

But George was eager to talk. "We've been having the greatest conversation, Dovey. I bet you know plenty about it, too. She's a graduate student in comparative literature," he explained to his companion. Peter Chook didn't look impressed and I couldn't blame him.

I managed to avoid the fish-dead eyes. "Nice to meet you." To George I said, "I'm going home now."

"Hell, the party's just starting," Peter Chook rumbled, big fist wrapped tightly around a Budweiser.

"Well, if you've got to –" George, as always, radiated interest and good humor, but it was difficult to tell exactly what he was thinking. Unlike his companion, he was not the least bit drunk.

Trying to hide my disappointment, I shook Rob Robbins's hand at the door, though I knew it was really Sheila I ought to be saying goodbye to. But she had gone back to the kitchen and I didn't want to walk past George and Peter again.

Outside it was even colder than before. There was frost on the Bel Air's windshield – this was mid-July, mind you – and my teeth chattered as I got in.

"Psst!"

From the open front porch Old Lust beckoned me urgently. "You! I forgot your name."

"Dovey."

She looked small and forlorn on the front porch. "Give me a ride home, Dovey, would you please? My daughter has left without me."

"Sure," I said.

Swathed in a red wool serape over her sari and a force field of scent, Old Lust climbed in the passenger side of the Bel Air. I started up the engine and pointed the car down the dark mesa road. Old Lust rolled down her window all the way and lit up a cigarette. I cranked up the heater, but it didn't help. For a long time neither of us spoke. It did not seem polite to ask why her daughter left without her.

Finally I said, "James Harrier isn't our neighbor."

She waved her hand impatiently. "Yes, yes, I know that."

"Have you met him? Our real neighbor, I mean."

"The man who brought the drunk? Yes." Something in her tone indicated clearly that George was not her type. Was he too old, or not famous enough? I wondered if George had ever returned the cassoulet pot to her. "Tell me," she said suddenly, facing me. "Does he have animals? When I asked him, he said no, but I think he is lying."

"Animals?"

"Yes! They are driving poor Barkley crazy at night with their crying and shrieking. And in the morning all the dirt outside the fence is clawed up."

"I don't think he has animals. I haven't seen any."

Old Lust shrugged contemptuously.

I turned onto our street and stopped the Bel Air in front of her house. "Thank you," said Old Lust, getting out. She gave the door a resounding slam, as if she were mad at me rather than grateful. Then she leaned back in the window, which she had left open. "He has animals," she hissed.

As I drove up the hill, I said, "*Ghost* animals," and permitted myself a tiny smile.

7

You read in stories about people "gasping in surprise" and I had always wondered what that sounded like in real life. As I strolled past the living room window with my cup of coffee the next morning, a small, sharp noise issued from my mouth. The rear compartment of the Volkswagen station wagon parked in the driveway next door was occupied by a strangely familiar lump swathed in olive green synthetic fiber. Before I could stop myself, I ran over to George's front door and knocked quietly.

There was a long wait. At last a soaking wet George opened the door with a towel wrapped around his waist. Did his eyebrows lift ever so slightly at the sight of me? I tried not to look directly at his big chest, covered with fine brown hair that didn't match his thick salt-and-pepper beard and hair. Or the two knobs of flesh that protruded from each of his hairy shoulders like miniature dowager's humps. How weird was that? But it wasn't polite to stare at deformities, so I didn't.

"Oh, sorry," I said.

"Come in," he beckoned, stepping back. "Half a mo." He walked down the hallway to the bathroom, shaking his wet head like a dog. A few minutes later he emerged in jeans, wriggling a black T-shirt over his head.

"What's up?"

I pointed at the station wagon.

"Yep," he said calmly. "It was too late to find a room last night, so I brought him home."

"Why is he still in your car?"

"It's his power spot. Said he'd had strong visions the whole time he was rocking around back there when we drove him up to the mesa." George laughed when he saw the expression on my face. "I'm taking him to town this morning. Had your coffee yet? I'm making some."

I looked at the bulky shape in the station wagon, thinking it might stir any moment. "No thanks," I said, and retreated back to my aunt and uncle's house.

Half an hour later I watched from the safety of my living room as the two drove away, Peter Chook's angry Roman emperor profile in the passenger seat overlapping my neighbor's own prominent beak.

Once the coast was clear, I strolled back outside. And sniffed.

An acrid odor hung in the air. It came from George's empty house. I walked to the back and stood under the kitchen window. Something was burning inside.

I went around to his front door and tried the knob. The door opened and I went in. Walked down the dark hallway to a cramped kitchen.

On the stove an empty pot sat on a glowing red burner. I turned off the burner and set the blackened pan in the dingy little sink streaked with orange stains, where it hissed angrily. Fussy nylon curtains, grey with age, framed the single small side window. The floor was littered with candy-colored styrofoam pieces. A trail of them led to a door standing half ajar at the other side of the kitchen. I was about to peek around it when I noticed for the first time what lay on the kitchen table.

A massive object that looked like a book. Its freshly varnished wood covers were fastened with metal door hinges.

This was the giant's album I had seen in the garage through my peephole. Slowly I reached out and touched the slick varnished surface. Pulled my hand quickly back. Laid my hand on it again.

The shiny new hinges squeaked as I opened the wooden cover. There was no title page. The first sheet of thick paper was covered with a forest of scratchy black marks. No margin, no white space. Just this strange crabbed script in no alphabet I had ever seen before. Some of it looked like pictures, but not of anything recognizable.

The hairs on the back of my neck rose as I reached out my hand to touch the page. The heavy parchment was clammy, the script deeply incised. I turned the page over. The next page and all the fat pages after it were crowded with the same angry scratches. They were bound together with wide stitches of red cotton thread like a flesh wound clumsily sewn up.

"How do you like it?"

I jumped a foot. George stood smiling at my side.

Once again he'd caught me somewhere I shouldn't be. And scared me so badly I couldn't speak. Finally I motioned at the pot, still steaming in the sink. "Sorry, I smelled smoke and came in."

George glanced over. "Wow, thanks. Peter must have left that burner on." He looked back at me.

Avoiding what lay between us on the table, I managed a little laugh. "Then I looked up and there you were."

Another silence while we regarded each other. Then he motioned at the open album. "You can see that, Dovey?"

Of all the things he could have said, I least expected this.

"Of course I can see it!"

He shook his head in mild disbelief.

I said, "You *made* this thing?"

"Yep." Slapping the big book shut, he hefted it easily in one hand. "Those covers are real teak, varithaned so they won't swell up and buckle. The paper I got in an art store over the hill. Rag stock, super expensive."

George laid the book carefully on the table and we stared at each other some more. His big round eyes with their dilated pupils held no expression.

He waited.

Finally I said, "The writing."

"Like it?"

I didn't. "What *is* it?"

He shrugged. "Shorthand, I guess you'd call it."

"You understand what it says?"

"Sure do, cause I wrote it myself. That's what writing looks like where I come from."

"You wrote all that since you got here?" I found myself comparing it to the empty black notebook. In spite of myself, I was impressed.

"You could almost say it wrote itself, Dovey." He picked up the book and opened it. "Want me to read some?"

"No, thanks," I said quickly.

George gave a little smile and set it down. "Didn't think so."

Abruptly I moved away and pointed at the styrofoam trail. "What's that?"

"Packing." Something in this word caused George a moment of private satisfaction as he nudged the door to the garage shut with his toe.

"What'd you do with Peter?"

"Fixed him up with a room over Smiley's."

I was edging out of the kitchen as we spoke. "That ought to make him happy."

"Maybe not." George followed me down the hall onto the porch. "They said he couldn't come back in the bar."

We were outside the house now. It felt very good to be in the fresh air, away from that book.

"Are you upset with me?" I asked.

"What for?"

"For coming in your house like that."

"Are you kidding? The whole place might have burned down. And I'm glad you saw my book, Dovey.

I was showing it to Peter, but"– he shot me a sideways look – "it's your opinion I really care about."

"Really?"

"Really."

I felt warm all over, or at least I wanted to. George valued my opinion about something that was special to him, even if that something was extremely odd, not to say repulsive. But my neighbor's mind had already turned to other things. "Hey, I'm going to hike the trail at the end of the mesa road. Want to come?"

The change of subject took me by surprise. For a moment I couldn't think what to say.

A little smile broke through George's beard. "Oh, c'mon."

"When?"

"Right now."

Without waiting for an answer, he headed for the station wagon.

"Wait." I walked over to lock my aunt and uncle's kitchen door. My aunt kept the key in a special compartment on the underside of a little plastic rock she had bought in some boutique. This rock sat right on the doorstep; all you had to do was turn it over to see the key. I was pledged to follow the house rules and they included this little ritual.

George watched me turn the key in the lock, stick it into the plastic rock, and put the rock back on the step. "People have the funniest ideas about how to protect themselves," he commented as I got in the station wagon next to him, in the place where Peter had sat.

He started the engine and off we went.

8

George steered the old VW confidently up the mesa road. He drove intently, full of pleasure in the act. As we barreled along, I kept sneaking looks at his rugged profile.

He caught me looking. Smiled. Then said, "What do you think of Peter?"

I made a face.

"Really?" He looked disappointed. "I could listen to him for hours. I've learned so much already."

"Like what?"

"The native spirituality of this region. Legends and stuff."

"If you ask me, he's making it all up."

"What makes you so sure?"

"He's not even from around here. The only ones who really knew that, and believed it, were the Miwoks. And there's just a few of them left. White people get that stuff out of books and then they embroider on it any way they like."

George laughed. "You're a pretty opinionated person, Dovey. What's wrong with people reading up on that kind of thing?"

I was glad George had granted me the dignity of being an opinionated "person" instead of an opinionated "young woman," which was what people – older men – usually called me.

"It doesn't matter if you get the details wrong," he went on. "It's the spirit of the thing that counts."

"What is the spirit of the thing?"

"Well, for instance, Peter got it in his head that he wants to call up all the dead souls circulating all around us here."

I laughed scornfully. "What for?"

George looked over at me with his guileless brown eyes. "He senses there's a lot going on in West Marin, Bolinas, that people don't know about. Says it's good training for him. Wants to become a seer. Someone with spiritual power."

"How are the dead souls going to help him do that?"

"In Peter's case I'm not sure."

We passed decayed Victorian farmhouses with tin-roofed outbuildings. Rusty dead trucks with bare axles sat propped up in front yards. Dogs sprawled on the side of the road next to clumps of brown-edged calla lilies past their prime. Bright orange nasturtiums with green leaves the size of dinner plates carpeted the hard dirt under the spreading bay laurels.

"What do you do for a living, George?" I said finally, to break the silence.

His eyes didn't leave the road. "Manage family holdings."

Somehow that wasn't the answer I expected. "Your own family?"

"I wish. Other people's."

"In Oregon? Is that where you're from?" I was thinking about what he'd said about the funny writing, how that was the way it was done where he came from.

"Previous owner of the car. One of these days I've got to get those plates changed. But," he laughed, "I have to say it's great to park anywhere I want and not have to worry about paying for the tickets."

We jolted along a narrow road bordered by manzanita and scrub pine; the station wagon had no shocks. Under the mirror the little bathing beauty danced madly at the end of her string. She had a blue swimsuit and a rubber orange body, but no face. It upset me that the string, which had obviously been broken several times, was no longer attached to the back of the doll but looped carelessly around her neck. George followed my look. "Previous owner." Now that I thought about it, the vehicle seemed pretty marginal for someone who managed family holdings. But wasn't it to George's credit that he didn't care about appearances, material things?

He gestured at a small sign on the left marking the turnoff to the Point Reyes Bird Observatory. "Ever been there?" I shook my head. "We should stop in on the way back. It's the raptor center."

"What's a raptor?"

"You don't know?" He clucked his tongue. "What's your favorite bird?"

I shrugged. To me a bird was a bird, unless it was something uncommonly beautiful, like the snowy egrets who nested in Audubon Canyon every spring. George seemed mildly shocked when I told him this.

He pulled into a dirt lot on the cliff overlooking the ocean, where several other cars were parked. We got out of the station wagon. Far below us pale blue seawater broke in long white triangular sweeps that crashed against the rocks. Icy wind whipped over the sheer bluff, filling the air with salt mist from the surf. I'd never been here before. Zipping up my down vest, I felt a sudden jolt of happiness. The hot sun, the misty surf in the shadow of the cliffs, the trail unfolding ahead. It was only an afternoon's outing, but oh, what a rare feeling. Was this what I'd been expecting would happen to me? Was my life, the real life I'd always been waiting for, finally about to begin?

The trailhead was located above the lot in a dense grove of old pines. As we approached the trees, all the birds hidden in the foliage shot up in a single dark cloud, as if someone had fired a gun. George stopped, shifting from one foot to the other, his big eyes fixed on the flock as they flew away. Then he joined me in the trees and we stood swallowed up in the sudden hush. In here under the tangled boughs you couldn't see or hear the ocean even though the cliffs were close by. The clean aromatic smell of pine needles filled the air.

"This was a dairy ranch once," George said. "There used to be a house here."

"How did you know that?"

Pride filled his voice. "I've been up here a lot. I read everything and I've explored the whole of Point Reyes, even off the trails."

"But you only just got here," I objected. The fact was, I was barely listening. Sadness, my own memories, were already crowding out my bliss. A house used to sit in this overgrown place, a family house. Now there was no trace of it.

We had owned two houses, the brown-shingled Maybeck in the north Berkeley hills and the modest midcentury ranchhouse in the little town of Inverness up the road from Bolinas, nicknamed Inwardness by the wits who observed the number of college professors and other contemplative souls who kept summer homes there in the old days. I liked the Berkeley house better because my mother's bohemian friends and my father's students were always streaming in and out of it. In Inverness we were shut away all by ourselves, a situation that tended to escalate my father's drinking and his fights with my mother.

A vanished life. I walked rapidly out of the trees.

George caught up with me farther up the trail. "What's the matter?"

"My father was a professor," I heard myself say. This bald fact bore no relation to that faded giant forever frozen two feet taller than me no matter how many inches I added to my height.

"Professor of what?"

"Literature."

"Just like you're studying to be. You want to be a professor like your father, don't you, Dovey?"

I said nothing. I was hearing my mother's exasperated voice say, "You worship him!" It had never occurred to me until now how that must have made her feel. Painting, needless to say, was something I had zero interest in. Once she walked in on us when he was at his study desk and I was sitting in his lap, all of six years old, reading along with him the arcane text he had open, pretending I understood it. She waited till she had me alone to deliver this accusation, then added, in an entirely different tone of voice I didn't understand, "And *he* worships *you*!" Even though I could picture her feeling hurt that I didn't love her as much as I loved him – not being loved was a big complaint of hers, where my father was concerned – it was almost beyond me to imagine that she could have been jealous of me. Or the other way around, a little voice inside me said.

George woke me out of my reverie. "Do you have brothers or sisters?"

"No," I said ruefully. All of a sudden tears rolled out of my eyes. It was a strange sensation because I rarely cried. I felt like I was being sucked down into a horrible place I'd never been before.

George just stared. He did seem extremely interested, in the way everything interested him; he had hung on every word I said. But he made no move to comfort me now and this time his cool response did not please me. In fact, I found the very impersonal look he gave me deeply wounding. Pushing down the unwelcome hurt, I was overcome by a terrible shame for my female nature. Of course men, and my father in particular, didn't like emotionalism in women, it put them right off. ("Drama queen" was one of his frequent epithets.) But they didn't seem to like its opposite, either. That's what I found so confusing. If, as a female, you tried to have a serious intellectual discussion without any feeling in it – a skill I had precociously picked up from my father – many men were just as put off as if you screamed and cried. It was all a painful mystery to me.

These reflections, though not very pleasant, at least got me out of the even darker place I'd been in. We walked on in silence, feet crunching the Park Service gravel that filled the jeep tread ruts on the trail.

We stopped in front of a large green metal sign with a raised relief map of the Point Reyes National Seashore. George traced his finger along the trail we were on, called Palomarin, that ran by the ocean and stopped at one spot. "The beach waterfall," he said. "That's where we're going. But it's not my *favorite* place."

There was something almost touching about the way he said this, like a little boy living in a private fantasy world who only comes truly alive when you accidentally stumble on some point of reference to it.

"What is?"

"Mud Lake. Farther up this trail. But it's shorter to get there if you go in from the north."

"What's so special about it?"

"I'll take you there real soon and you'll see why. But not today." George's voice held a note of determination. "Today we're going to the waterfall." He moved away from the sign and took off up the trail at a brisk clip.

Absurdly happy that my tears hadn't alienated George, I found myself trotting docilely after him. As the inevitable corollary to the crush, my old obedience thing was kicking in. I made a conscious effort to slow up.

A series of rounded headlands unfolded before us and my spirits lifted again. The contour trail wound in and out of these not-quite valleys breaking open at the coast. The hillside grass was half green from winter, half brown from summer. Aromatic sage and the last purple lupine from spring crowded each other in the gullies next to the trail.

George looked out to sea. "Today you can see the Farallones." The rugged little islands, usually shrouded by coastal fog and haze, stood sharply etched on the horizon.

"I'd love to visit them."

"They aren't so romantic once you get out there," he laughed. "Solid guano from top to bottom."

"I thought only park rangers went there."

George pointed to the bottom of the cliff. "What do you think of that?"

I looked where he pointed and gave an involuntary cry. A naked female body lay sprawled and lifeless on a towel on the sand.

A moment later, the body rolled over on its back.

"You mean – what do I think about nude beaches?" I said with an embarrassed laugh, but he only smiled.

I must have started walking very fast then because George, catching up again, placed his hand briefly on my shoulder. Terribly aware of it, I made an effort to fall into step with him. At first the synchronizing felt self-conscious, but when I stopped paying attention we got into a kind of rhythm. The spot where his hand had rested still tingled.

Then he touched my shoulder again. "Here we are."

We stood over a sheer drop where a stream fell fifty feet to the beach. The water thundered down on the grey sand and spilled into the advancing sea foam, creating all kinds of minor eddies and confusion that were quickly swallowed up by the urgency of the tide. The wind blew droplets, fresh and salt, back in our faces. George shook himself joyfully in the mist.

Watching the waterfall, I could feel something exactly like that opening up inside me. I was helpless to stop it. The beach we looked down on was very like the first beach of my young life in Inverness.

I shut my eyes and suddenly I was right there, a short little person planted upright on the sand at the cove right below our house. The only path down to it was on our property and since, thanks to the tides, people rarely came strolling around the bend, we considered it our own private spot. My mother loved this beach and took me down every day the sun came out. I always stood right where the sliding water buried my feet, uncovered them, buried them again. Each time my toes popped up, I shrieked with pleasure. And because the child takes her mother's presence supremely for granted, I waded in fearlessly all the way to my stomach, secure in the knowledge that I was watched, protected, bobbing in the enveloping attention of the unseen person behind me, safe inside her magic circle, as I faced the waters of Tomales Bay.

Now I was a grown up again on top of the cliff, and my heart sank. Was there any place in the world where I could just turn around and there she would be, my lost mother? Turn around and see her again? One more time. Mother?

I twirled around and opened my eyes. George's face was right up close to mine. This time it wasn't scary. He caught my arm to steady me.

"Afraid of heights?" he teased.

"Yes," I nodded, for lack of a better explanation.

George gripped my shoulders and looked deep into my eyes. "Gentle little Dovey," he whispered, using that name for the first time and pulling me close, "I have a confession to make."

It was thrilling to be in his arms and called by this wonderful name, but what did he possibly have to confess?

"You know, my book? The one you saw just now?"

I nodded, feeling a shiver of apprehension.

"It's about you."

Looking up at George, I thought: But how could that be?

It was very noisy here. All the water sounds – stream, waterfall, ocean – drowned out everything. Dizzy, I leaned against his chest. He wrapped his long arms around me.

Then, very softly, he kissed me.

9

The phone rang just as I dumped the mushrooms into sizzling olive oil in the sauté pan. I looked anxiously at the clock. The stew would take another hour to cook and George was due at seven.

"Dovey?"

I didn't recognize the voice. "Yes?"

"It's Sheila Robbins."

"Oh, hello."

"I'm so sorry there wasn't more time to talk at the party! Did you have a good time?"

Yes, I said, I had.

"Actually, Dovey, one reason I'm calling –"

For a moment her invincible poise seemed to flag.

"Yes?"

"Well, I'm in kind of a bind. We had our 'Words in the Body' workshop scheduled for Noddy Dyer's, and now her teenage son's come down with the measles. I

know this is a lot to ask, but I was wondering if you
might let us hold it at your place. Sally told me what
a lot of room your uncle's house has and I thought
maybe if I twisted your arm a little –"

I was silent a moment. When no good excuse
came to mind, I said, "When?"

"Friday, nine to five. You wouldn't have to fix food or
anything," she added quickly. "That's all taken care of."

"Well – okay."

"*Bless* you," cried Sheila.

Thinking of Peter Chook, I wanted to add,
"No auditors." Instead I asked tamely, "How's the
conference going?"

"Super, Dovey! We're having a panel discussion
down at the community center tonight. Why don't
you come?"

"Oh, no, thank you. I'm busy." As I said it, I
realized it was probably the first time since I came
here that when I said I was already doing something,
I was telling the truth.

"You're a doll!" Sheila hung up.

I turned the burner back on and glanced out the
side window, checking for signs of activity in George's
house. Nothing, as usual. He lived there so lightly it
was impossible to tell when he was home and when he
wasn't. The Volkswagen station wagon's presence was
misleading, I now realized, because it seemed he often
took very long walks up on the mesa.

After the waterfall it was settled very quickly
that George would be coming over for dinner tonight
and then – my stomach did a flip-flop of fear and
excitement. I was pretty sure, after all the fantasizing,

that I was delighted, but how had it happened so fast? That had been my problem in college, too, of course – I put up an impenetrable shield around myself that kept men away, but all it took was an accident, a touch, a chance remark, to collapse the whole house of cards and send me hurtling down the path of blind submission – especially if I'd managed to cook up a crush ahead of time. It was so damn easy to have me, I thought in disgust, nobody realized quite how easy. It was as if once a man, any man, took the incredible trouble to get right up next to me, I lost my power to say yes or no. He was simply there and that meant I had to surrender. And surrender I had, once or twice, to some pretty unsavory fellows. Now, even as I'd been dreaming about it, George had gotten up next to me. The moment had happened and here we were.

To make matters worse, Sally Finch had been out in front watering her hydrangeas when we drove back from Point Reyes in George's car. As I passed her on my way to my own back door, she had given me a happy, conspiratorial wink, clearly delighted from the bottom of her good-natured soul that George and I were "getting acquainted." And, I had no doubt, she would give her wholehearted approval to tonight's interaction on the grounds that at last I would have a real boyfriend, not some young punk but a solid, older fellow like George, just the type for a serious young person like me.

Part of me – the same part, I realized with an odd start, that wanted me to be studying German and Latin every day – agreed with Sally. Sex would be good for me. It was physically hygienic, it cut down on the isolation, and it would prove, finally, that I was a real, live, hundred-percent female, not some nebulous entity floating over, around, off to one side of the rest of the world.

So I tried to put a cheerful face on it and look forward to the evening. I wasn't at all frightened, not the way trivial things like meeting new people or walking in the eucalyptus grove behind the house frightened me. Even though I couldn't quite connect my tangled feelings about George with the strange moments of anticipatory bliss that had fallen on me at the start of our hike and at other times during the summer, it did seem nice that this incredibly attractive man, a man everyone noticed, was so keen on me.

I took a bath, changed the sheets on the big bed, and set the kitchen table while the stew meat was in the oven. I was adding the mushrooms to the somewhat dried-out result when George knocked on the back door. He had changed his clothes, too. His hair was wet from the shower; feathery tufts curled up on his forehead. As he sat down at the table and looked around, he seemed his same old curious self, asking me questions about this or that feature of the kitchen, all very bland and impersonal. We both acted as if nothing was about to happen, but the air was heavily charged. Without much ceremony I opened the bottle of cheap red wine he had brought and plunked down his dinner in front of him.

George started eating even before I sat down, spearing big hunks of meat with his fork and gulping them down without, it seemed, even bothering to chew them. "Good," he grunted with his mouth full.

"I forgot to ask if you were vegan."

The response was muffled. "Unh-uh."

The kitchen window framed a nail clipping of red sky, all you ever saw of the coastal sunset over the tree cover in our little hollow. Some of this reflected glow fell on George's wet black hair and clean workshirt as he kept forking the tough stew meat into his mouth and for a moment he was all lit up in radiance. I barely touched my food.

George pushed his bowl away and wiped his mouth on a napkin. He gave me that sharp, direct look with those big gold-flecked eyes, then became ingenuous George again. "How many famous poets do you suppose are in Bolinas right now?"

I was still reacting to his look, which had either thrilled or chilled me, I wasn't sure which. "You mean for the conference?"

"Think of all of them sitting down to write a poem this very minute!"

I thought of Peter. "Sitting down to get good and drunk, you mean."

"You know what I mean. Just imagine all the creative energy concentrated in this one little area of Northern California. It's really exciting, isn't it? Maybe I should try to write poetry after I finish this book. Peter thinks I should."

Now that everything George said seemed terribly special to me, I focused all the mental powers I could muster on his dilemma. Finally I said, "Isn't writing poetry a pretty specialized skill, like brain surgery or pole vaulting? You don't just take it up like a hobby. You have to practice your whole life to be able to really do it."

"Naw, you just spill it out straight from the gut," said George. "Peter says that's the real poetry. You don't need a lot of elite rules and things if you're in touch with your true center."

I wished he wouldn't keep bringing up Peter, but in the grip of my crush – it was part of that whole process of giving in I knew so well and was now in the throes of – I immediately adopted George's point of view. It was true I was elitist, I told myself, that was my trouble. What a lot more fun in life I would have had so far if I'd just stayed in touch with my center, wherever it was. Tonight was the first step in that direction, too, even if it was a bit like those other times in college, the times that never worked out. If George said so, it had to have some merit. Maybe, I even found myself hoping, this theory about poetry was his own idea and not Peter Chook's at all.

I was ambivalent about George, I realized. Here my inner clinician nodded emphatically. That means it's healthy. It's real, not some idealized fantasy. Fear of intimacy always makes a person look for flaws in the love object. True, my real-life therapist Dr. Moseley had never quite said this to me, but it was what I imagined her thinking about me because it was what I thought about myself.

Something continued, in a nagging, subliminal way, to trouble me.

"Your book."

"Yeah?" He looked up brightly.

This had been bothering me ever since the waterfall. "How can it be about me when we only just met?"

"It's because your story is so special to me, Dovey," he said solemnly.

I felt a big letdown. It was the Tragedy, of course. George had heard all about it from others before we'd even talked about it. He was just another stupid crash scene voyeur. There were a lot of them out there, morbidly interested in the spectacle of the orphan freak who'd lost both her parents in such devastating ways. The disappointment on my face must have shown, because he said quickly, "Don't worry, it's never going to be published. That's the whole point."

"The whole point of writing your book is not to publish it?"

"That's exactly why I get to write it," he smiled gently. "Because no one else, especially you, is ever going to read it."

"But –"

Here came another look from those compelling eyes and I forgot I was going to say this made no sense. Why wouldn't I be able to read it?

Now George was asking me what, out of all the books I had ever read, my favorite, *favorite* was.

Frowning with effort, I mentally reviewed titles. Finally I said, "I don't have a favorite." And then: "I've read too many books. Too many!" And to my own amazement I started to cry, not just little tears like on the trail to the waterfall, but loud, uncontrollable sobs.

Even as part of me bore appalled witness to my grief, I half hoped George might try to comfort me – was that why I did it?

He reached up and pulled me down on his lap. His wiry beard brushed my face.

In a steadier voice I repeated, "I don't have a favorite."

He kissed me gently. Then he drew back and smiled.

Now, I thought, George is going to ask me why I got so upset. Instead he said, "*My* favorite book is *The Prophet*, by Kahlil Gibran. Have you ever read that one?"

A little flabbergasted, I shook my head.

"'For life goes not backward nor tarries with yesterday'? You never heard that?"

"No." As a matter of fact, an aunt of mine on my father's side had owned that book; I remembered seeing it on her coffee table. Behind my aunt's back my cultivated mother, of course, made cruel fun of this work of "Oriental wisdom." In a flash I pounced on myself for having this thought: That's the way you are, always judging, always critical. Here's a guy who likes something mostly women read. Doesn't that show at least that he's sensitive? Besides, the voice went on – now it held a new, faintly threatening note – it'd better be all right because you don't have a choice. You're his.

I was his. Somehow this truth surfaced fully grown in my heart just as George hoisted me into a more comfortable position on his lap. I looked down, embarrassed to meet his eyes. "What are these?" I said, touching the two lumps on either side of his shoulder blades that protruded faintly through his shirt.

George laughed. "Bunions."

"Bunions?"

"Work-related calluses."

I tried to imagine what kind of work this could be. Lifting barrels? Yoga instruction involving frequent shoulder stands? And how did managing family holdings factor in?

He was touching my hair, first patting it absentmindedly, then stroking it more insistently, then patting it again. His thoughts seemed temporarily elsewhere. He started to say something, then stopped. He smiled and kissed me, then murmured, "Let's go in the other room." I got out of his lap and stood beside him. He rose from the chair and led me into my aunt and uncle's bedroom.

Because of my aunt's bad back they had a king-size bed, one of those super-deluxe Posturepedic models that must have cost a fortune, covered by about an acre of white chintz. I had debated about leaving this awful bedspread off when I made up the bed, but decided that would be too obvious. Now I pulled it down. George began taking off his clothes and I took off mine. He said, "Isn't this wonderful, Dovey? You and me?" It was the right thing to say. Although that first look was almost too intense, now he seemed so welcoming, so beautiful.

We entered the enormous bed from opposite sides, under the blankets – it was always freezing in the bedroom – and George took me in his arms. At first it felt very good but after a while I stopped feeling anything. George put in a certain amount of time and attention trying to correct that, but it didn't help. I had had the same problem with the guys, men, whatever they were – my classmates – all those fellows I couldn't say no to after my boyfriend Nick and I broke up and were just friends. I never had any problem about it with Nick, but he and I had always been just like friends anyway. We liked going to the same movies and hiking and it was all pretty natural and everyday, not romantic at all, not like those novels I read furtively all along, wondering what I was missing. Theoretically at least, my current situation

– going to bed with a handsome mysterious stranger –
was very romantic, so what was the matter with me?

George's whole body fluttered and shook. Low
cooing noises issued from his mouth. Finally he rolled
off, sweating and satisfied.

I felt a little depressed, lying there in the darkness
next to him. I thought it would make me feel more
"real," but this had felt less real (and less fun, in a way)
than reading *The Secret of Rowena Manor*, which, silent
witness to all it chastely banned from its own pages,
lay directly beneath us this very moment, under the
bed where I had hastily kicked it while cleaning up
the bedroom this afternoon.

He pulled me over on top of him. "Next time," he said.
"Next time you'll make it." We lay there a few minutes until
I realized that next time meant now, and the whole process
started up again. Unfortunately, for some reason I felt even
farther away from it this time than before, and we ended up
the same, with George shaking and flapping in that peculiar
way and then the two of us lying breathlessly side by side.
Besides feeling frustrated, I was beginning to be a little sore.
Unfazed, George lay back, hands crossed under his head.
Neither of us said a word. All I could think of, stupidly,
was: I'm George's now, I'm his.

"But you're not *really* mine," said George, "until
– you know."

My heart gave a terrible jump. "I was just thinking
that."

"You deserve to feel everything I do, Dovey." He
reached over for me. "Let's give it another try."

I was starting to make a weak protest when the
window above the bed glowed amber. Voices, the sound

of a running car engine, came from outside. George leaned over me and lifted up the curtain.

"What is it?"

"Somebody at my house. I'd better go see." He got out of bed, pulled up his jeans in the dark and left the bedroom. I rolled over to the window and peeked out. A blue taxi labeled "Muir Woods Tours" was pulled up in front of George's. People were talking, but I couldn't see them. First a deep voice disputed with a high one. Then George's voice joined the exchange. After a few moments, the taxi pulled away, revealing a large shambling form I instantly recognized. Dismayed, I let the curtain drop.

About an hour later George was back. I was still wide awake. "Sorry," he said. "It was Peter. He didn't have enough money for the cab."

"What does he want, in the middle of the night?"

"They kicked him out of his room down at Smiley's. He wants to stay with me."

I was silent a moment. "Are you going to let him?"

"He's out of money. He hasn't got anywhere to go."

To counteract my immediate reaction, the lecturing part of me said: See how compassionate George is? To him I said, "You're giving him your bedroom?"

"I don't use it much anyway."

"Where do you sleep?"

"Out in the garage. I fixed it up."

"Does he know you're over here?"

"He's passed out now." George began moving his hands up and down my back. "C'mon," he whispered.

"I don't think I can."

But George would not take no for an answer.

99

10

"George!" Somewhere between a bellow and a whimper, the hateful voice violated my sleep the next morning. "*George!*" It came from outside. "Hey, man!"

Lying several yards from me on the far side of the Posturepedic, George opened his eyes. "Gotta go," he said wearily and climbed out of bed. In the pale light of day I watched him put on his clothes. His flesh looked used, like an old man's. Liver spots mottled his pale skin. Those strange lumps on his back were haloed with fine brown hair. Once again it struck me how different in color and texture his body hair was from his salt-and-pepper beard. Was it something genetic, like having one blue eye and one brown eye?

George left the room without looking back. "Oh," the voice exclaimed with heavy irony as he came out my front door. "*Oh*."

Two pairs of footsteps retreated in the direction of George's house. A door slammed.

I rolled on my back and stared at the ceiling. I felt achy, exhausted. My private parts were swollen and uncomfortable. And even though my most pressing desire was to get up and pee, I was unable to move. Sore as I was, I wanted George right back there with me – *this* time it would be different – but he had just left me for the company of a middle-aged drunk of his own sex.

I hauled myself across the bedroom into the chrome universe of my aunt's overly remodeled bathroom. Turning on the light switch triggered a great deal of alarming activity: the overhead light and the big vanity bulbs lining the mirror leaped on, a circulator fan whirred at a deafening volume. One look in the mirror and I stepped back in horror. Who was this unnaturally bright-eyed creature, features cast in a faint aura of corruption? The next minute she turned into me. I gave the strange face a few brisk splashes and turned on the shower.

Under the stinging pellets I tried to consider my situation, but that was already a lost cause. The thing in me that panted, George, George! drowned out all the other voices. And there he was right next door, hobnobbing with that disgusting derelict. I couldn't, mustn't, go over. I must just sit quietly and wait. Wait till George got rid of his guest and – I hoped – came back to me.

I got dressed and went into the kitchen where, tensely poised, I sat sipping coffee. Every noise from outside had to be instantly processed: did it, or did it not, have to do with George? With great difficulty I resisted the temptation to sit in the living room, which had a clear view of next door. Though I could see everything from there, I could also be seen, and that, according to the protocol of female waiting, was not desirable. Besides, I felt sure they were sitting in George's little kitchen, so why not sit in my kitchen too?

Forty-seven minutes passed in this manner. Desperate, I returned to the bedroom and fished under the bed. Paperback clamped safely in my paw, I climbed back under the covers with all my clothes on. Right away that made everything better. I opened my Bible of Love to the place I had left off at a few days before – all too close, alas, to the end. With a feeling of impatience I reread the scene with the kiss. Ordinarily all this was mother's milk to me. But real life had imparted a flat and bitter flavor to these pages, like a drink of grapefruit juice after brushing your teeth. It was very hard for me to picture George in Randolph's role, even though the heroine, at least in her inner feelings, fit me well enough. The main point was always that this very bad man who was so sexually exciting had to turn into a very good man *after*, not before, he kissed the heroine – otherwise the kiss wouldn't sufficiently titillate.

Well, I had had my kiss and a good deal more. So why, now, wasn't I as happy as darling Cathy? Like Randolph, George was passionate and persistent. And I suppose you would have to say attentive to my needs. Unlike Randolph, he was the opposite of Satanic and sinister. But in spite of his bland personality, his handyman skills, and his demonstrated generosity toward the down and out, the air around George did not look quite right. His sturdy body did not quite mesh with his Georgeness, and sometimes it seemed to shake like a badly built lean-to.

A blank slate. But George's book was not blank. I thought of him writing about me in that weird chicken-scratch script. It was creepy, the kind of thing obsessed loners did. But the truth was, on a minute-by-minute basis he didn't seem that obsessed with me at all; if anything, it was the other way around. I was displaying untypical behavior, too. All the men I had ever been obsessed with I was in the habit of engaging in long imaginary interior conversations. I felt them watching my every act, approving or disapproving, commenting on this or that. But with George's advent, a deep, echoless silence – like the silence that had fallen in the stand of trees on the trail when George and I had walked into it, like the silence in that sage bush on Highway 1 – yawned inside me. Around George I felt in the presence of – nothing.

You repressed little bookworm, that inner voice scolded me. This is what you were waiting for, but you'd rather be off diddling yourself and reading romances. Give life a chance, Dovey! Put that trashy novel away. Open up to this man. Finally you've got something real, not make-believe.

I stuck *The Secret of Rowena Manor* back under the bed, though I might just as well have thrown it away; once you read the scene with the kiss a few times, you were through with the book and never wanted to look at it again unless it was really well written and you could forget enough of how they got to the kiss to go through the whole interminable buildup again.

Since the situation next door was clearly hopeless for the next few hours, it was time I got hold of myself and did something else. Like get out of the house. Reluctantly I climbed out of bed again. A few minutes later I was pulling the Bel Air out of the driveway, headed for town.

As I walked up the Bolinas bakery steps, someone called my name. Sheila and Rob and a third person with his back to me were sitting at a picnic table outside the little cafe next door. Sheila beckoned me and I walked over.

"Dovey, have you met Bill Grebe?"

The poet William Grebe looked to be in his fifties. He had thinning grey hair around his ears. Behind wire-rimmed glasses his sharp blue eyes peered up at me and nodded briefly.

"We're taking Bill up to Hawk Hill after brunch," said Sheila. "Want to come along?"

I hesitated. All I wanted was to be with George, but I couldn't bear the prospect of going back to more sitting and waiting. Home, in short, was no longer my sanctuary from the world but another place where too many things were happening, to be avoided until I had some time to myself to sort things out a bit.

I gave a reluctant bob of my head.

"Great," Sheila beamed.

A thought struck me. "We could go in my aunt and uncle's car. It's really big and roomy."

"That'd be a lot better," Rob said at once. "Thanks, Dovey."

I blushed. A warm feeling of usefulness, a sensation I did not often experience, washed over me.

Next to me Bill Grebe was cutting his omelet in little pieces with a knife and fork. He ate with precise, finicky movements. The convict look of jeans, denim jacket, and white T-shirt seemed totally at odds with the extreme sensitivity this middle-aged man radiated. He seemed very austere and self-contained and I wondered if he was gay. Whatever he was, you did sense that, physically, Bill Grebe did not very much care for young women or, if he did, had long ago given up trying to do anything about it. This gave him an aura of safety that was very appealing – to a young woman like me, anyway.

"You don't write poetry, I hope?" he asked after he had finished his toast.

"No," I said.

"Good."

Rob laughed. "Did you think she was going to try to pick your brain on the way up? Network your connections?"

"You never know. No offense," he mumbled to me without looking up. I did not feel at all offended, but the opposite. I thought Bill Grebe was very nice.

"Dovey's letting us use her house for Words in the Body," Sheila interposed, trying to repair a social rift that had not occurred. Bill Grebe politely inclined his head. "He and Jimmy are giving it jointly," she explained to me. "One after the other," Bill Grebe corrected.

When we finished Rob picked up the tab, including my coffee and orange juice. I wondered if he would write it off on his taxes. I knew he was a poet, too, and put out some kind of small literary journal, but somehow Sheila had the stronger, more social personality and I only knew Rob – the times I went in the food co-op to pick up some flour or beans or carrot juice – as an auburn-haired man of few words who was always checking to make sure the Tofutti machine was properly turned off.

Nobody said much as we strolled lazily down the sunny street to my uncle's car. I opened the front door of the Bel Air. Bill Grebe got in on the passenger side, Sheila and Rob sat in back. Executing a cumbersome U-turn, I headed us for Highway 1.

When we came to the junction, Rob showed where the local folk always tore down the BOLINAS sign to discourage yuppie tourists as well as crasser types in Winnebagos (though hip Europeans were always tolerated). No road marker to Bolinas ever stayed up more than twenty-four hours, he said proudly. Bill Grebe grunted.

"North is Point Reyes," said Rob as he turned south toward Stinson Beach.

"A place of mysterious incidents. Headless hikers and whatnot."

"Shark attacks are *really* unusual," Sheila said quickly. Like most West Marinites, she was sensitive about the region's downbeat reputation.

"Ah, but you're forgetting this bit of land is the furthest point west in our great country."

"So?" I said.

"So in most western places bordered by an ocean – I'm thinking of Wales, but I'm sure there are others as well – people believe that's where dead souls jump off the cliffs into the water to get to the underworld. Not surprising that unexpected things happen there."

Out of the corner of my eye I could see Sheila and Bob exchange a glance. Though we had never discussed it, I suspected that they, too, were thinking of the Tragedy, especially when Sheila said firmly, "I'm sure I never heard of any story like that around here."

Following a long line of holiday beachgoers hoping for sunshine, we inched south down the winding lagoon road through Stinson Beach.

"We aren't going to see that many birds," Rob was saying. "Southern migration's barely started. The ranger told me the first ospreys got here last week."

"Like me," said Bill Grebe.

"Where are you from?" I asked.

"Jersey." Pronounced with impressive finality.

"These north-south ridges create a natural funnel," Rob soldiered on. "The birds fly the following winds. Sometimes they get lost in the fog."

We drove through forested uplands of fir, live oak and laurel onto the narrow spine of the ridge that led directly to Hawk Hill. I had to keep dodging helmeted bicyclists in the new style of shiny skintight black shorts and garish yellow shirts; there was not enough room for them and the Bel Air on the narrow road at the same time. I always thought those racing shorts were hideously ugly, and said so. Bill Grebe gave me a look that might have indicated guarded approval.

Suddenly we entered a dense fog that swallowed the trees right up to their bristly tips. In the midst of the swirling greyness – for it had also gotten very windy – bare brown hilltops flashed in and out of sight. It made me think of the "stinking fogges" Sir Francis Drake complained of in his ship's log as he hugged the Point Reyes coastline some four hundred odd summers earlier. I was about to mention this when Bill Grebe spoke up.

"How can one place be so wet and so dry at the same time?" His voice was full of irritation. "I wake up every morning doubled over with arthritis. Then I look at my skin and it's shriveled up like an old fencepost. Yesterday I got a nosebleed."

"I'll lend you our humidifier," Sheila offered promptly.

"Humidifier?" He waved his hand angrily at the fog, which was now so thick I had turned on the headlights and the car heater. "Are you trying to kill me?"

"Maybe we'll see a golden eagle," Rob said, trying to steer the conversation in another direction.

"The only way we'll see anything," Bill Grebe retorted, "is if it gets on the road two feet in front of us. So I think I'd rather *not* see a golden eagle, thanks just the same. All this is much more Harrier's thing, you know," he added gently. "You should have brought him on this outing, not me."

There was a little silence that I interpreted as meaning that the Robbinses had indeed asked James Harrier first, and he had declined, and that was why Bill Grebe was sitting beside me this very minute.

A small smile curved Bill Grebe's lips. "Eagles, oh my yes, Jimmy would whip you off a roundel in a nanosecond. Nature's a red herring for him, of course. Just like the amours."

When neither Robbins responded, I said, "What do you mean?"

"Jimmy would be a better poet if he wrote about the things that really bother him. He got locked into a successful public persona too soon. Now he's embarrassed to write about the awful stuff, so out comes *Field and Stream*. And the Casanova drivel."

"What awful stuff?" Sheila was eager to know.

"The awful stuff we all have inside us. Different for each person, of course."

"Case specific?" I offered.

Another tiny smile. "Yes."

I pulled into the paved lot on the edge of a steep cliff. To our right loomed the giant orange superstructure of the Golden Gate Bridge. Beyond it San Francisco was completely swallowed in mist. I shut off the engine and we all looked at each other.

"Well, Bill?" said Rob. "Up for a little walk?"

"I can see there's no escape." Bill Grebe made no move to get out. We all flinched as a blast of cold wind struck the Bel Air broadside and rocked the big car. Finally Rob opened his door and the rest of us reluctantly followed suit. Heads bent against the gale, we walked up a narrow road chained off to cars. Every thirty seconds the foghorns on the bay wailed through the mist.

Sheila and Rob forged ahead as Bill Grebe and I lagged at the rear, peering over the cliffs dotted with brilliant purple iceplant. Large black boulders rimmed in white and linked by frothy cobwebs of surf jutted up out of the ocean. Other rocks were darkly visible beneath the surface.

"There's a sea lion." I pointed at a bullet-shaped head poking out from under a wave. Bill Grebe made an involuntary exclamation. "Christ, it looks human!"

From a deep trough of water something that did uncannily resemble a person's face stared up at us. Then it sprouted black and white wings and flapped away low over the water.

"It *looked* like a sea lion," I said defensively.

"What a lumbering flight it has," he said thoughtfully. "Yet that's surely a hawk of some sort. Don't ask me which, please."

We had caught up with Sheila and Rob at the top of Hawk Hill, a bare little dome surrounded by a sea of boiling mist. "Such a shame there's so much fog," Sheila said. Bill wrapped his jeans jacket tightly around his thin frame and crossed his arms. "How long do we have to stay here?"

"We can go back right now if you want," Rob said gamely.

"We hoped we could see the Farallones," Sheila put in. "But there's no chance today, I'm afraid."

The Farallones made me think of George and suddenly I was dying to be home at my self-appointed post. "I really should be getting back," I said.

"Well, then, let's go." Sheila sounded relieved and disappointed at the same time. But just as we turned to walk down the hill, the wind shifted and the mist thinned. A burst of sunlight revealed the great white city on one side of the colossal bridge, the sparkling ocean on the other, and the Farallones set like little craggy jewels on the horizon, all of it spread out before us in a glittering panorama. The vision stopped us in our tracks.

"Last but not least –" Rob pointed upward, where at least fifteen large birds were now visible riding the thermal updrafts. "The hawks of Hawk Hill!"

"I can't resist," Bill Grebe said. He cleared his throat and recited:

"Saynt Valentyn, that art ful hy on-lofte,
Thus syngen smale foules for thy sake:
'Now welcome, somer, with thy sonne softe,
That has this wintres wedres overshake.'"

I spotted Chaucer, but Sheila put her finger thoughtfully to her head. "Don't tell me, let me guess." Then, after a moment, "I give up."

"You don't know what that's from?" He sounded incredulous. "Funny, when I got your invitation I was sure you did. Main reason I accepted."

A rare note of annoyance entered Sheila's voice. "I have no idea what you're talking about."

"It's a very old poem about some birds who come to a conference just like yours."

"Aren't you going to tell us the title?" she asked with strained playfulness.

Bill Grebe sighed. "They don't seem to teach anything before Shakespeare anymore. Pity."

The mist had risen again and the vista evaporated as quickly as it had come, along with our sudden collective good mood. Without another word the four of us turned and trooped down the trail to the car. Just as we reached the road Bill Grebe said sharply: "Look! That's a hawk."

A big bird with a coal-black breast was perched, alarmingly still, in a scraggly wind-twisted pine next to the Bel Air. Reddish feathers mantled its stumpy legs. Rubbery yellow feet ended in outsized talons that firmly grasped a thick branch. Its round eyes were fixed on us.

"I tread her wrist and wear the hood, talking to myself, and would draw blood." Seeing my blank face, Bill Grebe added, "Robert Duncan, you ignorant thing." Almost perfunctorily, he went on:

"She would bring down the little birds.
And I would bring down the little birds.
When will she let me bring down the little birds,
pierced from their flight with their necks broken,
their heads like flowers limp from the stem?"

After a moment I said, "Golly."

"Golly is right, young lady."

The hawk stayed where he was, his unblinking eyes regarding us. Bill Grebe turned away; I could see the bird made him uneasy. "There's an old tradition that all birds are *angelos*," he muttered.

"Angels?"

"Messengers. The Greek word. They come bearing tidings from the other world."

"What other world?"

"Oh, the land of the dead, the otherworld, the world of true forms," he said airily. "Whatever. Fact is, we're all angelos, we just don't know it."

"We're messengers? What do you mean?"

"I mean, we all come into this world trailing clouds of glory, flapping our beautiful wings and clutching a message in our claws. But we forget the message, just like we forget the place we came from and go back to."

I pointed at the hawk. "What's *his* message?"

"To know that, my dear, you must understand the language of the birds."

"The language of the birds?"

"It's what they speak in that other world. It's what Adam and Eve spoke, before the Fall. Ditto St. Francis. Ditto all those people back when the line between human and animal, natural and supernatural, wasn't so clear. The language of the birds is the primal language. It's the language of deep reality."

The scratchings in George's book – *my* book, I corrected with a shiver – came irresistibly to mind. "Is the language of the birds something we could learn now?"

Bill Grebe laughed. "Anyone who claims to understand the birds these days is just plain cuckoo."

Before I could find out more on this vital topic, Sheila and Bob walked up, voices raised. With a loud flap of its black and white wings, the hawk leaped out of the tree. Soon it was a dot among all the other dots hovering over the hillside.

We made our way single file down the narrow trail toward the parking lot.

"Wait a sec." Bill Grebe walked to the low fence on the cliff's edge. "One last look."

Following him over to the rail, I didn't see what slashed down from the sky as he leaned over until it was right on top of him. Whap! Claws extended, the big bird landed full force on the poet's bald head.

Bill Grebe screamed loudly. Then he stumbled and pitched half over the fence. I grabbed the collar of his jeans jacket from the back as the hawk streaked skyward again. Now he was dangling, head down and choking, 150 feet above the jagged rocks sticking up from the ocean. I was slip-sliding after him, losing my grip on his collar. Behind me Sheila was screaming. Then Rob was there and together we hauled the poet back over the little fence to safety.

A small crowd gathered around us as Bill Grebe sat on the dirt trail panting for breath. Blood trickled down his forehead from the gashes on his head. Sheila was crying, "Oh God, oh God," when a ranger came up.

Sheila pointed at the sky. "That bird attacked him!"

"Quite a large hawk," Rob added.

The ranger squinted up into the grey. It was impossible to distinguish the culprit in the crowds of hawks wheeling and turning overhead. "Really unusual behavior," he commented. Then he turned to Bill Grebe, who was patting his bleeding head with a worn white handkerchief, staining it red. "Are you okay?"

"Yes, thank you." He put the handkerchief away and got to his feet. Rob tried to take his elbow. "No need, I'm all right." Bill Grebe said it in a calm voice rather than a cranky one.

The ranger was taking down his name and home address. "You need to get those cuts looked at."

"There's a first aid kit in my uncle's car," I said. I knew exactly where it was, next to the flares and "Get Help" sign he kept stowed in the trunk.

"Put some disinfectant on it right now," said the ranger. "Then go to the doctor. I'll file a report. Sorry about that."

In the parking lot I retrieved the first aid kit from the trunk, but the wind was so cold we all got in the

Bel Air immediately – though not before Bill Grebe
cocked a wary eye skyward as he closed the door
on the front passenger side. "Very Hitchcockian,
no?" he laughed. The Robbinses, rather uneasily,
laughed, too.

Inclining his head toward me, Bill Grebe winced
as I dabbed hydrogen peroxide on the triangular black
tracks crisscrossing his pink dome. They triggered a
stray link in my mind to something, I couldn't say what.

"Do hawks carry rabies?" he asked.

"I don't think so," Rob said from the back, "but
let's get you to the emergency room right away."

"Not necessary," Bill Grebe said, straightening
up. "I don't need stitches. There's some Bacitracin in
my suitcase."

No one tried to argue. As I started the car, I stole
a glance at him. Had a brush with death unexpectedly
mellowed his irascible disposition?

I turned the heater up high and Pureed the Bel Air
out of the parking lot onto the road. In markedly high
spirits now, Bill Grebe began telling us stories about
other poets – who said what to whom, who made an
ass of himself or herself, who slept with whom. Sheila,
I could tell, was committing every word to memory.
Now she was getting the real stuff (as opposed, I
reminded myself, to the awful stuff) and could forget
all the grumbling and bad temper before, though in
time that, too, would become legend: "Remember,
honey, when we took Bill Grebe to Hawk Hill and
the bird attacked him and he nearly fell off the cliff
and then told us all those funny stories – what was it
he said about X?"

Then, with no prompting, Bill Grebe began saying out poetry by heart. He seemed to know an endless amount of it, crowd-pleasing stuff, and not one word was his own, I was pleased to note. He recited "As I Walked Out One Evening," by W. H. Auden, Sir Walter Raleigh's "The Nymph Replies to the Shepherd," and Wallace Stevens's "The Emperor of Ice Cream" as we drove out of the fog into mottled sunshine.

"'O Rose, thou art sick,'" I prompted as I turned off the highway onto the Bolinas road.

"'The Sick Rose' by William Blake it is," he said.

"O rose, thou art sick!
The invisible worm
That flies in the night,
in the howling storm,

Has found out thy bed
Of crimson joy,
And his dark secret love
Does thy life destroy."

There was a little silence. "Thank you," I said. I wasn't sure why I had asked for that one. I didn't know much poetry, old or new, only the pieces we had to read in school. Listening to Bill Grebe now, I began to have a sense of what I might have missed. Something lay just out of reach under every line, something none of the novels or books of criticism I compulsively read possessed. For the first time I could remember, I did not feel superior but rather what I knew in my heart I really was – an awkward, untutored girl. I wanted Bill

Grebe to tell me more about the poem. But I couldn't just ask naively, "What does it mean?" because, for all that he was in a good mood and I had just saved his life, he would surely sneer at me.

"About the Blake —" I began just the same, but by now we were back on Wharf Road. Rob leaned forward from the back seat. "You can let us out here."

I stopped the Bel Air in the middle of the street and left the motor running as they clambered out. Pressing his hands together, Bill Grebe gave me a grave little Buddhist salute. "Young lady, I owe you."

Sheila came up to the driver's side and whispered in my ear, "My God, what an afternoon. You saved the day, Dovey!"

The three of them climbed into a little white Datsun and drove off.

I let the Bel Air pulse a little longer in the middle of Wharf Road. The adventure was over, I was back in my life again. For a split second, as its big chassis rocked me gently in place like a cradle, I wished mightily to be going anyplace but where I was bound. Then I put it in gear. "Blend," I commanded, and headed home.

11

The phone was ringing as I walked in the kitchen door.

George's voice came through bright as a shiny copper penny. "Want to come over for dinner?"

I looked out the window at the kitchen next door. He must have seen me drive up. The curtains were open and the bare overhead light bulb glowed in the squalid room. I hesitated. "Is *he* there?"

"Yep. We ordered takeout from Smiley's. I'm just going down to pick it up. Enchiladas. They're good."

I did not see how I could possibly sit through a dinner with Peter Chook, but I couldn't control my urge to be with George. I said, "I'll come over when you get back."

A few minutes later the VW station wagon backed out of George's driveway and headed down the hill. I paced nervously. Fifteen minutes passed, then twenty. Finally headlights reflected off my living room wall and I heard the noisy engine again. I hurried out the front door just as George was getting out of the car.

"Hey." Standing legs akimbo, George held a brown paper bag in one hand and a twelve-pack of Budweiser in the other. Dark spots were already spreading on the bottom of the brown bag. "How was Hawk Hill?"

"How did you know I was there?"

"Didn't you see me? Passed you guys on the road headed that way." He motioned toward the door. "C'mon."

We trooped down the corridor to the rear of the house, where my rival, the fat, chain-smoking puff-toad, sat enthroned on a wooden chair shoved against the kitchen wall. He looked no more pleased to see me than I was to see him. Peter's spiky, unwashed hair stood up like a grey halo around his head; his skin had the unhealthy cast of a dead cod. Having this *thing* – I still couldn't bear to think of Peter as a fellow human – look straight at me still filled me with superstitious dread. I barely managed to dodge the hideous leer he shot in my direction before he turned back to George. "Got the beer?"

My neighbor set the twelve-pack on the table and his guest plucked off a can like a ripe peach. "You're not seeing me at my best," he confided after he had drained it in a series of long, urgent gulps. "Hell of a trip getting out here on the Greyhound. *Hell* of a trip. But just wait till I get settled in. Basically I'm an up-at-seven, black coffee, work-all-day kind of guy." He reached for another can.

I made an effort to put a good face on it. "Want a glass for that?"

"Don't mother me," he snapped. Only George, I understood, got to play that role in his life. George had become his total, urgent focus of concentration. As he was mine.

I took a plate out of the cabinet and laid out the enchiladas. The warm, greasy stuffed tortillas were covered with tomato sauce and black olives. I licked a finger. Not bad. I set three more plates on the table and rummaged in the dirty counter drawer for some forks. "Do you have any napkins?" I asked George.

Peter snorted. "And don't forget the fingerbowls."

"How about paper towels?"

"Have a beer, pal," said Peter.

"Just water for me, thanks. Dovey?"

"Water."

As soon as we sat down, Peter began rocking and keening. Suddenly he jerked his head upright like a puppet brought to life. Grabbing my hand and George's, he bellowed at the ceiling, "Give thanks! Let's give thanks! Great Powers of the unseen world, we rejoice in thy bounty! Amen."

Once the blessing was over, Peter didn't release our hands. Coyly he mimed the attitude of one lost in thought. Then he turned to George. "Thank you for your naivete," he said.

Now the moment I had dreaded was here. Slowly the great head swiveled in my direction, the two dead eyes met mine. "Thank you for your fear of life."

Silence fell as George and I digested our character analyses. Peter Chook still held our hands clamped in his big damp paws. He pretended not to notice when I wriggled mine free. Instead he leaned back and shut his eyes. "This is a special place on the earth," he said. I thought so too, but didn't like hearing it from him. "Spirits, what's going on in Bolinas?" A portentous silence, then his huge body gave a galvanic heave. "Something big, folks." He paused. "Crimes. I'm getting crimes."

George leaned forward. "Wow! What kind of crimes? Everybody's talking about this missing hiker."

"That was a shark attack," I pointed out. *The Chronicle* had printed the coroner's conclusion a day or two before.

"Hush!" Peter frowned in concentration. "I'm getting a speeding ticket and something else. Some other violation. Can't quite make it out, but it's a biggie." His little eyes popped open and he shook his shaggy head. "Whew, the spirits sure are in a bureaucratic mode. A *speeding* ticket, for God's sake. How frigging trivial can you get?"

He stopped abruptly and turned to me. "You're afraid. Don't be afraid."

Peter was wrong. I wasn't afraid of him, I realized. What frightened me was the deep smoldering rage he triggered in me. Thinking *Filthy drunk!* I picked up my fork, cut off a slice of enchilada and washed it down with a swallow of the tepid tap water George had put before me. George ate with his usual speed, tearing off big bites and gulping them whole. "This is great," he said between mouthfuls.

Meanwhile a storm was brewing in Peter's corner. His eyes shuttled between us. The fact that our attention was fixed on our plates instead of him was causing him unhappiness.

For a moment I caught another whiff of the smoke, so to speak, rising from the mysterious bonfire kindled deep inside me. When I opened my mouth to speak, Peter pounced. "Be quiet! You'll disturb the atmosphere."

"Be quiet yourself." Seeking support, I looked over at George, who said blandly, "Now, Peter."

"That constipated kid."

"And you've got diarrhea." I had never talked to anyone this way before. Usually if I didn't like someone I simply withdrew to that place inside myself where I had lived out my life in inviolable privacy for as long as I could remember.

Peter shot George a look that said: See what I mean?

"What about your offering?" George prompted.

"It's hard in this atmosphere . . . with all this negativity. Never mind." Peter sighed deeply and raised his hands. Then he lowered them and turned to George. "This isn't anything Satanic. I'm not into *that* stuff. This is a prayer to the *white* magic forces, all those good spirits who can hear me out there." He raised his hands, then dropped them again.

I picked up my fork. "I'm going to keep on eating, okay?"

Peter looked at me. "As a great man once wrote, selfishness is shelfishness." Then he shut his eyes and crooned: "Spirits everywhere, all you flying souls, light down! Enter our hearts tonight, this special night, and tell us your secrets!"

He blinked once, opened his eyes and finished off the Bud. "This will all be meaningless to *you*," he said to me as his fat paw groped for another can. By this time he was eating, too, and the next words came out muffled in tortilla. "*You're* not part of what's going on here."

"Yes, she is," George said unexpectedly and I felt a ridiculous burst of gratitude. "Any more?" I asked him. I had finished my enchilada but I was still hungry.

"Have the rest of mine." Peter Chook shoved his plate of mashed-up food toward me. "Don't be uptight, take it."

I looked at it and turned to George. "Mind if I raid your refrigerator?"

He hesitated. "I moved the fridge into the garage. The door's a little hard to open and shut. I can tell you what I have in there and get it for you. Yogurt. Pickled herring. Applesauce."

Now that I had seen the book, I didn't get why George still had to be so possessive of his garage. Peter gave George a dreadful wink that I was meant to see. To me he said, "Isis and Horus," in a stage whisper. Peter, it seemed, was determined to keep rubbing in the fact that he knew something I didn't. I didn't much care what this something was, but just the same I felt unbearably provoked. I sat back feeling very cross. "Yogurt, please." I began to wish very hard I was back in my own house.

George disappeared through the door and shut it firmly behind him. That left me alone with Peter Chook. The silence that followed was broken only when he cleared his throat with dreadful thoroughness.

A few long minutes later, George was back. He closed the door behind him and set a pint of blueberry-flavored yogurt on the table. "This okay?"

"You shouldn't eat that mass-produced stuff with the celluloids in it," Peter said as I took a spoonful. Then, roguishly, to George, "You aren't going to tell her, are you?"

"Tell me what?"

Another one of those big winks. "Sorry, only for the initiated."

"If it's such a big secret, why brag about it? That's no way to keep a secret."

"In African tribes," Peter said pointedly, "the men prohibit the women from watching their dances because they know the woman's mockery profanes the atmosphere and drives away the spirits."

George nodded amiably but didn't answer. Still discovering just how slow his host could be on the uptake, Peter looked over jovially at him. "Let's throw her out, shall we? Eh?"

In a way I saw his point of view – it was exactly how I felt about him – but in spite of my revulsion I folded my arms and stayed right where I was.

Catching my eye, George laughed. Peter grabbed another beer. "Look, man," he hissed, "I don't care if you're fucking this chick – just save the real stuff for you and me."

The way he said the word *fucking* made it sound like an activity he hadn't personally engaged in for quite a while and I was about to point this out when I glanced over at George. His face bore the expression of someone watching a moderately interesting talk show.

"All right, Peter," he said finally. "If it means that much to you, I'll write you into Dovey's book tonight."

Peter, triumphant, stuck out his tongue at me.

Tears of rage stung my eyes. "Filthy, filthy drunk!" I cried. I stood up and stormed out of George's house across the lawn to my aunt and uncle's.

After a few disoriented moments in the kitchen, I poured myself a small finger of my uncle's Wild Turkey and took it to the study. I couldn't stop thinking about Peter. His alcoholism, his pathetic fragile egotism, even his sheer size infuriated me. Such a very big man who was such a very little man.

All of a sudden I found myself thinking how good it would feel to put my hands around that thick, ugly neck and throttle the life out of him.

I shook my head to get rid of this deeply disturbing thought. Sitting down in the big easy chair and taking tiny sips of the Wild Turkey – see, Peter? This is how a person is *supposed* to enjoy alcohol – I calmed myself down. I began to feel mature and superior again. For confirmation I looked over at my father's picture. But only a vast neutrality, a kind of Georgeness, oozed from it.

Another thought came to me and for some reason I rejected it just as fast. Filthy drunk.

I wandered aimlessly into the bedroom. Undressed, got into bed. Picked up *The Secret of Rowena Manor*, then shoved it back under the bed when I remembered I'd already finished it. Would George even come over tonight? Maybe I should leave the back door unlocked, just in case. No, on second thought I wouldn't.

Loud voices rose from next door, then a noise that sounded like a crash. A quarrel? That was too much to hope for. More likely, George was being harangued on some minor issue of spiritual protocol. But surely such a polite, insatiably curious pupil as my neighbor would not be disputing the point back? Unless they were arguing about Peter's right to be in the book. *My* book. I listened hard.

There was another muffled thump. Peter tripping over a twelve-pack, no doubt.

I switched off the light and lay awake, rigid with anger.

12

A heavy object, cold and damp, was pressing down on me. I panicked but couldn't move a muscle. Finally I managed a pitiful croak, the kind of frustrating whimper you give in a nightmare when what you really want to do is let loose with a great full-throated scream.

A laugh in the darkness, then, "Sshh!" It was George.

Heart pounding, I pulled out from under him and switched on the bedtable lamp. George had all his clothes on. Bits of dry leaves clung to his shirt.

"How did you get in?"

"Kitchen door."

"It's locked."

A laugh. "Rock of Gibraltar."

Here was the place to read George the riot act. Reaching inside myself for the same righteous anger I had felt toward Peter, I met the familiar black hole

of my gentle obedience. "Kind of nervy, aren't you?"
I said weakly.

"Do you mind?"

Mind? I realized a little dully that from the black
hole point of view, I didn't have an opinion about
George freely entering my house. I looked up at him.
In the lamplight his placid bearded face held, as always,
no expression other than his unceasing interest in me.

"What's Peter up to?"

"Passed out."

Thanks to my early training, sarcasm was still
available to me. "I feel like he's the wife and I'm
the mistress."

George gave a bark of laughter. "Oh, come on."
He sat up and swung his legs over the side of the
bed to take off his shoes, which he hadn't bothered
to do before.

"So what did you learn at his feet tonight?"

George finished undressing and crawled under the
covers. "We got a lot of stuff settled, I guess."

I felt my lips tighten. "Did you write him into
the book?"

George gave me a beautiful smile. "No."

I was pleased to hear this, but I didn't want to
know the reason for it.

With a questioning look he reached over toward
the bed lamp. I nodded. George switched it off.

Now, in the dark, we were back to the night before
as if nothing had happened in the meantime. I forgot my
anger and all my scruples. Taking the key and walking
right into my house, didn't that show how much he
wanted me? "Oh, George. George!" I cried, hugging

him in relief. He hugged me back just as hard but said nothing and that made me afraid I might have put him off with this sudden display of affection. My emotions were so unpredictable, so little known to me, that I had no idea what shape they were going to take, the present case being a good example. Fury toward Peter, abjection toward George. And if my feelings surprised *me*, I told myself, it was only right to expect they could have had the same effect, if not worse, on other people.

George clearly had his mind on other things, as he was once again intent on arriving at our mutual goal. Once again my own desire dissolved like water. But thanks to his determination, after what felt like a very long time I opened up. I surrendered.

It was a miserable little half-opened bud of pleasure, wrenched out of me in spite of myself. George made a soft chipping noise of approval and rolled off.

My reaction wasn't so positive. I felt tarnished, soiled and strange. Like I was hurtling through a void to an unknown star. Then, just like the heroine in *The Secret of Rowena Manor*, I was possessed again by the seductive notion: I'm his. It was no longer scary, it was thrilling, despite the fact my physical response had been rather puny.

Out of the silence he said, "Now we can go to Mud Lake."

Even a hiking agenda from George failed to mar the bliss of this tender moment.

"What's so special about Mud Lake?"

"I told you. It's my favorite place."

Those everlasting favorites again. But by offering to share this spot with me, wasn't George offering up a bit of himself, too? This indirectness in expressing his feelings almost made me smile in the dark. A typical man. The thought filled me with a fragile joy. Imagine me, Dovey, making such a confident conclusion. And if he was a typical man, then it followed that I was no longer a creature floating off in the wild blue yonder but – a typical woman. How extraordinary, to be ordinary!

"Let's do it tomorrow, okay?"

"Do what?"

"Go to Mud Lake."

"Okay."

But later that night, in the limbo between sleeping and waking, I heard myself say out loud, urgently, "Your book."

"Huh?" George's voice rose immediately from beside me in the bed. He did not sound as if he had been anyway near asleep, either.

"What did you write about me? I want to know."

He leaned over me and switched on the bed lamp. I was fully awake now, and already regretting my words. "You want to know," he repeated. He cleared his throat gravely. "Wanna know right now?" The look he gave me was greedy, intense. "I can go get it." When he saw the naked fear in my eyes, he started to laugh. He cocked his head innocently. "Don't really want me to go get it, do you?"

"No." It was a whisper.

"Don't really want to know, either?"

Down in the black hole I shook my head.

"Then let's get some sleep," George said briskly and turned off the light.

13

Soon his snores rattled the room. It was such a human sound that I relaxed a little. After a while I must have fallen asleep too, because when I opened my eyes it was morning and I'd forgotten all about the book. But my first thought was not a pleasant one. When would Peter start knocking on the door?

I looked over at George, asleep on his back with his mouth hanging slightly open. The sight of him produced a constriction, a little nervous spasm, in my body. I lay back and looked up at the ceiling. Don't worry, I told myself, everything's okay.

Easing gently out of bed, I tiptoed into the kitchen and took the coffeepot out of the dish drainer. Then I glanced out the window and froze.

The driveway was empty.

I was not imagining it, though I wished I were. My car keys lay on the kitchen table where

I had left them the day before, but the Bel Air was gone.

I ran back into the bedroom. "George, George!" His eyes flew wide open like a doll's. He stared at me blankly.

"My uncle's car – it's not there."

He got up, padded naked after me into the kitchen, and peered out the window. "What's that on the driveway?"

"Where?" I couldn't see what he was looking at.

"Some kind of writing. Let me go put my clothes on."

I rushed outside as George went back to the bedroom. My aunt and uncle's driveway was an old-fashioned two-treader with a weedy center divider. On the cracked concrete strip nearest the house two words were scrawled in messy pink block letters: MAL AIR. The MAL was underlined three times.

George came out the kitchen door buttoning his workshirt. He touched the writing with his finger and sniffed. "Lipstick."

"Lipstick?"

"Peter," he said.

I followed George over to his house. He called in the front door, which stood ajar: "Peter?" We went in. All the rooms were empty. From the kitchen, littered with beer cans, George poked his head quickly in and out of the door that led into the garage. When I tried to look in after him, he pushed me back gently. "Not there," he said.

I still couldn't believe it. "How could he take my car without the keys?"

George laughed. "My God, do you know all it takes to start one of those big old American cars? Just stick a quarter in the ignition and turn it on. I said you should keep it locked up, remember? That's how he got in it the first time."

I put my head in my hands. It went without saying that my uncle kept his beloved vehicle locked at all times, even in the safety of his own carport, though it was difficult to imagine him chaining the hood down with a bicycle lock to protect the battery, like some safety-minded people I knew did with their old cars. The Bel Air, so out of place now in Bolinas, was my uncle's most cherished possession; he washed and waxed and detailed it himself in an elaborate ritual he had worked out over the years. And though he was too stubborn to admit it, the truth was that my uncle was just as out of place in Bolinas as his car. In his own youth Marin County had been a summer retreat for the San Francisco and East Bay well-to-do. In the psychedelic sixties, however, Bolinas had gone through a convulsive transformation during which enough pairs of eyes winged out on LSD had stared so long and so intently at the landscape that they had altered it as permanently as their own psyches. No amount of Johnny-come-lately gentrification could eradicate the entrenched counterculture presence he so despised.

Now I, through my own carelessness, had let an alcoholic maniac who, though not a resident, embodied everything about Bolinas my uncle loathed, steal his baby. I had let Peter Chook profane my uncle's beloved car with his dirty drunkard's hands and drive it off into the night, or morning, or whenever it was he had done it. That raised another question. "How could he drive off without waking us up?"

"He put it in neutral," George said promptly, "let it coast down the driveway, then turned on the motor once he got far enough down the road."

I wouldn't have given Peter credit for so much savvy. "What should I do now?" I asked, then answered myself. "Call the sheriff's office and report it missing."

"Want to use this phone?" George pointed to the ancient wall receiver.

"I'd better go back to my house. I have to look up the license number."

We trudged back across the strip of lawn, still soaked with dew. In my mind the questions began. It was only about seven o'clock, and George had come to me in the middle of the night. I wondered when Peter had sneaked out to the car. I wondered if he had watched us through the bedroom window. More questions bubbled up. "Does Peter always carry around tubes of lipstick?"

George looked thoughtful. "He must have got into some of my mother's stuff."

"Your *mother's* stuff?"

"I keep it stored in the garage."

I tried to remember what else I had seen in the garage besides the book and the big packing crate, but too many things were going on, I couldn't concentrate.

"He probably took the car for a liquor run. If you just wait, I bet he'll bring it back. "

"The market closes at seven every night."

"Once you call the sheriff, Dovey, everybody will find out. It'll be a big story. If you wait a day, maybe he'll come back. Then nobody would know it was ever gone."

Thanks mainly to my police phobia, I found this reasoning attractive. My uncle wouldn't have to know, either, as long as the sharp-eyed Finches did not spot Peter Chook going or coming back in the Bel Air. Although the thought of Peter behind bars was very appealing, I would be ridiculously grateful to have the car back and pretend nothing had ever happened. No trials, no testimony, no upsets. And forever after, I promised the gods, I'd lock it up tighter than Fort Knox.

"Go ahead and call the sheriff now if you want to," George said. "In fact, that's probably the smartest thing to do."

We were at the Dutch doors. "No," I said. "Let's see what happens." He followed me into the kitchen. I made a pot of dark French roast in my aunt's Mr. Coffee machine and we sat at the table. George said, "All ready for our hike?"

"Our hike?"

"Mud Lake, remember?"

I stared at him. That was the last thing on my mind. "I don't know, George. This has got me a little upset. I feel like I should be doing something about it."

"Oh, c'mon," he said reproachfully, looking deep into my eyes.

"No, I don't think I'd better."

"Look," he sighed. "There's really nothing you can do about the car right now. We can keep an eye out for Peter on the way to the trail. He might just bring it back this afternoon if he thinks nobody's after him." George stood up. "I'll go get my pack ready."

After he had gone, I sat at the table a while longer, then prowled the house restlessly. Made the bed, washed dishes. Without the Bel Air I felt strangely stripped of power. I refused to consider the possibility that Peter would not return it; the consequences were simply too awful to bear thinking about. What I hadn't expected was how much I missed the old dinosaur, how naked I felt without it. It was as if that car had been a kind of magic chariot that shielded me from harm, family protection operating on a level I had never been consciously aware of even as I enjoyed its sheltering power. My amulet. Nor had I been aware, as mutually alien to each other as we were on the surface of life, of how much it linked me with my aunt and uncle, of how much hidden energy passed back and forth between people linked by blood and so little else.

A search in my uncle's filing cabinet uncovered the Bel Air's car registration and another poignant document: the original 1964 owner's manual, in mint condition. I took it into the kitchen and sat down to read it. On the front cover was an airbrush drawing of a Platonic ideal Bel Air ringed by a smiling four-headed Platonic ideal family. Tears rose in my eyes, whether for my relatives or myself or the poor old Bel Air I couldn't say, it was all so mixed up inside me.

George's big head surfaced abruptly over the Dutch door. He held his arm up and pointed at his watch. "We should get going."

"I'm coming," I said, but George was already gone.

I started to get up and suddenly found myself on a planet with heavier gravity. My body felt leaden, rooted to the chair. I sat back and took a breath. I didn't want to go to Mud Lake, it seemed. Then, with an effort, I hauled myself up. Instead of going out the door I picked up the phone and dialed. "Hello, is that Rob? Yes, it's Dovey. Is Sheila there? Oh, nothing. Just tell her we're still on for Friday. Thanks."

I hung up. What had given me this need to make contact with someone, anyone? I thought wistfully about calling Nick in Montana, but I had no idea of how to reach him on that farm. Betsy was off the map. Everybody I knew in Berkeley was away on summer jobs.

The phone rang under my hand and I jumped. "Dovey?" The tinny voice was nearly swamped in a sea of static.

A disorienting moment later, I recognized my aunt. "Hi! Where are you?"

The voice squeaked something that might have been "Brussels." That city, I knew, was on their itinerary. "Dovey," she went on, "it's about the Bel Air."

I sat up with a hideously guilty start. "Yes?"

"Your uncle wants you to be sure to have the oil changed when the mileage hits –" Static drowned out the rest of the sentence.

"I'm sorry – what?"

Bzzz, bzzz. "One hundred seventy thousand miles on the odometer."

"It's not there yet," I said faintly.

"What? I can't hear you."

"Not there yet!" I shouted into the receiver.

"This connection is terrible. I'd better hang up now. Hope you're having fun, Dovey. 'Bye." More crackling, followed by the dial tone before I could say any more. I let out my breath and set the receiver gently into the cradle. Goodbye.

Back to the situation at hand.

Mentally pulling up my socks, I reviewed my feelings about George. On one hand, he was what you might call an ardent lover. On the other, it seemed a little mean spirited of him to keep teasing me once he realized how much his crazy book freaked me out. But you hardly know him, I told myself. You have to get to know him, get used to his way of doing things. He's bringing you out of your isolation, and you don't like that, do you? The inner clinician again. Surely it was because I'd been by myself so much that I couldn't instantly adapt to George's ways. In fact, wasn't he being no more or less than a "typical man"?

Somehow the phrase had a much hollower ring now than it had the night before. I had to admit honestly I hadn't the faintest idea how a typical man behaved. In the silence that fell after all this internal chatter stopped, blind instinct seized me.

Run.

Praying that Al or Sally would not accost me with unwanted questions, I sneaked around the far side of the house to the empty driveway. The ugly pink words mocked me from the pavement. I scuffed them out with my shoe. Then I started walking as fast as I could down the road.

In front of Old Lust's house I stopped short. Where did I think I was going? As I stood there in a quandary, the dog began barking inside the fence. A latch was noisily undone from the other side and the gate flung open.

Before me stood Old Lust in all her womanly glory, resplendent in a full-length Indian-print gown. Her electric red hair glinted in the sun. "Oh, it's you. I thought you were the snoop."

"The snoop?"

"Someone's been prowling around here. At night."

Could it be Peter? I wondered, but just now came the sound of a car engine. At the top of the hill the powder blue Volkswagen station wagon sat idling in the road. Before I had time to register the fact that George had been watching my escape attempt, Old Lust said, "Your boyfriend's waiting."

How did she know about George and me – had Sally told her? More likely Old Lust's own impeccable erotic antennae had simply picked it up out of the atmosphere.

Smiling, he waved at us.

I waved back and thought: A person's life has certain deep, unavoidable patterns. Trajectories even. George fit into mine in ways that weren't visible to me yet but were no less real for that. The summer had tilted into an unknown direction. Mud Lake was the next step.

"See you," I said to Old Lust.

Something like pity flashed across her face. Caught in the old spider web, aren't you? her eyes seemed to say before she slammed the gate shut. She didn't say goodbye.

When I got back to the cul-de-sac, George reached over and flicked open the passenger side door. "I put your pack in the back," he said. "It was lying by the side of the house. I guess Peter didn't want it in the car."

He looked at me. I looked at him. The Volkswagen's rusty body shook impatiently.

I got in, slammed the door and we drove off.

14

At the Bolinas junction George turned north on Highway 1.

I did not often drive the Olema road, as everyone called this portion of Highway 1 that cut through the rift valley above the lagoon, because my father had died on it. According to the autopsy report, the only thing truly unusual about that single-vehicle accident was that he wasn't drunk when it happened. That stuck in my mind always because there had barely been a single moment after my mother's disappearance when my father wasn't drinking. In the English department Gina and his other TAs had to cover for him all the time to keep his classes running.

In any event, that hairpin turn he failed to negotiate was farther up the road near the town of Olema, well past our destination. As we passed the scatter of houses and barns called Dogtown and moved into open country, I suppressed my growing unease and let my mind boil away on other matters.

If Peter had no money, he couldn't get very far in my uncle's car – couldn't, for example, try to drive it back across the country with no way of buying gas. The Bel Air's miles-to-gallon ratio was not very impressive and Peter Chook looked as if he had said goodbye to the world of credit cards a long time ago. It occurred to me that I should have called Sheila right away to ask her to keep a lookout for him at the poetry meetings. How like him it would be, I thought bitterly, to make some brazen appearance after taking the car. I had a vivid picture of Peter schmoozing up to some poet with a complicated tale of woe: it would end up being my fault, of course, that he had been forced to take my car.

Finally I spoke out loud. "Where could he go without any money?"

George laughed. "He's probably sleeping in it somewhere, just like when we found him the first time."

"But he has to eat."

"Mainly, he has to drink. He can skip the food, but he has to get alcohol. You'd be surprised how guys like that can cadge drinks for weeks without a dime to their name."

"Everybody around here knows my uncle's car. Why hasn't someone spotted it?"

George frowned as if making an effort to put himself in Peter's shoes. "He'd probably stash it off the road out of sight and use it as his bedroom. Somewhere in walking distance of a store or a bar."

"I should ask the people at the market and Smiley's to watch for him, then."

"That's a good idea." His voice was light and easy, but George seemed uninterested in Peter or the car. He gave me a deep, direct look. "I just can't wait to show you Mud Lake, Dovey."

I welcomed George's attention in the midst of my turmoil and felt for the first time what it might be like to have a grown man wholly engrossed in me. It was part of the strange mood of this whole day. The car gone, my need to talk to other people, trying to run away, our excursion – somehow, some way, it all fit together.

At the Five Brooks stables sign he turned off down a gravel road. "I hope there won't be lots of people on the trail," he fretted. "That's why I wanted to go early." He pulled into a dirt parking lot next to the trailhead. The lot was empty except for a faded red Plymouth Barracuda with sandblasted doors. In the back seat an open cooler perched unsteadily on a mound of loose clothing. A pudgy blonde girl with tattoos on her arm leaned against the car smoking a cigarette. She did not look up at us as George parked nearby.

"Saw them here yesterday, too. They're camping against the rules," George said in an undertone as he locked up the Volkswagen. "I bet the rangers chase them out." Then he laughed. "Somewhere out there Peter's probably doing the same thing."

We put on our packs. Mine held a bottle of water, two apples, and cheese. George's was much bulkier.

"What have you got in there?"

He held it out from his side. "Camp shovel, climbing ropes and hooks, etcetera."

"What are you planning to do, scale Mount Everest?"

"On a longer hike a person should be properly equipped."

"How long is it going to be? I don't want to be away too many hours."

It hit me suddenly, like a bolt of lightning. Going on this hike was all wrong. I shouldn't be here. I needed to be doing something about the Bel Air, I should be on the phone to the sheriff's office, all those things.

"Don't worry, it's not more than five hours there and back. Plenty of time to be home before dark."

At the trailhead we encountered a cluster of signs showing various iconic objects – dogs, cigarettes, fires, tents – with red diagonal slashes through them. National Park Service sympathetic magic, like the hex symbols on Pennsylvania Dutch barns, meant to ward off the undesirable. Ahead of us flat meadow gave way to a steep set of hills running in a straight line to the ocean. George pointed to the map. "We go up this side of Inverness Ridge. Mud Lake's right on the other side as you go down. If you kept on another five or six miles down to Palomarin, you'd hit the trail we took that comes out on Bolinas mesa."

"It says part of the trail is paved."

"Yep, an old stagecoach route ran up along the ridge. They paved it later, before the highway was built down here. It's called the Bolema road. That must stand for Bolinas and Olema, don't you think?"

It was just the kind of dumb self-answering question George liked to ask, though his knowledge of local lore continued to impress me. A story popped into my head, no doubt set off by his talk of stagecoaches.

I had heard it from another waitress in the lodge I worked at one summer in the Sierras, a skinny, sexy local girl who wore lots of makeup. One day an old timer who hung around the coffee shop invited her to go see an abandoned gold mine in the foothills. They drove up to the deserted shaft and sat in his car while he kept saying, "Let's go look inside," and she kept saying, "I don't want to." Finally he started up the car and drove her home. When she got out, he said, "I'm glad we didn't go into that mineshaft."

"Ready?" asked George.

Listening to that Sierra waitress tell her story, I understood that whatever the guy had an itch to do to her, he didn't – just because she said, "I don't want to," and stayed in the car.

But I was so tired of being afraid of life. I was so tired of saying no. I took a deep breath and said, "Yes."

As we started down the trail, I glanced over my shoulder. The blonde by the Barracuda had been joined by a skinny youth with a thin moustache and a cowboy hat. Loud voices carried on the wind. They were arguing.

George watched me watching them. A smile played around his lips. "Do you know what I noticed first about you, Dovey?"

"What?"

"This whole looking back business. You're always looking back."

"Looking back?"

"Like just now. You're always doing that. Remember Gibran? 'For life goes not backward nor tarries with yesterday.' That's good advice, don't you think?"

I felt a deep sense of outrage. "I am not always looking back!" In the matter of the Tragedy I had built my whole life on doing the exact opposite.

"Yes, you are!" he said gleefully. "You pretend not to, but you are."

He was in front of me on the narrow paved road. "Look, this is you."

George swiveled his head all the way around on his neck.

I gave a loud shriek. George's face was grinning down at me while his body marched straight ahead.

With a grunt of laughter, he twisted his head back to its normal position.

Reality had just hiccupped. After a shocked moment I said hoarsely, "What was that all about?"

George kept his head pointed straight ahead and didn't answer.

Trembling all over but still denying what I had just seen, all I could do was repeat mechanically, "I am *not* always looking back."

George's response was a muffled snicker.

I stopped in my tracks, very upset. The image of that mocking face perched on his broad back danced in front of me. "I want to go home."

"Oh, come *on*." George turned around properly this time. "Can't you take a joke? You're too serious, Dovey. That's your problem."

My first reaction was pure annoyance because people were always telling me that. "No, it's *your* problem," I answered heatedly. "*I* don't have a problem."

"Oh, yes, you do," George said smugly. "You have a real big problem."

"I do not! And I don't want to go with you on this hike. I want to go back." I ran over to the edge of the trail and grabbed onto the trunk of a spindly pine.

George walked over and stood next to me. "We're going to Mud Lake."

"No! No!" I was crying now and hugged the tree harder.

"You're acting like a kid, Dovey. Cut it out." Unhooking each of my arms from the tree, he spun me around, then marched me forward down the trail. To my intense shame, I let him do this. I went along with him.

Why was I meekly submitting, why was I not running away screaming, when the world had just split open?

Because it all felt so familiar.

Why did it feel familiar?

Because I was used to accepting the unacceptable and asking no questions, a voice in me said – one I'd never heard before.

Once, in her eagerness to get me to diss my father, the therapist had overstepped her boundaries by quizzing me if he had ever overstepped his boundaries. Meaning abused me. Well, there was the lap sitting past the age I should have been doing it, maybe. There was all the hugging. But as near as a kid like me could judge, it felt mawkish and overpossessive, not sexual. And he had died just as I was reaching puberty. No, I told her firmly.

The real abuse, the voice said now, was teaching me to obey if I wanted love. To obey no matter what. And unless a person was really hiding from love, that left the door wide open for anyone and anything that came knocking.

I'd been hiding, all my life. Until now.

So all things considered, it wasn't that big a jump to accepting – even this.

My tears dried. I walked blindly in step as the good student in me, aloof and disconnected as ever to dire reality, reflected calmly on a passage from my biology textbook about the "hunter's message," an invisible communication from the predator that first delivers fear and panic to the central nervous system of its prey and then, mercifully, serenity in the moment before the kill. I wasn't serene, exactly. It was just, as I said, somehow familiar. Almost comfortable. To go along with something that just couldn't be. Acceptable, unacceptable, no problem – if all you wanted was to be loved and this was the only way you knew how to do it.

After a while, when he saw I had calmed down, George let go of my arm. Wrapped in our separate silences, we walked on.

The trail steepened up a thickly forested hillside. Spanish moss hung on the long branches of the bay laurels. Banks of ferns sprouted from stone outcroppings. Blackberry vines choked out the foliage under the trees. As we trudged over the faint pitted remains of pavement – the Bolema road, this must be – I kept hearing the sound of a dog with a jingling collar behind me. The possibility that some kind of animal might be following us I found deeply alarming. After a few furtive glances over my shoulder – I most definitely did not want to get into the "looking back" thing with George again – I realized the noise was coming from a loose buckle on my daypack.

The only little doggy here was me.

After an hour or so we reached the top of the rise. Where the trail forked in a dark grove of redwoods we stopped. The grove was still and damp, like the bottom of a well. Dusty green sunbeams crisscrossed the heavy branches. A shard of piercing blue sky shone through the treetops like inlaid metal.

"We want the Lake Trail," George said. I followed him down the path that branched to the left and we walked into a bright meadow full of wild irises and cow parsnips with big white flowers.

"At least the trail wasn't crowded," he remarked. "So far we haven't passed a single person. Hey Dovey, check out that view."

By the position of the sun it was about mid-afternoon. Spread out behind us was a soft landscape of the rolling hills that surrounded Point Reyes Station. Behind the little town Black Mountain rose like a clenched fist. Ahead a series of deep canyons lay between us and the ocean.

I looked at it with all the enthusiasm of a prison road crew worker. "What's so special about Mud Lake?"

"You'll see. We're practically there."

We walked down the ocean side of the ridge under redwoods whose massive rust-colored trunks blushed green with moss. When we came out on a clearing dotted with gopher holes and a few ground-hugging clumps of orange poppies, George stopped and danced a little jig on the trail, flinging out his arm. "We're here!"

Below us, set like a bulging eye in the side of the hill, was a wide pond about three hundred feet in diameter. A large island of bulrushes in the center was encircled by thickly growing watercress and miner's lettuce that gave way at the edges to drifting sheets of green scum. Close to shore a few mossy boughs stuck out of the water. On the far side a pine forest bristling with bright green new shoots stood just inches from the water's edge.

Like someone watching a tennis match, George looked back and forth between me and the pond. He was torn, I supposed, between seeing his favorite place again and wanting to watch my reaction, but it held unpleasant echoes of the way he had swiveled his head on the trail. "Well?" he demanded. "What do you think?"

From deep inside my black hole, I shrugged.

In fact, you had to say there was something extremely *organic* about Mud Lake. "Teeming with life," a National Geographic caption would probably put it, but a clogged, choked life trapped below the surface, forever decaying, regenerating, decaying again, relentlessly impersonal. Chock full of microbes, but hardly inspiring you with optimism about the life cycle the way the *National Geographic* wanted you to be. Mud Lake made me think of things that rotted and died, not things that lived and grew.

George motioned toward the lake's edge. "Let's have our lunch here."

We sat down in a grassy clearing among the reeds. I took off my daypack and offered George an apple and some cheese. He ate with his usual crude efficiency.

"Don't you have any food in that great big pack?"

"No." George gulped down the rest of the apple. "Dovey, there's something else I want to show you. Two things, actually."

But my mind was drifting. I was hot and tired and without hope. As the sun beat down on the shining waters of Mud Lake, I watched the scum and plant beds slowly drift, merge, and split apart like clouds. Dragonflies cruised the pond's still surface. A minnow flashed under the water a few inches away from my foot.

Eyes bright and unblinking, George took it all in, too.

We sat in silence a long time.

Then, suffocated with drowsiness, I lay back on the grass and fell asleep.

15

A tangle of confusing images resolved into a scene. I was walking with my father in an open field, holding hands. We were happy. Suddenly my father sat down on the grass. I tried to help him, but he waved me away, tearing at his collar. It seems he was changing into something and it was dangerous for me to stand too close. His body glowed with light. His face turned into a Halloween mask. He kept screaming at me to escape, yet I was rooted to the spot. He was a regular supernova shooting off comets and stars by the time I woke up.

Surfacing from my terror, I sat bolt upright at Mud Lake. I was alone. The grass beside me held the mold of George's body. His big backpack lay on its side.

Slowly I got to my feet and looked around. The sun had dropped behind the treetops. Deprived of light, the pond looked drab and dull, like a dead animal's eye.

When I shouted his name, the late afternoon woods swallowed up my voice. Trail, forest, grassy hillside – all empty.

It dawned on the little doggie, whose dream had frightened her far more than the "incident" (as I was already calling the little matter of George's rotating head), that this might be a good thing.

Shaken out of the hunter's trance, I felt like myself again, and that self was terrified. All I wanted was to find the quickest way out of here without running into George.

Shouldering my daypack, I half-ran up to the fire road, where the thin paving had given way to gravel. A small overgrown path led into the trees on the other side of the road. It looked as if the rangers had driven their jeeps over it because the grass held the impression of tires. If rangers were around, I wanted to find them.

I followed the path through a clearing in the trees. It stopped abruptly at the very edge of a ridge overlooking a deep crack in the land that held a thickly forested valley. Below the dropoff a trail zigzagged down the steeply eroded hillside. The orange sun, still suspended over the far ridge, had turned this valley into two fingers of land, one bright and one dark. On the bright side, directly below me, something like a house window flashed and glinted in the trees – a ranger's cabin?

I started down the switchback, taking fussy little steps to keep my balance on the steep trail. As I dropped out of line with the sun, the object in the woods gave up its glint and I lost my sense of where it was. I came out on the valley floor in a damp little cluster of live oaks laden with Spanish moss. The uneven ground was choked with blackberry vines and orange-leafed poison oak. I looked around for the trail, but there was nothing, not even an animal track. Scrambling back to the eroded sandstone above the woods, I found what I'd missed before. Flattened bushes and the mark of tires, off to one side of the trail, running straight down the fifty-foot slope. And the glint in the trees at the bottom.

I didn't recognize it until I was right on top of it. Another impossible, completely impossible thing, but there it was. Tires flat, all four doors hanging open, hood wrenched up like a gaping mouth, cruelly smashed front end embracing a sturdy pine.

The Bel Air.

With a strangled cry, I slid down the rest of the slope to my uncle's mutilated car and pressed my cheek against its faithful flank where the paint was still intact. Tears rose in my eyes. No more Puree, Blend, or Grate. More like Crush.

From inside came the sickly sweet smell of alcohol. I peered through the cracked rear window. An empty vodka bottle lay in the back seat next to a battered paperback copy of Carlos Castaneda's *Tales of Power*. I moved around the side. Directly above the driver's seat a round hole in the windshield the size of a cantaloupe radiated a sunburst of fracture lines. In a daze, I leaned far over it – I could not bear to sit behind the wheel and stare at tree bark through that terrible hole – and retrieved the registration papers from the glove compartment.

Bolema, Olema. A car wrapped around a tree.

So many backward echoes.

Inside me the tectonic plates shifted hard, splitting bedrock. My body was shaking as I stepped back from the door.

I looked up the steep incline. The Bel Air had rolled, or been driven, over the drop from the ridge. This was where it had ploughed to a halt. I tried to think rationally – how had Peter Chook gotten the car here? Answer: the main trail, though steep, was a fire road all the way. A vehicle could get to Mud Lake. Then, somehow, the car had rolled down that steep embankment to crash here.

But why? Why had he driven it out here, and where was he now?

It was hopeless, I just couldn't reason it through; my mind kept skittering off the track like the panicked animal I now was.

In one burst of adrenaline I charged back up the switchback, not stopping for breath till I reached the top. The crumbled place at the cliff's edge marked the spot where the Bel Air had gone over. I bent down to examine it. The tire tracks that led directly to the dropoff had been scuffed over.

I retraced my steps down the overgrown path through the trees. When I got to the main trail, Mud Lake lay deep in shadow.

What now?

Run, run, run.

The flight instinct made my whole body twitch as if I had bitten down on a live power line. Run, but where to? I forced myself to hold still.

I might have stood paralyzed like that for hours if a new element had not been introduced.

"Dovey!" Pause. "Hey, Dovey!"

It was George.

An eyeblink later, I was crouched behind a thicket of flowering yellow lupine. Cautiously I peered through the branches.

On the far edge of the lake a man stood with one hand cupped to his mouth. I watched and waited. He called a few more times, then picked his way through the horsetails and low-growing scrub around the shore to the place where we had been sitting. There he called out to me again, waited, then bent over and opened his backpack. He took out some pieces of metal that he screwed together with workmanlike efficiency into something like a giant boathook. Then sat down, took off his boots and socks, and rolled up his pants.

Holding the long tool in his hand, he waded into the pond.

George had a destination. He splashed through the scum and watercress straight to the bulrushes that grew in the middle, where mud and sand had built up a kind of island. He stooped over and prodded something in the rushes with his boathook, pushing and pulling it this way and that. This operation was concluded, apparently satisfactorily, in a matter of moments. He stood up, shouldered the hook, and marched back to shore, where he methodically unscrewed the three pieces of metal and stowed them back in his pack. Then he dried off his feet on a corner of his flannel overshirt and put on his socks and boots.

He stood up facing the trail, backpack in place again. I ducked lower as he walked straight toward me, calling, "Dovey! Dovey!" Cowering behind the bush, I prayed the orange of my daypack did not show through.

"Dovey?"

The voice came from only a few feet away. I held my breath as the sweet-smelling lupine flowers tickled my nose.

When his voice came again, it was fainter. And oddly distorted.

I risked a look. With the light gone from the sky, I had a hard time making out the figure that was moving rapidly up the hill in the direction we had come, scanning both sides of the trail with terrible intentness.

Now his head was hunched in the most peculiar way and his neck was no longer visible. Something was wrong with his shoulders, too, the way they sloped so steeply.

With his big hook-shaped head swiveling back and forth like a bobble doll's, George disappeared over the rise.

16

I held still right where I was until half a moon made itself present in the pale blue sky over the circle of treetops. By the time I crept out from behind the lupines, the air was full of frog and insect croakings.

I hesitated, took a breath, then waded into Mud Lake. The water around me erupted with fleeing creatures as I ploughed knee deep through the rushes. By the time I got to the overgrown hump of vegetation in the middle of the pond where George had been poking around, my nerve began to fail. I took one tentative step, then another, on the quivering mass of reeds and grass, then made a quick circuit back to where I started.

Out of the corner of my eye I registered movement. Near where I stood a white branch was slowly rising and falling underwater. It was stuck beneath a large clump of rushes. I touched the branch with my foot.

It was soft. Fleshy. Connected to a trunk. Thick-growing bulrushes cast complicated shadows. I pulled the Bel Air flashlight out of my pocket and shone it on the water.

Through a foot of murky pond water Peter's wide open eyes stared up at me.

I screamed and turned to run. Tripped and fell face first in the water. A flabby hand brushed my shin. I screamed again and thrashed wildly. Legs bleeding, out of breath, I half crawled, half jumped back to shore, boots streaming water. I wanted to keep on screaming but I was terrified that George had already heard me. I bolted for the trail and ran flat out for five minutes in the opposite direction. Then I stepped behind a tree, gasping for breath, to listen.

Nothing, only the sound of my own panting. But I knew he'd heard me. I knew he was coming back, every cell in my body knew it.

With a loud explosion of leaves, I dove into the dense, dark woods bordering the trail, plunging from tree to tree until I came to an enormous fallen redwood trunk carpeted with green moss. I clambered over the log and positioned myself behind a fan of new branches sprouting from a swollen bore on its side. Through the fringe I could just see the trail, whitened by moonlight.

I didn't have long to wait.

Crunch, crunch! I spotted the dark shape on the trail just in time to duck back down. But not before I had gotten a quick disturbing glimpse of the big misshapen head shrouded in shadow. Draped over the backpack was an enormous garbage bag with something wet inside dripping water along the trail. I knew what was in it. Keeping a buoyant step under this impossibly heavy load, the figure radiated the preoccupied air of intense purpose.

Crunch, crunch! Silence. Crunch, crunch! Silence. Then, softly: "Dovey."

George spoke my name in an easy, friendly way. Picturing the swiveling head, the eyes glaring one way and the other, I clutched a ridge of rock-hard shelf mushroom on the log so hard my hands bled.

"Dovey. Dovey?" The voice died away down the trail.

In another moment he was gone.

Long after the crunching stopped, I stayed frozen in place where I was. An endless hour passed before I felt brave enough to crawl out from behind the log and survey the trail.

Empty.

Safe for now. But there was no telling where he might have stopped to lie in wait for me.

My best move was no move at all, I decided. I would stay where I was and make my escape in the morning. But I was soaking wet and the temperature was dropping on this chilly Northern California night. Through the tree trunks I spied what looked like a squatter's ramshackle hut. It was a wood rat's giant nest, about five feet high, made from haphazardly piled dead branches. I'd seen these abandoned nests before out here; some were over a hundred years old.

Beating my way through the underbrush – poison oak seemed quite a minor threat by this point – I crawled inside it. I barricaded the opening with dead tree limbs as best I could and curled up in the damp humus. Even after mounding piles of leaves over myself, I could feel the deadly cold. Noise after noise issued from the night forest as I lay there shivering in the wood rat's nest. The underbrush rustled. Far-off branches broke like gunshots.

From a nearby bay laurel came a sharp noise like a dog barking. I jumped, then realized it was a screech owl calling out. Another owl answered back.

All the while my mind kept skittering away from the big questions: Why had George killed Peter? Why was he after me? And most important, what was he?

Instead, images rose up, over and over. A dead face underwater. A body in a garbage bag. A wrecked car.

Mirror, mirror.

The gap in the tectonic plates of my life widened into an abyss.

Instinctively, I backed away from the edge of that giant crack. But backing away only made me tumble into a different pit, a pit of deepest hopelessness. The brown, earth-caked leaves heaped over my body convinced me I was lying in my own grave. The unknown direction of my life had now been revealed. I was dead, just like the other two members of my family. George was not my lover, he was my dispatcher. Or he was both, and that was why he had brought me out here.

In some unknown way that made perfect sense, my whole life since the Tragedy had been one long trip, with many postponements along the way, to Mud Lake.

A noise just outside the wood rat's nest brought me back. Something was taking jerky steps in the leaves a few feet away. Claws scratched angrily in the dirt, a body bumped against my barricade. Back and forth the unseen creature paced, circling the nest. Whatever it was sensed something was inside but didn't know how to get to me.

I lay still as death. The sound my heart made seemed thunderous.

Krkk, krkk!

Something jabbed at the tight latticework of the nest. There was a small commotion in the leaves.

Krkk, krkk! A long silence.

Then the sound of wings beating, *whoosh!* and it was gone.

I closed my eyes to calm down. After a while, the low, keening chorus resumed overhead. The owls were back. Baby owls whishing for their food, adult owls hooting back. But now, it seemed to me, the owls were reciting bits and fragments of George's book. How I wished they would be quiet. Their screeching took me somewhere far away, a place I'd never been before that was also somehow familiar.

My father's reddened face, contorted with rage, screaming, "Shut up! Shut up!" at my mother. She, screaming back, "Stupid fucking pig!"

Why did the men in uniform ask him all those questions? "One more time, please, Professor Eagleton?"

They asked me questions, too. "You stayed at your friend's house all afternoon?"

On and on the owls went.

The thought came. Not a trick current in Tomales Bay. Not a tidal bore.

And just as quickly, the second thought. Not a trick curve on the Olema road.

Then both thoughts passed and I went far away, farther than mind or heart could follow.

I must have dozed off, because when I opened my eyes again the woods were filled with mysterious grey light. Mist steamed out of the humid ground. I moved my body cautiously. Damp and stiff but definitely alive.

I sat up abruptly in a shower of leaves and a large white doe feeding a few feet away galloped off, shaking her black tail. I waited and listened. The night owls had given way to wrens and starlings who shut me out of their complicated early morning chatter. But just like an owl I had swallowed a bitter berry during the night. A mysterious seed had lodged in my gut and the first thorny shoots were sprouting down there in the darkness, piercing my innards.

I checked my watch. Five thirty. Was it safe yet to move, or would George be waiting? Broad daylight was better, after the trails were open to the public and other people would be about. But to sit here several hours fully awake would be unbearable. The damp rot of the forest oppressed me. My grave-bed clutched at me, pulling me down.

Shedding leaves and twigs like an uprooted plant, I crawled out of the wood rat's flimsy house, rose shakily to my feet and walked out of the woods.

At the middle of the empty, fog-shrouded fire road I stopped and looked up and down. The logical place for George to lie in wait, I decided, was somewhere between Mud Lake and the trailhead at Five Brooks. Though it was much farther, my best bet would be to keep walking south until I hit the Palomarin trail that came out at the other trailhead on the Bolinas mesa.

I took a deep breath and broke into a light run.

Jogging like this was heavy going in my wet hiking boots, but I managed to fall into a rhythm. Though the back of my neck felt horribly exposed, slowly I grew more confident. The sound of my own breathing, the comforting thunk! of my boots on the packed dirt, kept my fear from taking over. The trail wound up and down a few valleys to a fork. It was still too dark to read the trail marker. But the moment I ran my fingers over the embossed letters on the metal sign to make out what they said, the strange sensation possessed me that I was touching George's book and I snatched my hand back. I guessed left and took off running again.

The sun rose, but the air stayed cold; my breath came out in misty puffs. Color streaked the treetops and high meadows. Under different circumstances it would have been a beautiful dawn. By this time, however, because my socks had also gotten wet in Mud Lake, my boots had turned into instruments of torture. One heel had developed a major blister; the other had just given birth to a second. I took the boots off and stashed them behind a rock; no point leaving gratuitous clues for George. I tore the T-shirt I wore under my wool overshirt in two and bundled my feet in the pieces. Pulling my damp heavy hiking socks back on, I was ready to go again, shoeless. This new regime jarred my arches, but the T-shirt wrappings cushioned my battered feet against the hard surface of the trail.

Now, over my own rhythmic breathing – one *two*, one *two* – came the sound of a car motor. I had a brief heart-stopping vision of the smashed Bel Air rolling after me with something dreadful in the driver's seat. Then reality took over: the only legitimate, and likely, vehicles on these trails were ranger trucks, those big, gas-guzzling SUVs the Park Service favored. In an open stretch with a view down the ridge I stopped and listened.

Far below, a narrow white ribbon wound around the base of the ridge. It was the continuation of the trail George and I had taken to the waterfall. On this lower fire road a patch of olive green flashed by, trailing a cloud of dust. Useless to shout or wave, I was too far away. I started running again. Except for the fact that the bottoms of my feet ached, I was starting to feel better. The running warmed my chilled body and even calmed me down a little.

As I jogged along, my mind circled obsessively around everything that had happened. I couldn't take it in. All I saw was a never-ending unspooling of those images: dead face underwater, body in a wrecked car, body in a garbage bag – for it was Peter George had carried out on the trail, that much I was certain of.

A far, far too heavy corpse for a mere human being to lift and carry unaided, of course.

Two hours later I limped down the last switchback and passed through that pine grove above the Palomarin parking lot I had first visited only the week before. My feet were bleeding through the socks and I was now very sorry I had left my boots behind on the trail.

Just the same, I realized with a deep feeling of triumph, I'd made it. I had made it out of the park alive.

Now what? Get home, call the sheriff. Report the car, the body, George. But what if an unpleasant surprise awaited me back at the house? What if he were there and the Finches were gone, say, to the market? Don't be an ostrich, I told myself, home is the least safe place. Call from a public phone and wait it out.

I scanned the lot for an emergency phone. There wasn't one. Three or four cars sat where George and I had parked two days before. All their occupants must have taken the lower trail, since I had passed no one on the less-used path I had taken. One car I did recognize: the decrepit red Barracuda from the Five Brooks trailhead.

The blonde sat in the front seat just like she had the day before, legs slung over the side in the open doorway. This time she was leisurely smoking a cigarette and looking out at the ocean.

I limped over. Her little ferret eyes, set like plastic buttons in her broad face, took in my rag-wrapped feet.

"Going down to Wharf Road?"

"No."

"For twenty dollars?"

"Let's see it."

I pulled out the folded-up bill I always kept tucked into a pocket of my woolen shirt.

"Deal." She snatched it and swiveled behind the wheel while I hurried to get in the other side. When she unfastened the wire that held my door shut, it fell open on one hinge. With one sweep of her hand she cleared the seat of clothes, beer cans, used paper plates. I got in and held the door shut with my hand.

We took off in a roar of unmuffled exhaust. "Gotta do this fast," the girl cackled. "Shane'll kick my butt if he comes back up the cliff and the car's not there."

As the Barracuda skidded on two wheels around each hairpin turn, all the junk on the back seat sliding from one side to the other, the blonde kept eyeing me. Finally she said, "He's looking for you."

My heart leaped. "Who?"

"Your boyfriend. He comes around last night at Five Brooks asking all these questions and Shane goes, 'Hey, buddy, we ain't seen nobody.'"

"Was he carrying a big bag?"

She ignored the question. "That guy, he was zipping all over the place. First he pops up in the parking lot. Next thing you know he's back at the trailhead, then we turn around and his car's gone." She gave me a shrewd look. "Trying to ditch him, aren't you?"

After a pause I said, "Yeah."

"Good luck." She laughed shortly. "Guys don't like being ditched. I've got the scars to prove it."

We got to the edge of the mesa and she steered the old car down the curving road to the bottom of the hill. At the turnoff to Wharf Road the Barracuda ground to a halt.

She glared at me. "You gonna sit here or get out?"

I got out and lifted the door back in place while the blonde, one hand on the wheel, wired it shut again.

She turned around and roared back up the mesa. I hobbled toward town.

17

The phone in front of the market took coins.

I borrowed a quarter and a dime from a wizened hobbit in a baseball cap (when they weren't hallucinating, Bolinas street people tended to be far more generous than the well-heeled newbies) and dialed 911. The operator patched me to the sheriff's department. I hadn't thought about what I was going to say. After a moment, I spoke up and reported the Bel Air's location up in the park, gave my address and hung up.

Then I trudged slowly up the hill to the cul-de-sac like the little homing pigeon I was. Where else in this world did I have to go to but there?

At the top of the hill George's house stood still and shuttered. The driveway was empty.

I let out a long breath. Climbing up my own back steps like a very old person, I unlocked the kitchen door, taking both the key and the fake rock with me. I relocked the door from the inside and checked to see that all the windows were locked, too.

In my overnight absence a curious transformation had taken place. My aunt and uncle's bungalow had shrunk to the size of a dollhouse. A musty smell filled all the rooms. I sat down at the kitchen table to wait for the patrol car that the officer in San Rafael assured me would be there shortly.

I picked up the phone and dialed the Finches. Now that the matter of the missing Bel Air was, so to speak, out of the closet, I didn't have to dodge them. But how much could I say about the rest of it? The whole episode at Mud Lake was starting to feel like a dream.

"Why, Dovey!" Sally tried not to show her surprise. Almost always she had to call me and not the other way around. "I thought you must be over in Berkeley."

I got straight to the point, or one of them. "Did you hear my uncle's car start up two nights ago?"

Sally thought. "I don't remember. I'll ask Al. Why, dear?"

"Somebody stole it."

"Stole it?" she cried.

I heard a car pull up outside and looked out the window. My heart jumped. A sheriff's car in the driveway, another eerie moment of *déjà vu*. "I'll call you back," I told Sally and hung up.

At the firm double knock I undid the latch and forced open my stiff, scarcely used front door to a large young uniformed deputy with a deeply tanned face and almost invisible blonde eyebrows.

"You're reporting a car taken two nights ago?"

"Yes."

"Why didn't you report it then?" His voice was neutral.

I explained that I thought the person would bring it back. That I found it in the ravine near Mud Lake. That I was very frightened of my neighbor, which was why I stayed out in the woods all night.

I didn't say a word about the body in the lake.

He listened to all this without expression. "Did you know there's a call out on you as a missing person? We've been looking all over the park for you."

"Who reported me?"

"Mr. Peregrin."

"Who?"

"Your neighbor, the one you've been telling me about." The ranger flipped through his notebook. "Eight thirty p.m. last night. He called from the phone at Five Brooks. Said you'd been hiking together. Have any idea why he reported you missing?"

"We got separated. That was when I found the car. I thought he might have had something to do with it and I got scared. I spent the night in the forest."

To judge from the cluck of sympathy that issued from his lips, the deputy was a goodhearted soul. Trying to sort it all out, he stuck to the obvious. "Mr. Chook's permanent address?"

"I have no idea. Maryland somewhere?" A vague memory of something Sheila had said.

"And this gentleman was a friend of your neighbor's."

"Yes."

"Where was Mr. Peregrin the night the car was stolen?"

I blushed. George would be sure to tell them himself. "With me," I said in a low voice.

I was glad his aviator glasses shielded me from any change of expression in the deputy's eyes. "He stayed with you," he repeated in a neutral voice, and wrote this down in his notebook. "The whole night?"

"From about 2 in the morning on. The car was gone when I woke up in the morning."

"Would you have heard him take it before 2?"

"I think so. He wouldn't have had the time to drive it all the way out there and get back by 2."

"The vehicle might not have been driven into the park that night. Has Mr. Peregrin threatened or abused you physically or verbally?"

Ah, abuse. I thought a moment. "No."

"Let me go over and see if I can talk to him."

I followed him across the yard. "I'm not sure he's home."

The big deputy rapped loudly on George's front door. There was silence inside. "He might be in the garage," I volunteered. We walked around and he knocked again on the reinforced garage door. No answer. The deputy flipped shut his notebook as we walked back out to his black and white patrol car. "We'll contact the Park Service about your car," he said, looking over at George's house. "I'll be back to talk to your neighbor."

I thought of George's station wagon and got a desperate idea. "Parking tickets!"

"What?"

"He's got a ton of parking tickets."

"License number?"

I shrugged helplessly.

"We'll get it when we talk to him and run a database check."

I felt a surge of hope. In California too many parking tickets got you in jail faster than murder or incest and I knew they didn't let you write a check to settle the fines. It was doubtful that George, or anyone else other than a drug dealer, would have enough cash on hand to cover them all.

As the deputy drove away, I walked back in the house. My mind had gone strangely blank again. I found myself wondering idly if the missing Bel Air would rate a "Sheriff's Calls" notice in the *Point Reyes Light*, the local equivalent of a gossip column avidly read by all West Marinites.

That was only a distraction to keep me from wondering why I hadn't told the deputy about Peter's body.

He wouldn't have believed me, I told myself. It would have cast doubt on all the rest of my story. Now the body was gone from Mud Lake, but who was strong enough to carry a dead fat man out of the park slung over his shoulder? And so on. All true, but what about the next victim on the list – me?

Why had I kept silent?

That voice in me said: Because that's what you do, no matter what. Because you deserve whatever happens to you.

I reached for the phone, which rang under my hand the same moment, making me jump.

"Hi, Dovey."

I recognized the deputy's voice before he identified himself. The fact he used my first name did not give me a good feeling. It was that kind of law enforcement familiarity designed to put you in your place in the parent-child relationship and did not reflect well on their opinion of your credibility.

"Just got a report from the Park Service," he went on in his bland monotone. "The car turned up right where you said it was." A pregnant silence followed while I digested the implied question: Had I been attempting to cover the tracks of my own misfired teenage prank, joyriding on the Point Reyes fire trails?

"The rangers are having quite a time getting it out of that ravine," he went on. "And they can only tow the car as far as the edge of the Park. We'll call the Bolinas Garage if you give the OK. The garage can tow it from Palomarin, but they'll charge you for it. They'll need a credit card number, too."

"I'll call it in."

There was a little pause when I could have said something. Something like, "There's been a murder. I'm in danger. Help me."

I didn't.

A whole universe of thoughts was whirling inside me, and I couldn't express a single one. The old free-floating guilt, that ancient toxic cloud around the Tragedy, had risen in my throat like bile, choking the truth. Don't tell, don't tell.

I'm going to die, I thought. And I deserve to.

"We'll be in touch," the deputy said.

An hour or so later, I heard a car pull up. A door slammed. Then came the sound of men's voices. Pushing myself up on one elbow, I peeked through the curtain. Al Finch, his back to me, was talking to a man on his front porch whose head was just visible over Al's bald pate.

George.

I dialed the number on the card the deputy had given me. "He's back!" I cried into the phone when he answered.

"Who?"

"George. Come out here and get him!"

"We already pulled your friend over for questioning just now in town, Dovey."

"So why isn't he in jail?"

"There's nothing to charge him with." The deputy's voice ticked off reasons into my ear. "He couldn't have taken the car because you say he was with you. You say he hasn't threatened or harmed you. He says he doesn't know what became of Mr. Chook and so far this guy hasn't turned up."

"What about his parking tickets?"

"Ma'am?"

"I thought you were going to check for tickets."

"That vehicle's licensed in Oregon in someone else's name, but it's not listed as stolen. There's no way we have of knowing if he's accumulated traffic violations here in California. Lots of times that's why people hang onto out-of-state plates." This last piece of information afforded him a cynical chuckle.

I pulled back the curtain again. Al and George were still locked in earnest conversation. Once or twice Al, following George's motions, looked dubiously over at my house.

"We're continuing to look for Mr. Chook," the deputy went on.

"Well, that makes me feel just fine."

His voice did not change tone. "We can't hold people on circumstantial evidence. There's nothing to suggest your neighbor was involved. It looks like Mr. Chook might have driven the car out there, wrecked it, and wandered off somewhere in the brush. We found some tracks down there. Now all we do is wait till he shows up on the side of the road somewhere. Don't worry, we'll find him and charge him."

I could see they fully expected Peter, in that indestructible manner of drunks, to turn up bedraggled but miraculously intact, ready to be slapped with a laundry list of charges and sent for a nice long dryout at the county's substance abuse center up in Lucas Valley.

My silence prompted him to a final piece of advice. "Get a good night's rest. And if your neighbor makes you feel uncomfortable, just stay away from him. Tell him no and lock your door. If he does give you any trouble, call us."

I thanked him and hung up. Then I dialed the Finches. When Sally answered, I didn't waste time saying hello. "What's George talking to Al about on the porch?"

Sally hesitated. "Why, your car, I imagine. What's the matter, Dovey?"

I took a breath. "The car's been found up in the Park. It was totaled. They've been questioning George. Listen to me – George is responsible for all this!" I started crying. "Sally, he's very dangerous. I think he's going to kill me. What am I going to do?"

Just as I feared, this was way too much information for Sally. She sputtered, "Call the police, call the police!" When I explained that this process had already run its course, she lapsed into a monotone of confused questions: "Are you *sure*? How awful. They let him go?"

"Of course they let him go, you stupid woman! He's standing on your porch!"

The silence that followed showed me how deeply I had offended Sally. It also showed me for the first time just how much I detested her. "I think you are upset, Dovey," she said primly. I hung up.

George and Al stayed at it a few more minutes, then bid each other what was, from my point of view, a heartbreakingly cordial goodbye. Quickly I let the curtain drop. Footsteps sounded around the front of my house, then up his front steps. His door opened and shut. That was it. I sat stock still on the side of the bed.

The phone rang. I picked it up.

"At least you ought to hear his side of the story," Sally's voice said.

I slammed the receiver down. When the phone rang again, I picked it up ready to deliver a stinging reply. "Thank God you're all right." It was George.

I said nothing.

"Dovey?"

I replaced the receiver gently in its cradle. Then I got up and walked into the kitchen, just in time to see George walking around the side of my house to the back door. The knob lock was set. I threw the little cross latch as well, and the bar that connected the top and bottom of the Dutch door.

When his knock came, I stepped to the long side window, where I had a full view of George standing on the stoop. He turned eagerly when he saw me. In answer I held up the key and the plastic rock.

"I wish you'd give me a chance," he said. That was for the Finches' benefit. They would be very relieved to think of all this as nothing more than a lovers' quarrel. Then he turned around and walked back to his house.

Because he had me where he wanted me, of course.

18

And would be coming back. At some point during the night George would try for a visit, I knew. I didn't have a car to get away in – unless I tried to pull a Peter and steal one of the Finches' cars, and I happened to know that Al, like my uncle, kept his Datsun and the old Citroen securely under lock and key in his garage. As for just plain running, my feet were flayed. And part of me – not the rabbit part, I hoped – said quietly, Where are you going to go that this thing can't get to just as fast?

I wish I could say this was the moment I sat up on my hind legs and bravely prepared for a fight to the death without quarter. It wasn't. But just the same a tiny determination anchored itself inside me.

Whatever horrible thing was going to happen was going to happen here. I would just have to do the best I could to defend myself.

I got up and went into the study in search of protection of a different order. Unlike my parents, my aunt and her husband professed to be Christians, but I was pretty sure they didn't have a Bible. And a crucifix, I knew, would be way too papist for their tastes. I scanned the top bookshelf. *The Golden Book of Sunday School Tales* and a book club edition of *The Greatest Story Ever Told* was the extent of their devotional literature. The Sunday School book had a picture of Jesus on the cover that, except for lighter-colored hair, bore a faint resemblance to George. I put it back quickly. The ancient spacemen books, which riveted the interest of these conservative old people far more than the religion they had been born into, did not seem much help, either.

Since I didn't know what I should be praying to or against, I did neither. I went into the bedroom and lay down on the acre of bed. As the room darkened, I shut my eyes, but sleep was out of the question. Because I was at the scene of another crime, of course. Lying on the bed, the fresh memories that aroused, made me feel sick and excited at the same time. Whatever this creature that called itself George was, I had slept with it. Slept with it, here! So what did that make *me*?

In blind distress I marched into the bathroom and drew myself a large tub which I sprinkled liberally with my aunt's Helena Rubinstein bath salts. Ordinarily I never used them because the perfume was so overpowering, but I desperately wanted to get Point Reyes, and George, off me. If that meant smelling like a sixty-five-year-old matron with a permanent wave, fine.

I stepped into the garishly tinted bathwater –
Forest Glade, the scent was labeled – and settled in up
to my neck. But the water was *too green*. At the other
end of the tub my dirty swollen big toes poked up
through the surface of Mud Lake. Instead of purifying
myself, I was only getting in deeper, so to speak.

I yanked the stopper out of the tub and stood up.
Turning on the shower, I blasted myself with the hot
spray until my skin turned red and the last of the neon
green water swirled down the drain.

Emerging from the bathroom in a cloud of steam,
I felt slightly calmer.

I put on my aunt's robe and headed for the study,
looking for solace from Dad. In front of the desk I
stopped dead. There were bare spots in the thin film
of dust where the photographs had been. Then I
thought of my father's handkerchief, which I'd stopped
using since George's advent. I ran into the bedroom
and pulled open the night table drawer. Something
had clawed the fine linen into a mass of pitiful shreds
barely held together by the heavy stitching of the
narrow hem. I dropped the mutilated cloth back in
the drawer.

The last of my amulets were gone.

Wandering back into the study, I realized I was
pulling at my hair. I sat down on the couch and put
my head in my hands. Inside me was a hard little
something I kept snatching at, something that could
turn this nightmare around and change everything.
The bitter berry I swallowed in the night forest.
But it kept slipping through my fingers and finally
I gave up.

It was dark outside when I finally got up and headed for the bedroom. In the hall I caught a whiff of varnish. I walked in.

George sat in the middle of the big bed, cheap drugstore reading glasses perched on his aquiline nose. The enormous book with the varithaned wooden covers lay open in his lap. He perused it as a scholar would, frowning in concentration. Looking up at me, he smiled and scooted over to make room. "Front door. You forgot to lock it."

I had pushed the door shut after the deputy's visit. And no, I surely hadn't locked it.

"Kind of a Freudian slip, wouldn't you say?"

I fought the impulse to tear out of the house and into the night because out there I would surely lose. Instead, crossing my index fingers one over the other, I held them out in front of me the way I had seen it done in the movies.

"What's that you're doing, Dovey?"

I said nothing but held my fingers high, wrists shaking slightly.

George closed the book, got up from the bed and walked over to where I stood. "You don't believe in that," he said, lightly kissing the center of my finger-cross.

In spite of myself the old joke leaped into my mind, what the Jewish vampire said to the maiden who had tried the same thing. *Kann nicht helfen.*

He put his arms around me. I tried to scream, but what came out was a big, dry cough. "You took my photos," I said in a hoarse voice I didn't recognize. "You ripped up my father's handkerchief!"

"Yes, Dovey." He held me firmly. "I did those things."

I struggled and tried to push free. "That was all I had – all I had in life to protect me!"

After a moment he said, "Protectionwise, I think maybe you've been putting your money on the wrong horse."

I pushed harder against his chest and let out a real scream this time.

George didn't budge. "Those old fools next door aren't going to hear you over their TV program and their third martinis," he laughed.

I tried to scratch his face. "You killed Peter. You're going to kill me!" George grabbed my hands. "Dovey, listen. I didn't *kill* Peter. Word of honor. And I'm not going to kill you. Nothing's going to happen as long as you don't try to get away." He smiled down at me. "We're just going to make love, that's all."

This time I screamed to the rafters. "Let go of me, you monster!"

The air around his head seemed to buckle. "Okay. Guess I better say the magic word." He paused, then intoned in a mock-scary voice that was in fact very scary, "Woo-hoo, Dovey – do you want to *know*?"

On cue my body sagged. The fight went right out of me. Whatever he was about to tell me I didn't want to hear, period.

With a grunt of satisfaction, he pulled me down urgently on the bed under him. Kissing my neck and my face, tearing off my aunt's robe, he was in a big hurry.

And I – I was back in the black hole of obedience. The place I had lived for so long, the place where I was used to because it was better than *knowing*.

But now I found I couldn't be there anymore. Somehow I fought my way out in my head, and then I bucked him off my body. Crossed my arms and locked my legs together.

"Oh, c'mon." He looked exasperated.

"No." I was coming back, slowly, into myself. Or, more accurately, into some unfamiliar new version of me.

He looked over and stroked my hair gently. "Okay, we don't need to do this now," he whispered. "Because you already belong to me." Then, reproachfully: "But you didn't let me show you Mud Lake."

"You *did* show me Mud Lake."

"Not the little island in the middle. You fell asleep before I could take you out there. But you found that on your own, didn't you?"

"You showed Peter Mud Lake. You *killed* Peter. I saw him, remember?"

"He isn't exactly dead, Dovey." George gave me a sideways look with those big opaque eyes. "But don't pretend you aren't happy about it."

"Happy about what?"

"Admit it, Dovey. Deep down you wished he was dead, didn't you?"

"Is that why you did it?" I screeched.

"Peter wasn't supposed to take the Bel Air," George reflected, almost to himself. "That was something he did entirely on his own. I would never have wrecked your uncle's car, Dovey. I sincerely hope you believe that." He squeezed my hand earnestly, then gave a short laugh. "You know, it's funny. Peter couldn't wait to get written into the book and go to the other state, but I don't think he realized exactly what all was involved. When he did, let me tell you, he freaked. Next thing I know he's vamoosed with the car. But what does the crazy guy do? Drives it up to the park, gets around the gates God knows how, and homes in on Mud Lake without my saying one word about it! That's what I call pure instinct."

He looked for my reaction. I said nothing. "Then," George continued, "when he sees me coming, he guns that baby right up the trail and off that side path before you can say Jack Robinson. In the dark I don't think he saw the dropoff coming."

"But that didn't kill him, did it?"

"No."

"You did."

George laughed again. "You keep saying that, but it's not true."

"I saw his body in the lake. Then I saw you with it on the trail."

"Mud Lake doesn't have anything to do with you, really," he went on as if I hadn't spoken. "It's not your portal. I just love Mud Lake because it's a field of rushes that reminds me of home and I thought it would be a great place to –"

He stopped.

"To what?"

"Never mind. It was just a thought."

I said quietly, "Where's home, George?"

"The other state."

"You mean Oregon? Where you drove from?"

"It's a very big place. Got all kinds of folks, you'd be surprised. My particular spot, it's like a deep, dark desert. And it's not Oregon, hahaha. As a rule I stay right there. I like it. But sometimes I get called. As soon as I get sucked down a portal, I find me a walk-around first thing. Like this Sierra Club body." He gestured at himself like a suit of old clothes. "Get rid of the head, fork mine in, good to go. But I never come, Dovey," he added with a meaningful look, "unless I'm called."

"Who called you?"

"Who?" He burst out laughing. "Are you kidding? *Who*?"

"I never called anybody!" I cried, though I knew this wasn't true. Hadn't I called out for a wondrous love as soon as I got out here? But George wasn't quite what I expected by way of an answer.

"I heard you while I was up in Oregon. I came right down soon as I finished my business there. Your portal was wide open, Dovey. Just like your front door. Could have driven a tank through it. Three guesses where it is."

I had a pretty good idea by now, but it was still off limits for discussion.

"I don't know as much as I should," George went on. "I mean about what it is I do, exactly. The whys and the wherefors. That's why it was so great to run into Peter. He's *into* this stuff! He told me what the Egyptians do and you know, that actually rang a bell. And I loved hearing about those Miwoks and Yankees – is that how you say it?"

"Yankees?"

"You know, Carlos Castaneda and the shaman Don Juan. Boy, that Castaneda! I really wanted to meet him, but Peter said he flew away a while back."

"What do you want, George?" I cried. "What do you want from *me*?"

"Dovey, it's not what *I* want. It's what *you* want."

Under my terror I felt a twinge of honest exasperation. Was this like one of those movies where Al and Sally would swear the house next door had always been descrted, there had never been an old powder blue Volkswagen station wagon, and they had seen me talking to myself out the kitchen door? "You mean" – and I actually managed to say this sarcastically, lying next to him in the bed – "you're only a figment of my imagination?"

"Oh, I'm real, all right," George said. "Ask Peter. Ask what's-her-name in Oregon. Ask that gentleman I encountered on the mesa trail while I was scouting your location a couple of weeks ago. Only a figure of speech," he corrected, laughing. "You can't ask them, can you? They're not in askable shape anymore."

The Sierra Club body. A moment of silence while I registered the missing hiker's fate. Then I asked, "Was that you or him I hit with the car?"

"Both of us. Boy, did that hurt! I just wanted to get your attention, Dovey. Rock your boat. Get you in the right frame of mind."

"For what? What is it I'm supposed to want?"

"Actually, it's what you *don't* want."

"And that is?"

He gave another little laugh, as if to indicate it was self-evident. "To know. You don't want to know what's in your book." He tapped the big varnished album. "That's why you called me. It's only natural you don't want to know," he added. "Nobody does."

"But I can see the book. You said that was unusual."

"It is, Dovey. You're my first to do that. But you still can't *read* it. Look," he said patiently, "All the stuff a person doesn't want to know gets written down in two places. In your body someplace where you can't see it, and in the other state. The *real* state. This book."

Out of all that I pounced on a single word. "Stuff?" For some reason it made me think of what Bill Grebe had said about James Harrier. "You mean, awful stuff?"

"Yes, Dovey. Your stuff *is* awful. It's so awful you can't stand it anymore. So awful you decided you better fly away with me instead of dealing with it!"

George guffawed. Then he winked. It was a very upsetting wink because one eyelid went all the way down while the other stayed wide open.

I grabbed the book away from him. "Don't you bully me with this anymore! I can read it, I know I can!"

Defiantly I rested the heavy book on my knees and opened it. Frowned again at the ugly strokes covering the pages. "What kind of stupid code is this, anyway?"

Just as I was saying this, I heard the owls back in the forest at Mud Lake.

Not the tidal bore.

On the page the spiky black script rippled ever so slightly. I looked closer. "Hey, it's changing!"

"Give that back!" George grabbed the big book out of my hands. "Want to spoil everything? It's not *supposed* to get translated."

As he hunched protectively over the book, his whole body began to twitch and shimmer. His neck receded and his nose hooked over his mouth. His arms stirred restlessly, making a soft noise. When they curved against his sides, the book dropped on the bed. A line of saliva ran down the side of his rapidly thinning lips. "Don't call me George," he screeched in a terrible high voice. "Call me" – the noise he started to make was a sound no human should have to hear. Somehow I knew this was his name in the other state and that if I heard another syllable I would be gone to that other state myself.

The situation was turning very bad. I screamed, and kept on screaming.

A voice, barely recognizable, said, "Stop!" I didn't know if he was addressing me or himself, or both of us, but I stopped screaming and he stopped turning into whatever he was turning into.

As soon as he looked like himself again, George jumped out of bed. "Enough of that," he said briskly in his normal voice, tucking the heavy book easily under his human arm. "We have to go over to my place now."

"Why?" I said faintly.

George grinned. And the words he uttered then, I'm told, are what every young woman dreams of hearing.

"Dovey, I want you to meet my mother."

19

"I don't usually bring her along," he was saying as he force-marched me across the yard. "Once I got here and saw how it needed to go, I went back home and fetched her asap."

We entered George's house and trooped down the hall to the kitchen. At the door to the garage, he turned to me eagerly. "Excited?" When I said nothing, he scolded, "Well, you ought to be."

"I don't want to meet your mother," I said. I'd met the newly rendered Peter, hadn't I? And, it seemed, I'd also met the missing hiker – all of him below the neck, that is.

"You saw me bring her in from the portal that night," he snorted. "I saw you spying on us. But you still don't get it about the portal, do you?"

No, I didn't get it. He pushed me into a darkness that smelled of freshly sawn wood and fumbled for the switch by the side of the door. The harsh light of a bare bulb hanging by a cord revealed an unremarkable space with lots of new wood where he had reinforced the sagging walls and boarded over the garage door. I stood by the refrigerator he had moved in from the kitchen, a huge old mumbling Amana of about the same vintage as the Bel Air. Near the door was a pile of lumber and a power saw with a thick extension cord.

He guided me over to the long packing crate resting on two sawhorses in the far corner. Next to it a rumpled sleeping bag was spread out on the garage floor. A crudely painted picture of a woman's head decorated one end of the crate's plywood cover. "I did that," George said. "Don't ask me why, it's just something I do when we're down here together. Peter said it looked Hellenistic, whatever that is."

Gently he lifted the lid. The crate was filled to the brim with the little star-shaped blue and pink styrofoam packing pieces I had noticed in the kitchen. The floor around the crate was littered with them, too.

"Hang on." George picked up a small Sunbeam blow dryer that was plugged into the same extension cord as his power saw and pointed it at the crate. Pellets showered us like colored snow. Slowly the blow dryer carved out a hand, the curve of a shoulder. Slender olive-skinned arms with ropelike tendons, jet black hair fanned out on either side of the head. A tiny body, less than five feet tall, awkwardly clothed in a too-large khaki safari dress I recognized as having been recently on sale in the Banana Republic store over the hill in Mill Valley.

The crate was a coffin.

Never taking his eyes off me, George aimed the blow dryer at the last of the pellets covering the head. Thin lips were slightly parted over odd little square-shaped teeth. An abnormally large space between the mouth and the nostrils gave her a monkeylike look.

"Why doesn't she smell?"

"She's not dead."

"Like Peter's not dead?"

"No, no, big difference. Peter can go in earth or water because he's still got his heart. Mom's more fragile, she has to stay away from the elements. She doesn't breathe or open her eyes, but she's not dead. Feel that." George grabbed my hand and forced it to touch her forearm. The cool skin was moist. He heaved a deep sigh. "A long time ago somebody took her heart and vital organs, that's why she's this way. We communicate in the other state, but not here. I really miss talking to her."

I could feel a new something stirring inside me. Rage. "Somebody?" I hissed. "You mean you, don't you? *You* killed her, didn't you? Back when you were human?"

"I already told you, Dovey, I don't have memories. I'm not a person anymore. Maybe I never was one, I don't know. Anything that went on down here was a really, really long time ago." He smiled wistfully, this handsome man. "At least I get to have my Mom. That's more than you can say." Abruptly he laughed. "I guess some people would say she's better this way, because then she has to do what I tell her to. No backtalk. Sound familiar?"

George's face wore the maddeningly smug expression of the ignorant person who thinks he has finally scored a point off his betters. "Hint, hint. What other mother engaged in backtalk? Look where it got her." He chuffed and chortled. "Mirror, mirror on the wall. It's not *exactly* the same, our stuff. But close enough. It'll do, all right. It'll do!"

"What's close enough, George?" I asked belligerently. "What?"

He choked back a snigger. "We're laying eggs in your nest and you can't even see it, can you?"

"No, I can't. Sorry."

"Well, here's how it's going to be," he announced. Whenever I heard a man say this, it was always when he felt he had to take charge, usually in relation to a woman. Lay down the law. I sensed George felt I hadn't reacted sufficiently to the show and tell. Here's how it's going to be, sure. Give it your best shot, mister.

"You'll fly away with me," he went on, "but your body will stay here. Don't worry, it won't look beat up like Peter. And it won't be like Mom, it'll move by itself and all. But someone down here will need to take care of it." He paused. "You do have family, don't you, Dovey? They're pretty well off, right?" When I didn't answer, he said, "Don't worry, your relatives will see you get the right care."

"You mean I'll be crazy or catatonic or something?"

"Just the part that's here. Not the rest of you. Not the part that goes with me."

"Will the rest of me still think?"

"Still *think?*" George laughed uproariously and slapped my back. "Dovey, you are too much!"

"Well?"

"Sure, you'll *think*. Same as always. Well, almost the same. You will have a new outlook, that I can promise." His outline quivered with excitement. "'Cause the rest of you, the real you, will belong to Mom and I."

I know it sounds ridiculous, but all I heard was George's grammar mistake. "Me," I muttered under my breath.

"What?"

"Me, me, me, you jerk! 'Mom and *me*.' Object of the preposition. Only Midwestern hicks say 'belong to Mom and I' because they think it sounds educated. Don't you know *anything*?"

George removed his hand from my shoulder. "You're an awfully strange person, Dovey."

I stepped away from him. "And I don't belong to you, either." I don't know where I got the gumption to say this. Up until this evening, it seemed, I had more or less agreed with him about who I belonged to.

Now I didn't.

He decided to ignore this little flutter of rebellion. "There isn't a sacrifice. Peter kept thinking there had to be a sacrifice, but it's not necessary. All you really have to do is say yes."

He stopped and waited.

"No," I said.

George didn't miss a beat. "Fact is, Dovey, you already have said yes, ninety-nine percent of the way. Just by – you know, by being with me. All you have to do now is say it out loud."

"No." Then I said, for no particular reason, "Not a tidal bore."

He looked at me intently. "Now I wonder, what little birdie started telling you that?" He pondered this a moment. "Doesn't matter, there's still plenty you don't know. Call me –" He converted suddenly to the other voice and uttered a terrible guttural sound, something like *Goerge*, and started chortling when I flinched away. His head began to melt in the glare of the garage light. More chortling. "Not I, me. *Goerge*."

Things were getting out of hand. "Can't we go back to my house?" I begged. "It's really cold in here."

"Yes!" said George with the sweeping dramatic gesture of a circus ringmaster. "Yes, we can go back to your house." To my relief his form stabilized. "Mom doesn't mind waiting," he explained as he left the packing crate uncovered and guided me to the door.

We walked back across the wet midnight lawn. The Finches' house stood dark and silent next to my aunt and uncle's. George made a show of opening the kitchen door for me. As soon as I turned on the light, I plunked myself down at the table.

"What are you doing?" he demanded. "Let's go to bed."

"Wait a minute." I went into the study, took out a fresh bottle of my uncle's Wild Turkey with the seal still on it, and brought it back to the kitchen.

He eyed me curiously as I took out two juice glasses from the cabinet. With a shaking hand I poured myself a stiff shot, but when I offered him the same, George shook his head. "Bad for you," he counseled. "Look what it did to Peter. Look what it did to somebody else."

"Look what *you* did to Peter."

Victoria Nelson

"Look what somebody else did to somebody else. And to you."

I ignored him and sipped the drink. Warmth and hope seeped into my bones. Now I realized, in one big empathetic flash, exactly what it was those people in the West Marin bars – and my father – were after. But as George had pointed out, look what happened to them. Went searching for a little warmth and hope, got turned into toads. How incredibly unfair. I took another sip. The Wild Turkey gave me the courage to say, "Where's your book, George? What's *your* story?"

"Dovey, like I said, I don't really have a story. Nothing you could look up, exactly. I bet you'd like doing that, wouldn't you? Researching it in the library."

I glanced up at the clock over the sink – 3 a.m. – and poured myself another shot. The Wild Turkey was acting on me like pure adrenaline. I felt calm, alert, bolt awake. Not passive. Ready for anything. Except what to do next.

"C'mon," George made an impatient motion toward the bedroom.

I stayed put. "I'm not tired yet."

"That's not the point. I want you to say yes while we're – you know."

I tried to distract him. "Do you really sleep?"

"What?"

"When you close your eyes and lie there – are you really sleeping?"

"I can do all that stuff," George said proudly.

"But do you *need* to sleep – like we do?" I rubbed my finger along the side of the juice glass. The Wild Turkey glinted amber at the bottom. "I thought maybe you could dispense with sleeping and eating and so on."

George shrugged. "Sometimes."

"Aren't there things you can't ever do, like crossing water?"

"We're very free-floating these days, that's why it's all so confusing. Oho," he wagged a playful finger. "I see where you're going. All right, Dovey, here's a tip for you." He stopped, baiting me. "Don't you want a tip?"

"Sure."

He leaned across the table and stuck his head up close to mine – closer, in fact, than seemed physically possible. His face glittered like an icon. He said in his other, squeaky voice: *Tricks don't work!*"

Lowering my eyes, I whispered, "What tricks?"

He sat back and crossed his arms smugly. "Old tricks, new tricks. Any tricks. None of them work. Know why? Because they're not sincere!" He sounded comically righteous. "It's not like some fairytale where you draw a circle or wave a magic wand and make me go away. You don't get to wiggle out on a technicality. You have to use all of yourself, and I happen to know for a fact *you* can't."

"Why not?"

"Because you can't read the book, Miss Smarty. Correction. You started to read it, you naughty thing, but then you backed down. You're two people, Dovey. One knows what's in the book, the other doesn't. The one that knows comes with me, the one that doesn't stays here, and never the twain shall meet." He sat back triumphantly. "Now, are you coming to bed?"

I said faintly, still looking down, "I believe not, George."

George scraped his chair back and got up, indicating by his manner that, as before, he was prepared to be a gentleman.

"Then I guess it's time I saw to Peter."

And he was gone.

20

In the early hours of the morning I sat in the empty kitchen alone with my Wild Turkey and my self-contempt. The brief flush of bravado that swept over me had long since evaporated. I could make smart remarks, be a tease, postpone the inevitable – I could stop just short of saying yes – but I was George's camp follower just the same.

Because I couldn't read my book of awful stuff.

Because I was two Doveys, soon to be in two different states, California and – I got up, refilled my glass, and went into the study. Sat down at the rolltop desk for the very first time and took out a piece of stationery. At the top I wrote in big letters, with my uncle's Schaeffer fountain pen, "What Doesn't Work Against George." And I made this list:

1. The police
2. Religion – Christian
3. Ethnic spirituality – cf. Peter
4. Alcohol (ditto #3)
5. Amulets, tricks of any kind

When I looked at what I'd written, a flash of lively satisfaction momentarily canceled out the seriousness of the situation. Didn't leave out much, did I?

Now wait a minute, I could hear a secular humanist – that would include every one of my professors – objecting. You've picked the wrong fight and that's why you're losing. You're not dealing with a creature, you're dealing with a delusion. Well, it had to be granted that the prospect of madness was something even George, my would-be delusion, had already brought up. What will set you free, my inner professor continued, is psychotherapy and a judicious sidebar of medication.

So as not to spoil the list, I began composing a lengthy response in my head. According to George, I argued, madness was on my trajectory, but according to him I hadn't reached it yet. What's more, according to me George was real. He lived in a body, even if it wasn't his own. (How that sounded gave me a little laugh.) A whole community had seen George and acknowledged his existence. And so on. The next thing I knew, my head was on the desk and someone was knocking on the front door. It was daytime.

Was George making a formal entrance for a change? Weaving through the house, I made the new-to-me discovery that a person could have a hangover while still drunk.

Flinging open the front door, I cried, "Welcome to Rowena Manor!"

"Hi, Dovey, can I come in? This is kind of heavy." A woman's voice.

My eyes, I realized, were shut tight. I opened them. There was Sheila Robbins on the porch, chin tucked over a big cardboard box she could barely hold.

The workshop. I tried to say something, couldn't, and ended up simply motioning her to enter. Sheila followed me down the hall to the kitchen, where the empty bottle of Wild Turkey sat conspicuously on the table.

"I'll put my stuff over here, if that's okay," she said hurriedly, setting the box on the counter. "The rest is still in the car." She gave me a bright smile. "Hope we aren't going to be a nuisance. I should have called to remind you yesterday."

I avoided her eye. "No problem."

Retreating to the bathroom, I vomited violently but efficiently in the toilet. Then I peered at George's buddy in the mirror: her disheveled hair, her puffy tear-stained face. I splashed water on the face, rinsed out the mouth, and combed the hair. Noticed she was listing slightly to one side and hastily straightened up.

I looked better, but I didn't feel better. I could hear Sheila bustling back and forth from her car to the kitchen. Another car or two had pulled up and she greeted the new arrivals outside.

As I made up the bed, people began gathering in the living room under Sheila's direction. I sank down on the white chintz vastness. How could I go out there and face them? Over the voices a knock sounded on the back door. Why, I wondered, did he even bother?

I plodded into the kitchen and opened up the Dutch doors. Sally Finch stood on the back steps with a bowl covered in plastic wrap. "I made potato salad for the lunch," she said stiffly.

I stepped back to let her in. "I guess you better put it in the refrigerator." On the kitchen table Sheila had already laid out croissants, napkins and coffee cups. Sally crammed her bowl onto an already crowded shelf in my aunt's no-nonsense avocado green Kenmore. "I'll go see if Sheila needs help," she said, heading for the living room. I could tell she was still feeling insulted. That was a blow. I hadn't been very nice to her on the phone, but she was a grown woman after all, and my elder to boot. Even if she hadn't believed me about George, somehow I imagined Sally would understand I had been upset, would not hold grudges. But now I could see she was wrapped up in her grievances. Instead of reaching out to me, she was acting like a little girl.

It registered on me that I was very disappointed in Sally. Because they were much more easygoing and informal than my aunt and uncle, I had always secretly thought of Al and Sally *in loco parentis*. Their white hair made them seem strong and responsible, but they weren't. They were kids. Aging, gullible kids who were no help to me at all.

Arms tightly wrapped around myself, I was digesting all this when the first workshop participants filed in for their coffee. A snowy haired woman in jeans was followed by another older woman who looked somehow familiar. She had auburn hair, very fashionably cut, and some kind of baggy shorts-and-shirt outfit that was far too chic for Bolinas. Her large haunted eyes briefly met mine. It was James Harrier's wife.

She smiled wistfully as I held out my hand. "I am Mara Harrier," her voice quavered, and I smiled back as our eyes met. Wounded prey. My heavy heart lifted a quarter inch. Kindred souls had recognized each other.

Mara Harrier and I helped ourselves to coffee and stood huddled in a corner as more people, mostly women, crowded in from the living room. Somehow an unholy connection had been forged; without a word spoken, it had been settled that we would provide each other a kind of sanctuary from the group. Even while my head throbbed, I felt a grateful relief. My aunt's kitchen packed full of chattering people was almost stranger than George's garage. Over the heads of the women I saw James Harrier with his back to us, listening as Sheila, her shining face tilted upward, spoke earnestly to him. Standing close to him, so close their elbows brushed, stood that sixteen-year-old from the party, wearing a lot of eye makeup.

"Pretty," Mara said in a light, cultivated voice that was only slightly cracked around the edges. She was looking at an ornamented tin of olive oil on the edge of the sink.

I said, "Sheila brought it."

With a well-groomed nail she traced the acanthus design, then looked out the window. "What's back there?"

She was pointing at the eucalyptus grove. After a pause I said, "Woods."

Mara nodded intelligently. My answer didn't seem odd to her.

Sheila clapped her hands and the buzz of conversation lowered slightly. "Time to start. Everybody into the living room, please!"

Students perched on the couch, the window sill, the floor as Sheila's voice floated into the kitchen. "Mr. Harrier asked you each to bring a copy of his book *Traducies* for the workshop. Does everybody have a copy? If you don't, you can purchase one from me at the conference discount."

James Harrier kept his head modestly bowed through all this, but I was thinking of my professors and how I always respected the ones who didn't assign their own books for the courses they taught.

I looked over at my new friend. She was gazing out the window at the trees.

James Harrier's voice came low and rich from the living room: "Would you please turn to 'To the Young Woman Who Asked Me Why' on page 10." A great rustle like dead leaves filled the living room. Sheila hovered in the kitchen doorway, sneaking troubled glances over at us two lost souls who wouldn't enter the church and take the sacrament.

Out of nowhere a deep rage consumed me. I glared at her. Even to me my voice sounded combative. "I thought this was supposed to be a class, not a reading."

Making a shushing noise that she sweetened with a little smile, she whispered, "He always reads from his poems first to set the mood."

I had a sudden vision of myself rushing up to the front of the room and snatching the book out of the poet's hands. Tearing it in two. Spitting in his face.

Startled at the violence of my feelings, I drifted back to the corner of the kitchen I had been sharing with Mara. With everything else that was going on, why should I hate this man? Had that sixteen-year-old reminded me ever so slightly of Gina, before my mother died and when she was just my father's graduate student paying supposedly friendly visits to our house in Berkeley?

The thought crossed my mind that it would not be good to let George know how I felt about James Harrier. I wasn't at all sure how he chose his targets (including, and especially, me). Did he only go after the people I hated, like Peter Chook, or – thinking of what had almost happened at Hawk Hill and putting two and two together – the people I liked, such as Bill Grebe? Or both?

Mara Harrier jerked her thumb in an almost waitressy way toward the eucalyptus grove. "Want to go for a walk?"

Somehow an inevitable request. "Sure."

As we crept out the kitchen door, Mara saw me recoil from the bright sunlight. She drew out a pair of sunglasses from her canvas shoulder bag and passed them over. "Please."

Mara Harrier's sunglasses were big as saucers and very, very dark. Putting them on was like entering some polarized antechamber of hell. She lit up a cigarette with a little ivory lighter and drew in heavily. "Do you mind?"

I shook my head.

Two somnambulists, we walked through the open space to the dense stand of shaggy-barked eucalyptuses. The air was full of their pungent smell. At the edge of the grove I paused, letting her go first. In Mara's company, I felt safe the way a deer feels safe watching an injured mouse hop into the jungle: Whatever's in there will get her first.

I must have made a noise without realizing it, because Mara Harrier said, "Yes?"

"Oh, nothing." It was very easy being around her because she didn't seem like a real person but more like some waiflike sprite who might dissolve into thin air at any moment. I was always attaching myself to, or letting myself be attached by, helpful aggressive women like Sally and Sheila, and they never failed to let me down. Mara was not the ambivalently helpful maternal type. She reminded me of my mother, only a lot more vulnerable and not so verbal. That sort didn't give you much either, maternally speaking, but then you didn't expect them to.

We stopped in a little clearing. "Let's not go too far," she said. "I *hate* to walk."

"The trail ends here anyway," I said. We sat down on a large stump.

Let me tell you something about eucalyptus groves. They may be scorned by environmental purists, but they are still pleasant to sit under. The trees, tall and skinny and unkempt, possess a kind of careless grace. Layer upon layer of peeling bark adorn their trunks; the silvery sickle-shaped leaves and withered brown buttons are aromatic.

All except this grove, in my case. I hadn't ventured to set foot in it after my mother died. Yet at this moment, sitting beside Mara, sunshine flickering through the branches as a small breeze stirred them, I felt neutral. No doubt because something much more pressing was on my mind.

Mara Harrier sighed and drew on her cigarette, an act that gave her a misleading air of assurance. "My therapist says walking might help calm me down. Then I wouldn't have to take the Elavil. I don't want to get addicted. That would be awful, don't you think? Getting addicted?"

I nodded.

She smoked some more and without saying anything gave me to understand that she knew something was the matter and that I could talk about it or not talk, whichever I wanted. That was why we were together, of course: something was seriously the matter with both of us. Also, her manner clearly indicated, the luxury of condescension having long since been dispensed with, I was not to expect anything as vulgar and practical as *advice* from such as her but rather the nonjudgmental ear of a fellow wanderer in the void.

Within these limits it was a little hard to think of what to say, but I still wanted to. Finally I got it out. "I'm scared of these woods."

She looked at me. For a moment I imagined I saw sympathy flicker in those large eyes.

"I'm –" I went on, and then started sobbing. Crying uncontrollably, I clung to the frail woman even as she awkwardly tried to switch her cigarette from one hand to the other so that she could pat me, feebly, on the back. But it was useless trying to make Mara into what she was not, and realizing this brought me to my senses.

I sat up and wiped my eyes with the back of my hand. Finally I managed to say, "I have a problem with someone who seems to have me in his grip."

Mara Harrier listened without expression.

"What does your therapist say to do," I asked, "when you're in somebody's grip?"

She offered no comment other than a loud and unexpected snort.

I plunged ahead in spite of myself; the urge to tell was overwhelming. "I don't think I can get away from him. If I just pick up and go, I have the feeling he'll be able to follow me anywhere." I grabbed her hand and leaned over desperately. "I think he's going to do something to me."

Mara Harrier began to tremble. A tear formed in one large, liquid eye. She gave her head a number of rapid little shakes, like a field mouse whose neck is being snapped by a terrier. She didn't speak.

I sat back and let go her hand. I looked at the ground, the leaves, the little hillocks of grass. A few feet away a big blue jay hopped over a branch. I said bitterly, "So what would your therapist say to that?"

"My therapist would say," Mara Harrier replied with surprising speed, "what drew you to this man who kills?"

Then she gave me a sad little smile as if to say: But we both know what a silly question that is.

I brushed myself off and stood up.

"Let's go back now."

Flicking her butt away in a shower of sparks and grey ash, she rose to follow.

21

Back at the house loud voices, laughter, rocked the living room. The session was still going strong. Sheila buttonholed me in the hallway. "Dovey, is everything really okay?"

I looked into her earnest face. Given Mara's reaction in the grove, I couldn't see trying again.

"It's been hectic." I watched Mara drift off in the direction of the voices. "Sorry I was a little spaced out when you got here."

Sheila beamed. "I know just how you feel. This has all been such fun but what a zoo, huh? Now I'm just going to set out our lunch. Don't lift a finger, I can do it. Jimmy says he's on a low cholesterol regime and I want to make up a special plate for him now before everybody comes in. Where's your darling neighbor? He asked if he could come to our meetings."

When I didn't answer she said, "Did he know he was welcome to attend?"

"I expect he did."

"As long as he knew. Hi there, Bill. I didn't see you come in."

Bill Grebe stood at the back door wearing a baseball cap – to hide the claw marks, I wondered? "I *didn't* come in," he said fussily. "A class is in session in the front and I didn't want to interrupt. So I walked all the way around here instead. Hello," he greeted me, then looked at his watch. "Is he still yakking? I thought you said lunch was at twelve."

Sheila bristled. "They're having a very lively discussion."

He fidgeted, nervously, the wattles of his middle-aged man's neck strained and tense. "Well, what am I supposed to do? I want to eat, and start my workshop. I don't want to wait around."

"You can come sit in the study," I suggested. "Right in here." I showed him the way. "At least it's private. I'll bring you some food."

"Thank you," he said curtly.

Sheila rolled her eyes conspiratorially when I returned to the kitchen. She was slicing a baguette on the counter.

Here was the opening I had to take. "Sheila," I said, "You know Peter Chook stole my uncle's car, don't you?"

The knife halted midstroke. "No, I didn't. Dovey, how terrible!"

"The wreck's been recovered out in the park."

A net of worry drew all the lines together on her face. "I am so sorry to hear this. After our party I never laid eyes on him again." Concern gave way to a certain blankness while Sheila seemed to be thinking intently.

"Were you going to say something?"

"No, it's nothing." She was tearing lettuce leaves now.

Back in the study, Bill Grebe was leafing through volume 1 of *The Man Without Qualities*. I wondered what George had done with volume 2. The thought of him carrying my paperback around now aggravated me out of all proportion.

"Do you like Robert Musil?"

Bill Grebe threw the book aside with an exclamation that suggested either it or the question, or both, was not worth commenting on. The mellowness brought about by his near-death experience had clearly not endured and his ill humor cheered me up a little. I started to sit down on the imitation leather couch across from the desk, then got up again. "I forgot to bring you something to eat."

He waved his hand impatiently and I sat back down. "I have a question for you," I said tentatively.

A wary look crossed Bill Grebe's face. "What sort of question?"

"Remember you were talking on Hawk Hill about the other world – the world of true forms? Could you just tell me what you meant by that?"

To my relief he took the question seriously. "People used to believe," he said, "there was more to the universe than just the material world around us. They thought this world was just an annex to the world we can't see. Plato said the invisible world was the only true world. Organized religions still believe that."

How I wished I had George's book – my book – right there to show him. "What about messages from the other world, the language of the birds? You said if modern people tried to understand what the birds say, they'd go crazy."

Bill Grebe squirmed a bit in his chair. "I was joking, really." He thought for a moment. "The poets are ambivalent about it, of course. Edgar Allan Poe – need I say 'nevermore'? Yes, the messages can be problematic. May I ask what your interest is?"

There was no getting into that point blank. "You said we're all from that other world but we just don't know it. So what happens, poetically speaking, if you get sent back? I mean, to the other world? Does it have bad places as well as good places?"

Bill Grebe frowned. "Going to the other world while you're still alive is not supposed to be a good idea. Think of all the bad things that happen in the ballads when people get swept off to fairyland. No, it's not good. Trailing clouds of glory we may all be, but where we belong is here, in this world. That's the received wisdom, anyway." He was glaring at me now. "I don't quite get what you want to know. You're not one of those silly neopagans, are you?"

I saw the tack I had to take. "No, no. I just meant, you know, what the hero does. In the literary tradition."

Instantly he was comfortable. "No, the message the birds bring is supposed to be for here. What's more likely to get the hero in trouble is refusing to understand it. That will keep him locked in its spell."

Locked in its spell! Was that what had happened to me? Bill Grebe seemed to be saying what George had hinted at, that not being able to read the book made me more vulnerable, more likely to go crazy. But if I was two people, like he told me, and the other me could read the book, how was I supposed to find that other me?

By now Bill Grebe had half-risen from his chair, but I was desperate to keep him there. "Do *you* believe in that? I mean, in some other place, some true place beyond anything you can see?"

After a moment he said primly, "I believe in Poetry." Sunlight from the window reflected off his glasses, firing them with light. The effect was unexpectedly impressive.

"So can you use poetry as – as a shield to defend yourself from something bad?"

"Let me see," he said indulgently. "In the old days people used to say charms and things. There are some lovely ones in Old English."

I motioned impatiently. "Tricks don't work."

He shot me a quick speculative look. "Are you asking if poetry can be employed in the battle between good and evil?" The way he pronounced the words made it sound like he was putting 'good' and 'evil' in quotation marks, which wasn't encouraging. "I suggest you reread your Milton."

"That's just *reading*. Suppose you had a real crisis and you needed to *do* something, make a stand. How could poetry help you?"

"I'm not Dear Abby, miss. I'm afraid I'm ill equipped to advise you about personal matters. All I can tell you is that great poems have wisdom you can't find in psychology or religion."

"But they all say different things! How do you know which poet to listen to, which one to follow?"

"I wouldn't *follow* anybody," he huffed. "I'm simply drawn to those other poets whose inner truth resonates with my own."

"Which is?"

"I beg your pardon?"

"Your inner truth – what is it?"

He clucked impatiently and did not answer.

"I don't really want to know my inner truth," I blurted. "I just want to be normal."

For the first time the light of real sympathy was kindled in Bill Grebe's eyes. "My dear," he smiled. "*Normal* is the big illusion. There's nobody normal in this world. Your only real duty while you're here is to become the one human being that you are."

There it was. One human being. Not two.

A tap-tap sounded on the door. Sheila poked her head in. "Workshop time!"

Bill Grebe got up. "Want to sit in on the never-ending battle between the worldly sophisticates and the innocent Hallmarkers? Pretty primal stuff."

I shook my head.

"Sure?" he gave a little smile. "You know what they say. Other people pray, Californians take workshops." Another brief look of inquiry. Then he turned away.

I watched him walk into the other room. He was not an old man, but he moved like one. His bowed back carried a heavy invisible burden. Bill Grebe might believe he worshipped Poetry, but his body, I now had the power to understand, was in thrall to something else. Bill had his own George and, like most people, had no idea what was in the secret book that creature had written on his body.

Nothing Bill Grebe had talked about – with the possible exception of poetry – was real to him, I realized. He didn't believe in messengers or other worlds at all. For him it was all just window dressing in the poet's department store. "The power of *metaphor*," I could hear him intoning with just the right note of irony.

I sat down heavily on the sofa. I was back where I started. But something Bill Grebe said had triggered a memory. A newspaper headline floated up in my mind, a classified ad, yes, from the *Pacific Sun*, where had I put that copy? I rummaged through the desk until I found the newspaper folded up under the mail I was saving for my uncle and aunt. I leafed quickly to the back, the "Personals" section, where everybody from chiropractors to aura readers advertised their services. And there it was in bold type, right in the center of the page:

DEMON WORKSHOP!

The small print said: "Confront your demons. Empower your life. Weekend marathon conducted by licensed therapist." With a sinking heart I saw the workshop had taken place the previous weekend. A Mill Valley phone number was listed. I hesitated. Outside the window the sun shone bright. I reached for the phone and dialed.

A deep, assured male voice greeted me.

It took me a minute to speak. "I'm inquiring about the workshop."

"We just had it."

"Are you going to have another one?"

On the other end of the phone the man sighed deeply. For a minute I thought he was simply impatient with me, like Bill Grebe. Then I realized he was wrestling with an inner conflict. "That *really* depends," he said gloomily, "on a lot of factors I can't totally predict right now." Then, in a twinkling, he turned brisk and businesslike. "I can take your name and number, though."

Despair squeezed my heart. "I was hoping it would be something I could go to right away. Could you . . . would you tell me what exactly you do in your workshop?"

"We visualize our problems – our demons – like they were a real, separate person." He spoke slowly, as if explaining car repair to a child. "We use Gestalt dialogue to confront them directly. We work through the issues, find out what our payoff is for having them."

A little silence fell. I said, "And then the demon goes away?"

Wariness entered his voice. "We don't conceptualize the resolution quite like that. It's an intrapsychic process we're dealing with." A rich chuckle traveled over the line. "I'm not licensed to perform exorcisms."

"But couldn't you just tell me what's the main way – the strategy, or whatever – how it is you conquer the demon?"

This time the sigh, quickly checked, was definitely aimed in my direction. "In the first place, you never *conquer* the demon. He – or she, or they – is part of you. In the second place the process is different with every individual, because the problem – the demon, if you will – is unique to each person. Naturally there are patterns. The *process* is what counts, you see." He began to wax enthusiastic in spite of himself. "In the processual dynamic you discover everything – who you are, what your demon is, how you got in it, and how you get out of it. How you resolve it."

For a moment, listening to him, I felt much better. "But did anyone in your workshops ever call up his demon and then get conquered, I mean *resolved* by the demon instead of the other way around?"

A longer, more definitive silence fell at the other end of the line. Clearly he had reached the limit for free consultation. Of course it had been nice of him to talk to me this way, but then talking intimately to strangers was his business. I thanked him.

"Thank *you*," the demon workshop leader said briskly. We hung up at the same time.

22

Bill Grebe's voice droned steadily through the wall from the living room as I took out my list from the rolltop desk and added, with a flourish:

6. Art, including poetry
7. Psychotherapy

Then I folded the paper in two and put it in a drawer where my uncle would discover it, to his utter bewilderment, a few months later.

Through the other wall came the snores of one of the workshop participants, an older woman overcome by lunch and prosody who had crept uninvited into the bedroom.

I wandered into the kitchen, checking next door from the window. If the absence of the VW station wagon was any indication, George had been gone all day. In my driveway Sheila was shepherding James and Mara Harrier into her Toyota as I watched. The poet's rugged profile pointed straight ahead – fixed on the serene horizon of his career? – but Mara's eyes flicked briefly in my direction as they drove off.

Out the back window a strange thick haze hung over the eucalyptus grove.

I looked closer. The haze resolved into curls of rising black smoke. I walked out the back door to the edge of the trees. A ground fire, burning low, licked through the dry brush under the trees. I ran back to the house and dialed the Bolinas Fire Department from the list of numbers my uncle kept posted over the kitchen wall phone.

I hung up and looked uncertainly at the closed living room door. Should I interrupt the session to tell them what was going on? A good hundred feet of bare earth intervened between the bay laurels the three houses sat under and the burning grove.

When in doubt say nothing, that was the family motto. I hooked up the hose in the back yard and began soaking the ground. What if my aunt and uncle came back to find that besides losing their car, their house had burned to the ground as well? That made me think I should tell Sally and Al, too. I went around to their front door and knocked. Al came to the door. I was watchful for how he would react to me, but Al did not seem to be looking at me any differently than before; he was the type of person who always seemed fed up about something. "There's a fire out back," I told him.

He followed me to the edge of the grove. Loose dry bark on tree trunks was catching fire.

"Ah, that's nothing," he said. "We could put it out ourselves."

"Our hoses won't reach that far," I pointed out.

"Those kids again," Al commented inscrutably. "Hey, I saw your uncle's car down at the garage this morning. They put it next to Sonja's bus." Sonja, I knew, was a Bolinas earth mother who lived in an old school bus on the mesa. "What a wreck! Does he know about it yet?"

"I'm faxing their hotel in Zurich," I lied.

"They better find that fellow so you can collect the damages from his insurance company."

"I don't think he had insurance."

Al didn't pick up on the past tense. "Then your uncle's insurance will pay for it. But they'll just total it. The blue book value on that car is zilch, I don't care how great it's kept up. He's going to flip, Dovey." He looked over slyly at me. "You and George make up all right? He told us how mad you were about it. Don't blame you one bit."

Sally had to have passed on to her husband what I'd said about George. That I thought he was going to kill me. And here Al was acting like everything was normal. I looked at him and said nothing.

Al leaned over and spat in the grass. "I don't care what he says, I think he showed bad judgment letting that fellow stay with him. It's really his fault all that happened. Maybe your uncle can sue George's insurance company," he offered helpfully.

I didn't try responding to this, either. Even I, with my minimal knowledge of worldly affairs, knew you couldn't do that.

Siren screaming, the big yellow Bolinas fire truck pulled up in the front yard. Someone yelled and the engine drove over the lawn and across the bumpy field to the edge of the trees. The fire chief followed in his jeep.

Now faces appeared in the windows of my aunt and uncle's house. The kitchen door opened; one or two people ventured out. I walked back up to the yard.

"We have a small brush fire out there," I told them. "It's under control now."

Bill Grebe stood unhappily in the doorway. "Will you *please* come back and let's continue," he begged his charges, who straggled reluctantly into the house.

I sat on the kitchen steps and watched the firemen squelch the modest blaze with professional efficiency. Sour black smoke billowed through the trees. Al stood in attendance by the fire truck. Still too offended to come out and talk to me, Sally watched from her kitchen window.

I heard another car pull up in front. Footsteps came down the driveway. I braced myself. But it was the friendly blonde sheriff's deputy.

"Hello!" I called cheerfully. It was a comfort to see him even though the encounter was not likely to be of any benefit. "How's the search going?"

"We called it off at noon today. But we're keeping our eyes open." When he saw me sigh and look down, he said, "Still scared of your neighbor?"

I looked up at this big, comfortable young man with the beginnings of a belly. A thick gold band rode on his left index finger. I smiled wistfully, more to myself than him. "Thanks for asking."

"Pardon me, I'd better go see what's up now."

Watching him walk easily out to the fire truck, I indulged in a brief fantasy: being this fellow's happy wife (for I didn't doubt, looking at him, that she was happy), having him come home every evening to me and our kids, feeding him, sleeping with him at night. What in the world would that be like? A very different fate lay in store for me, it seemed. But long before this summer, before any of this mess had begun, I had sensed that ordinary life was closed to me, barred totally with no appeal. But why? What was the invisible barrier? Was it because, as I often told myself, some parts of me were too grown up, others not grown up enough – forty years old in my head, twenty years old in my body, and forever nine years old in my heart? It was like seeing the world crystal clear through a glass window but never being able to reach out and touch any of the beautiful things on the other side.

And when I finally did reach out, what was the first thing my nervous, eager fingers found?

George.

The firemen coiled up the hose. They climbed on the engine, the fire chief got in his jeep, and both vehicles pulled away, leaving sets of deep treads imprinted on the field. Al and the deputy walked slowly back until I lost sight of them between the houses. A few minutes later, the patrol car pulled away.

As I looked at the scorched trees, a stray thought darted across my mind. Mara's rage.

I walked into the kitchen. Voices drifted in from the living room. It was hard to catch the sense, but members of the class seemed to be arguing among themselves, with Bill Grebe mediating. Would that be the innocent Hallmarkers and the worldly sophisticates? I didn't care. In the last two days I had slept only a few hours and exhaustion had finally overtaken me. I peeked into the bedroom. Empty now. I brushed a single iron grey hair off the pillow, turned it over and lay down.

As soon as I closed my eyes, I was right back in the meadow where I had left my father in my last dream, only now the meadow was inside the ruined grove behind the house. A bloodstained stone, idol of some primitive tribe, stood in the middle of the clearing. It got bigger and bigger as if it were moving toward me. Then I realized I was moving toward the stone.

Now I was right in front of it.

Bow down.

It was someone's voice, speaking inside me. My knees itched. I started to kneel but managed to twist my body and fall to one side. Then I jumped back up and put my hands on my hips. I'm *not* bowing down. I don't do that. So there!

Then I looked down at my knees. They were thickly crusted with mud and twigs, the accumulation of years. My proud response was exposed, a pathetic sham. I'd been bowing down all my life and hadn't even known it.

Now the stone was gone. In its place sat the wooden packing crate. The lid was open. The mother's hand stuck out.

If it wasn't a tidal bore, then –

My eyes flew open.

Without the familiar screen of my father's handkerchief the bedroom seemed strangely light, airy. I touched my face. Fresh, plump, living skin. *My* skin.

Noise came from the hall. Footsteps, loud voices. I got up and opened the door. The class was over. People stood around in little groups in the kitchen. Lifting up her box of leftovers, Sheila cried: "Time to go, everyone! Let's thank Dovey for the use of her house, shall we? Don't forget the potluck party at my place tonight at seven."

A puzzled smile crossed Bill Grebe's face when he glanced my way. "You look different."

"He means rested," Sheila intervened. "Poor Dovey, what a day! Us and the fire. Rob told me when I was downtown taking Jimmy and his wife home. The chief says it was probably cigarettes. I am just so thankful none of our group was out there. And Dovey, I saw your uncle's car down at the garage and I don't know what to say." She took me aside and said in a low voice, "I hope they find that awful Peter Chook and throw him in jail! But if they don't –" She hesitated. "You know, when your uncle comes back, he's going to be very upset about this, and I don't blame him, but – he needs to understand the Poets' Parliament can't be held responsible."

She sounded almost as apologetic as George, but I understood Sheila's alarm. In Bolinas my uncle, who wrote endless aggrieved letters to the local paper, was universally regarded as a litigious rightwing crank.

"I don't think you need to worry about it."

"Peter was only an auditor. He was never formally enrolled."

"I know."

"Just so your uncle understands."

"I'll make sure he does."

She heaved a grateful sigh. "Now won't you come to our party tonight, or have you had enough excitement for one day?"

"Can't make it, thanks."

"We should go now," said Sheila. "Bill, are you ready?"

Bill Grebe was still looking at me. "Still brooding on the vast abyss, Dovey?"

To my own surprise, I retorted: "What in me is dark illumine, what is low raise and support."

He gave a loud, surprised laugh. Our eyes met.

It was a moment.

But just as he allowed himself to see me as a woman for the first time – it was clear as daylight this was what was happening – Bill Grebe's own George rose up inside him and quickly snuffed out the spark. He dropped his eyes to the floor like a schoolboy and turned away.

"Goodbye," I said as they walked out the front door, but neither Sheila nor Bill heard me. "Goodbye," I said again. "Goodbye, everybody."

A minute later, the Toyota pulled out of the driveway and I was alone.

Or not quite. A familiar figure was striding up the hill, magnificent in a swirly gypsy skirt and magenta top, filmy scarves around the neck. "You, Dovey!" Old Lust called peremptorily.

I stood where I was until she reached me. "Last night your boyfriend was in my garden. I saw him crouching there like some disgusting peeping tom."

My first reaction, God help me, was a reflexive stab of jealousy. Was George now looking to bestow his sexual favors on this ageless beauty?

"At first I thought it was a raccoon. Then I looked out and there he was," she made a contemptuous motion with her hand, "rooting around in the dirt like an animal."

I came to my senses fast. "Don't let him know you saw him," I said urgently. "Go home and lock your door and don't come out until this is over!"

She caught the panic in my voice. "You are in danger," she said flatly.

I nodded.

"Why don't you go, then? Why are you staying?"

I hadn't known before, but now, suddenly, I did.

"To render justice," I said. I had no idea what the words meant, but they felt right the moment I spoke them.

She considered this. "I will call the sheriff and make a report."

"Please do, but don't leave your house."

Old Lust looked at me a moment. Then she took off a silver ring, one of many that graced her long, skinny hands, and placed it on my right-hand ring finger. "For protection," she said.

I looked at the ring on my finger. It was chunky and pitted, deeply incised with designs. Tears stung my eyes.

Old Lust had given me an amulet.

When I looked up, she was already on her way back down the hill. "Thank you!" I called, but the high garden gate had already swung shut.

I took a deep breath. Felt a strange unfamiliar purity envelop me.

Now I was truly alone.

23

More than purity, I had purpose. The bitter seed in my gut had sprouted and flowered. I knew what I had to do.

I walked over to George's house. The front door was unlocked, no surprise. I walked down the narrow hall to the kitchen and tried the door to the garage. Unlocked, surprise.

I flicked on the switch and stifled a scream.

Styrofoam, empty mineral water bottles, cardboard boxes, and trash littered the top of the cable spool. The big book leaned carelessly against the reinforced garage door. But the crate was empty. Next to it, instead, the body of George's mother reclined on a faded beach chair. Hands crossed behind her head. Khaki dress neatly straightened, feet bare. Was that some kind of carmine polish on the toenails? Dead eyes staring into the distance, impossible to meet.

Grotesque, unbearably grotesque. George had posed her like a department store mannequin. But what was he selling?

Mom and I lay our eggs in your nest, he'd mocked. Hint, hint. Copycat stuff. All along he'd been teasing me. He thought it was safe having these private jokes because he thought the Dovey who didn't know could never figure it out by herself.

Something inside me jumped tracks then. The man had a proper grave, I heard myself mutter. So should the woman.

Rage swept over me, Mara's fire. I ran to the beach chair and grabbed the mother's rubbery hand. "A decent burial!" I yelled at the all silent objects in George's garage. "She deserves a decent burial!"

I let the mother's hand go and walked over to the cable spool. With a single sweep of my hand I sent all the beer cans, paper cups and newspapers crashing to the floor. Then I turned the heavy spool on its side and rolled it careening into the sheet-rocked wall, which sagged under the impact. The big book bounced and fell on its face.

I wanted to tear down this garage with my bare hands. Rip out all the boards. Set it all ablaze. Bulldoze the remains and sow the ground with salt, like Carthage.

My whole body was shaking. I leaned against the wall for support. I needed to calm down. I could not let myself be distracted from my true mission. This time – I said it again, emphatically – this time a *decent burial*. No garbage bags. Or whatever.

Where to bury her was not even a question.

The eucalyptus grove, now and forever.

I would take her home.

A shiny new shovel sat upright in a corner. Hoisting it over my shoulder, I went back to the beach chair. Whatever she was, George's mother was neither large nor heavy. Still, it would be hard to carry her with dignity, as I was determined to do. Not slung over my shoulders like a sack of potatoes the way – well, once again it was an image reflected in multiple mirrors.

When I lifted the body into my arms, a gentle sigh escaped the mother's lips. I leaped in fright and almost dropped her. Had air collected in the body cavities? I listened hard, but no more sounds were forthcoming. I lifted her again. The head lolled against my shoulder, one arm stuck out awkwardly. The cold flesh was oddly flexible. After some experimenting I found that by keeping both my arms extended I could hold the shovel, too, though getting through the narrow door into the kitchen with both of them took some maneuvering.

We departed George's house, the mother and I, under a sunny late afternoon sky. Not a soul was stirring in the little cul-de-sac, not the Finches or Old Lust down the hill or anyone. We crossed the open space to the trees unchallenged.

I stopped in a blackened little clearing beyond sight of the houses. It wasn't *the* spot, the real right place – I knew that in my bones – but it was the place where Mara Harrier and I had lingered. Gently I laid the body down on a tangled bed of sickle-shaped brown eucalyptus leaves. The sightless open eyes were upsetting; I couldn't put her in the ground like that. But each time I tried to close them, they flew open again, dusty and opaque like a doll's.

I walked back to my aunt and uncle's house. In the bedroom, neatly folded in the bottom bureau drawer, was a gleaming white cotton percale bedspread that my aunt rated too good for everyday use. Thank God I hadn't put it out for George. I tucked it under my arm and headed back to the grove as the electric current of rage coursing through me discharged itself in random twitches, kicks and little cries.

But when I got back to the clearing and saw the body lying there so forlorn and exposed, a deep moan burst out of me. I was going to have to bury her in the ground and leave her and her flesh would rot until nothing but bones was left.

I shook out the percale bedspread, deeply creased from its long sojourn in the dresser drawer, and spread it full on the ground. I laid the body gently on the finely woven fabric and folded it over from both sides. Then I picked up the shovel.

For the next hour and a half I broke out the dirt from a hard, dry shell of a hole that refused to grow past three feet. Animals could surely get at such a shallow grave; I needed to go deeper. So I hacked and hauled, jumping on the shovel with both feet, and dug till both my hands were bleeding. At four feet, dirt showering back on my head, I stopped and climbed out of the hole.

The setting sun lit up the singed lower branches of the straggly trees overhead. Holding the bedspread at both ends, I gently lowered the body, bent like a drawn bow, into the grave. When the middle part of the spread touched bottom, I slowly let go the ends. They slithered down to rest on top of the white bundle. Using my hands, I pushed the dirt from all sides into the hole. Clumps and blotches fell on the bedspread until slowly all traces of the white disappeared. The hole was a third full, then half. Finally I picked up the shovel and heaved in the rest.

As I was tamping the top down firmly, a raucous noise made me look up.

Caw, caw, caw.

On a nearby limb two crows were disputing. Suddenly I was back in the Inverness house the day my mother disappeared. She in the living room doorway, smoking a cigarette in that indirect attention-getting way of hers. As usual looking at him, not me. Her delicate features already a bit haggard for a woman in her thirties. "I'm leaving." My father and I have heard this before, of course. He, deliberately misunderstanding: "Where to?" She doesn't answer. Takes a deep drag, exhales, puts the cigarette out. Walks over to me, sitting at the piano, where the music lies open on the rack, Bela Bartok's *Mikrokosmos*. Now she bends over and looks deeply into my eyes. I can see every pore in her lightly tanned face. Sometimes my neglectful mother, in a guilty charade of parenting, puts on a devoted expression, like makeup; I can spot it a mile away. This time it's the real thing, because this time she really means to leave. I see that right away, there's no mistaking it. In her eyes I see deep sadness and deep love for me, only for me. It is the first day of my life that I know, really know, my mother loves me. It is the last day of hers. "Oh, just go for a swim, honey. I'll come join you." This from my father. Mock downplaying of the situation. Everything A-OK. Red blotches on his long narrow face belie the calm words. She hesitates, still looking at me. "Go on. I'll run Dovey over to Beverly's." She looks from me back to him. The moment of love, love exclusively for me, is over. Later, as Dad and I get in the car, she comes out the front door in her swimsuit, beach towel over her arm. Marches down the path without looking back at us. Her narrow shoulders, the orange suit, recede from sight. Dad starts the car.

That afternoon, late, Dad picks me up from my friend's house down in Inverness Park. During the brief ride my usually voluble father says not a word. His face is ashen. When we enter the house, he calls out to her, something he never does. No answer. As night falls, I ask if Mother is still down at the beach. "Oh, you know Mama," he says. "She probably went over to Manka's." Sometimes my mother would spend the night at the local inn after one of their dustups. My father and I eat leftovers for dinner and retire to our separate bedrooms. I wake up very early next morning, just as light is breaking. In bare feet and flannel pajamas I walk outside into the chill dawn air. The back gate of our station wagon sits open in the driveway. When I see the bulky garbage bag inside, I scream once, loudly, without knowing why. My father, pacing in tight circles next to the car, jerks his head around and I look directly into the eyes of a guilty, cornered animal. "I'm taking some books over to your uncle's," he says. I know my aunt and uncle haven't opened up their house yet. The bag does not look like it has books in it; there's sand all over it. Quickly I look away.

In that instant something deep below my conscious self knows. And agrees not to know. There are just the two of us, me and my father. And two Doveys. The Dovey that doesn't know is the father's loyal subject.

Caw, caw, caw.

On the branch the winds riffled the crows' dusty black feathers.

I leaned on the shovel, remembering. At first I had fretted, in a very unfocused way, about the garbage bag. Then I had put it out of my mind, especially when the police asked me all those questions. Locked it down.

His was a weak and fragile nature but not an evil one until that moment – it must have been on the beach, when he saw in her eyes, as I had, that she was really leaving. It would have been an impulsive act, an accident of violence, to cross in a split second that fault line over which he could never return. But in the days and weeks to come – such were his powers of self-persuasion, his adamant refusal to see evil in himself – he would have commenced, to himself and others, to deny he had done it with such vigor that in time he would almost believe his own story. This knack of deflecting responsibility had always been the strongest feature of my father's personality. Other people, forces in society at large, were to blame. Not him. Not Albert Eagleton, Ph.D. (or "P.H. Dud," as my uncle had been known to call him).

Caw, caw, caw.

Killed her, the crows cried. Killed her. Then killed himself.

Yes, eventually it would have caught up with him. At some point a chink in the character armor opened up, just enough of a chink to make it possible for my father, in another fatal split-second on the Olema road, to turn the car wheel to precisely the right angle to let him embrace the distorted image of himself that rose up in front of the car headlights in the form of a rugged Douglas fir.

Not the Tomales Bay tidal bore. He killed her and buried her in the woods.

Not a trick curve on the Olema road. He killed himself.

That was it. That was all. That was the story of my childhood. There would never be any other story. Only that one.

The sun sank further into the trees and suddenly my mother came to me in the grove. She was with me, she was all around me, I felt her everywhere though I couldn't see her, her breath breaking over me like a wave. Mother. One pure second of love. Then she was gone.

I stood over the grave. My heart felt ripped down the middle. I was alone, again. Shovel in hand, crying bitterly, I walked out of the trees.

24

Two hours later, wincing from the new crop of blisters on my scrubbed palms, I walked into the kitchen after a long shower and turned on my aunt's vintage kitchen counter AM radio. The station was playing one of my favorites, the Platters' version of "Twilight Time."

I leaned out the Dutch door with a clear view of the back yard and the stand of scorched eucalypts. In the distance a dog barked. And lo, by royal command of the Platters it *was* twilight time, nine o'clock this high summer evening, and who should be walking across the empty strip behind the three houses in the gathering dusk but my old friend George. And what was that dripping, shambling thing he led behind him like a pet bear at the end of a long rope? Why, it was Peter Chook, larger than ever I remembered him, even with that heavy hawser looped around his neck. Peter Chook's grey skin melted into the darkening air, but his eyes glowed red. A purple bruise the size of a melon, edged in blood, covered his forehead.

They walked through the back yard to the foot of my kitchen steps. One hand resting on the rope slung over his shoulder, George looked up at me with his boyish smile. "Hi!"

"Hi."

Peter shuffled to a stop a few feet behind his master. My first reaction caught me by surprise. I tried to suppress it, but I couldn't. I wasn't sorry to see Peter like this. Did that mean George was right, that he had only done to Peter what I had secretly wished for? And did *that* mean I was somehow responsible? No, I decided, I was not. I hadn't asked George to come in the first place, no matter what he said, and I hadn't asked him to do this to Peter. I was angry, powerfully angry.

"For a while I had him planted in that nice sewage treatment facility pond up on the mesa," George was saying. "Did you know it's all natural and organic, no chemicals?" When I didn't answer, he went on, "Then I put him in the compost heap at the lady's house down the street."

"Like a crocodile," I said.

"Pardon?"

"You were ripening him."

"Yeah, but it wasn't as nice as Mud Lake, was it, Peter? I moved him out again just now while she was going to the restroom. Can we come in?"

"No."

George's shape shivered. "I don't have to ask," he said. "I was just being polite."

"Yes, you do have to ask. You can't come in."

"Then come over to the garage." Exasperation filled his voice. "Come on, Dovey. You can't get out of it like this. You're just postponing things."

"Maybe I am." I came out on the steps and closed the door behind me. "But sure, I'll come over to your house."

"That's more like it." George gave a tug on the rope and Peter lurched after him. Skin stretched tight as a drum, Peter's bloated body was bursting out of his clothes. Bits of dung and earth clung to his wet grey skin. His shoes squeaked with every step. I brought up the rear.

George motioned over at the trees. "What happened there?"

"Nothing serious. A little brush fire."

He shrugged. "It won't affect the portal."

We trooped single file up George's front steps, through the living room and kitchen and into the pitch-dark garage. George switched on the light. "Let's all make ourselves at home," he said cheerfully, dropping the rope. Arms puffed out at the sides, Peter's body shifted from one foot to the other, trampling the trash on the floor. George pointed a commanding finger. "Hold still!" Peter stirred uneasily but stayed put.

George plopped down in the beach chair. Amazingly, he still hadn't noticed anything amiss. Maybe that was because those big eyes were completely fixed on me. The hunter's gaze. "No point holding out now," he said. "Fact is, you've been saying yes to me for years and years. Want to know how?"

"How?"

"By saying no down here in this state!" he grinned. "You say no to *everything*! You thought saying no was keeping me away but the joke is, all it ever did was make your book bigger. Then this summer, all by yourself, you started to say a little tiny yes. Which I heard you getting ready to deliver. Now I'm a pretty possessive so-and-so, and I wasn't going to let you get away just like that. Said to myself, if she's going to say yes, it better be to me and nobody else! That's why I came for you, Dovey. So you wouldn't get away."

"I won't say yes. Not to you."

He leaned forward and tapped me on the knee. "Let me tell you one thing, young lady. If you try to get away from me that way, you'll have to keep saying no to everything until you can't stand it anymore. And when that happens – I don't care where or when, how many years from now – the first teensy little thing in your miserable life you dare to say yes to, I'll be right back for you." He touched my face gently. "You don't want to keep living that way, do you? Always saying no? That's more like death than what you'll get from me. All it does is postpone the inevitable."

The bravado was seeping out of me. I gulped and looked down. "I don't believe you," I said finally. "You say I belong to you but that's just your word against mine. I say I don't belong to you."

"Oh, yes you do."

"No, I don't. I know what's in my book now. I don't even have to open it to know what it says." I walked over to the book and laid my hand on it. "Killed her and buried her in the woods! Killed her and buried her in the woods!"

George jumped up and rushed over. "What are you doing? You're not supposed to be saying that!"

"See? *I know.* Everything. My father killed my mother. Then he killed himself."

George shook his head, exasperated. "Well, doggone you, Dovey!" He tried to push me away, but I opened the book triumphantly. "I can read it now, George. Look!"

I stopped cold. The first page was still covered with black scratches. So was the second, and the third. Heart sinking, I flipped through it, every heavy page. "If I know what's in the book, why is there still writing in it?" I cried. "Why are you still here?"

He shrugged. "You tell me."

"I think you're over with."

George laughed. "You *think* I'm over with? That's like being a little bit pregnant. Either I'm over with or I'm not. Fact is, I'm here physically and that's the only level we're dealing with right now." His big head closed in on mine and I had to struggle not to flinch away. "Let me tell you a little something about *knowing*, Dovey. I won't go away because of any little mental insights or revelations you may have had. What gets in by the body has to leave by the body. That's where my book is really written, you know. In that little stoop of yours. In the way you won't look people in the eye. That's Dovey saying, 'I don't want to know!'" He gave a shrill imitation of my voice.

"But I *do* know!"

"Sure you do. C'mon now, it's time to fly away. Don't worry, you'll still *think*," he laughed.

Stalling, I clutched the book to my chest. "I want to hang on to this. It is mine, isn't it?"

"It is, Dovey." Then George moved behind me where I couldn't see him.

There were grunts, cries, a loud tearing noise. Then, with a loud snap like sails catching the breeze, great black and white wings mantled me head to toe, shutting out the light. The air I was breathing inside this dark feathery tomb felt not of this world. As it passed through my lungs into my bloodstream, I felt my own turning begin. First the skin under my arms rippled. Then I screamed as my shoulder blades were yanked out of their sockets. My body was stretching and compressing like an accordion.

It was now or never. "Hey, George!" I cried from inside the blackness. "Where's Mom?"

"Right over here." The wall of feathers snapped back. Wings retracted, George spun around at the empty chair for the first time and gave an eerie squawk. His head swiveled around. "What have you done with her?"

Out in the regular air again, I could feel my conversion subsiding. I took a deep breath. My feet were feet again, my hands held the book.

"Don't you remember? You put her there for me. Hint, hint!" I taunted.

"*Where is she?*" he screamed.

Clutching the book, I ran for the kitchen door. George, screeching, was hot on my heels. I slammed it in his face, ran out the front door and sprinted for the trees. I had wanted to stay away from the grave, protect it from him, but somehow the little clearing with the fresh dirt piled up in the middle was the only possible destination.

The moon was just rising. With the underbrush burned off, the damp, charred grove offered few places to hide. Panting for breath, I ducked behind a tree.

Krk, krk, krk.

I whirled around.

A creature with a huge hawk's head planted on a man's body towered over me. There was nothing human in the unwinking tawny eyes. The yellow beak was the size of a fist. Stumps of wings had burst out of both shoulders. As the thing stepped toward me, I pointed at the mound of dirt. "She's there, you freak! I buried her there!"

With a shrill noise that morphed into a loud squawk of grief, it lunged screeing at the grave. As it clawed at the dirt, the beak retracted and the feathers flattened into skin. George's head reshaped itself. "Now you've really done it!" he screamed. "She's not like Peter! She won't last down there!"

"I gave her a decent burial," I screamed back, just as loud. "A decent burial!"

I should have run. Instead I stood riveted while the earth flew like a black river between George's legs. He got down to the body very fast. The white bundle looked strangely shrunken and collapsed. Whimpering, he dragged it out of the hole and unwrapped the filthy percale, exposing the still-articulated skeleton of a very large bird. Its bony wings, embedded in transparent skin, were awkwardly folded against a shrunken breast to which a few matted black and white feathers still patchily adhered.

"I've lost her! Lost her!" he keened. "Now she can't come back with me! She's gone for good."

He stood up and turned to me, his face contorted. "To heck with you, Dovey! I'm not taking you back with me now. I'm going to do you like I did Peter and you just see how you like it." Stooping to pick up the book with one hand, he twisted my arm behind me with the other and twirled me around. "We're going back to the house now and finish this in private."

"What about my mother?" I shouted as he propelled me out of the woods. "*My* mother?"

"Your mother, Dovey? Don't make me laugh. You didn't give two cents for your mother."

Wasn't that the truth. No, actually, I hadn't. Not while she was alive and, up until a few hours ago, not while she was dead, either. But now –

It took the fight right out of me, just as George knew it would. My shoulders slumped in submission and we walked in silence to the edge of the trees.

All three houses – the Finches', my aunt and uncle's, and George's – were lit up from behind like big sad Halloween faces. On the Finches' roof a dish slowly revolved, mournful as an unanswered prayer, as the ghostly spirits of satellite television flickered through their living room blinds.

Then I stopped short, making George bump against me. He couldn't see what I did.

My mother stood right in front of us, wearing the blue paisley sundress that always looked so nice on her. She looked at me with loving eyes, just like she had the very last time I saw her alive.

"I loved him more than I loved you," I told her. "I knew what he did and I didn't tell!"

I *deserved* what was happening to me, of course. That was why the writing hadn't gone away. That was why George could still do what he liked with me.

"What's that you're mumbling, Dovey? Why are your eyes shut?" George tried to push me forward, but I dug in my heels. I needed more.

"I forgive you," I imagined my mother saying, because the dead can't speak. "Now forgive yourself."

That was all and she was gone.

I opened my eyes.

"Dovey, for Pete's sake, get going!" I could feel George's hot breath on my neck.

"Let's go back to the woods," I said quietly. "I'll say yes, I promise. I won't make trouble. Only please, just do it in the woods. Next to her."

George thought about it. Then he said, a little querulously, "Okay. But don't forget I'm being nice about this." Keeping my arm pinned, he spun me around so that we faced the eucalyptus grove again.

"You don't have to hold my arm like that – I won't run away. There's no point anymore, is there?"

"No, there isn't." He let go and clasped my hand tightly in his. We marched hand in hand back to the clearing, for all the world like a courting couple if Al or Sally bothered to look out their kitchen window. In the light from the rising moon I saw his human face clearly. The black beard, the white skin, the teardrop moles under the eyes.

The grave lay open before us. He stepped back with a little sigh.

I tread her wrist and wear the hood, talking to myself, and would draw blood.

In the split second he let go of me – the way a moray eel does, the better to get a firmer grip – I jumped back and snatched the book away from him. As he whipped around and lunged at me, I lifted the book high over my head and brought it down on George's head so hard the wood cracked. He reeled back.

At this sign of his weakness, a strange frenzy possessed me. A heady Old Testament righteousness coursed through my veins. My guilt might be gone, but not my rage. I was a fierce avenger now. The skin around my mouth hardened. Claws sprouted from my fingertips. I darted behind George and grasped his throat with both hands. My talons pierced his neck. I clamped my foot-claws firmly in the flesh of his legs.

I hissed, "Eagle trumps hawk."

George screamed. His head spun around and the dark alien eyes met mine. The fear I saw in them gave me a thrill, the deep pleasure of the predator, a feeling I hope never to have again in this life. We wrestled. George pulled free and grabbed me in another armlock. I wormed my way out of his grasp and snatched the book from the ground. This time I banged him square on the head, splintering the wooden covers. Stunned, he slumped in the moonlight.

"Murderer! Murderer!" I screamed, whacking him again and again. George swayed a few moments, then toppled and lay still. I crashed the book on his head again, splattering us both with blood.

As I raised it high for the finishing blow, the voice came again. "Just like you know who."

I froze.

Birds of a feather.

I was about to commit a murder.

Aghast, I dropped the book. It fell open on the ground next to George.

The pages flipped in front of me. As if from a great distance, I saw the ugly black script slowly erasing itself from the pages.

I don't know how long I stood like that. When I came back to myself, my mouth was a mouth again. The claws were gone from the tips of my fingers. George lay unconscious at my feet, his head covered in blood. Pulling the belt out of his pant loops, I tried to fasten his hands behind his back, but my human fingers, shaking with urgency, kept slipping. I was afraid he might change into his other body when he came to, which judging by his moans would be very soon. I tied his hands as best I could. Then I pulled his pants down around his ankles and stepped quickly back. George lay trussed and barelegged on the ground with the shattered book full of blank pages beside him.

A noise came from the trees. Leaves crunched. Someone was coming.

I waited, straining to see in the darkness. Had Al Finch heard the commotion?

The footsteps stopped very close. A pair of red eyes glowed at the edge of the clearing. The frayed edge of a rope poked out of the shadows.

Peter Chook shuffled into the moonlight, looking for his master.

I pointed my finger at him and said loudly, "Stay!" Instantly he halted. "Good dog," I said, choking back hysterical laughter.

George groaned faintly beneath me. That sound made Peter stagger forward.

"Stay!" I commanded, and he stopped. I pulled off my T-shirt, tore it in half, and gagged George's mouth securely. Now Peter would have only one master to listen to.

"Take him!" I said firmly. Peter lurched over to George and stopped uncertainly. "Pull him by the heels. Follow me!" Peter bent over and grasped George's ankles clumsily. "Come!" I pointed where he was to go. With agonizing slowness Peter dragged the body through the trees, bumping it painfully over exposed roots. I followed, carrying the splintered book.

Behind my house Peter and his burden came to a stop. Wordlessly I pointed to the front, and we moved at the same snail's pace between my house and George's until we reached the blue Volkswagen station wagon.

"In the back," I pointed.

Peter's swollen fingers punched uselessly at the button on the tailgate. The terrible red eyes met mine, then lowered humbly. I reached over and opened it for him. He lifted George up and crammed him feet first into the small cluttered compartment, just as George had once done to him.

"Car keys," I said. Peter turned and shambled up the steps. After he disappeared inside the house, I took a deep breath. I was wearing only a tank top and shorts, but I wasn't cold. A grunting noise came from the rear of the station wagon. George was awake, straining furiously at his gag. His eyes bulged, his face turned red with exertion. I smiled and hefted the ruined book, taunting him. Contorting his body, he flopped furiously, like a fish. Then slowly, as if it were costing him a serious effort, he levitated off the floor of the compartment. Quickly I slammed the hatch shut. George's bound body began to bump gently against the windows, defying gravity like an astronaut.

Now that he was airborne, would he start to change into his other body? I looked over frantically at the house. Faint noises came from inside. Finally Peter shuffled out the front door, empty handed.

I groaned. The car key, of course, would be in the obvious place: George's pocket. I opened the door on the driver's side. "Here!" I pointed. Peter came around and crammed his bulk slowly into the driver's seat, his swollen skin bulging over the wheel. George had turned his body around in midair and now, over the seats, he was urgently butting Peter in the head with his feet. Peter sat stolid and unmoving.

"Good," I said to him. "Good Peter."

I went to the back of the station wagon and lowered the door. The next instant George's body came shooting out, but I was ready and caught him by the feet. With one hand I held onto his thrashing body, now in the process of befeathering itself, while I rummaged frantically through his pulled-down pants. At last I felt something metallic and fished out the set of keys. When I tried to push George back in, the body bucked and fought like a hooked marlin. I flipped him on his side and pushed him in, legs doubled over, just as yellow talons broke through the soles of his boots. With a loud ripping noise wings burst out the back of his jacket. The hands wriggled free of their binding. Claws seized my wrist.

I screamed. The head swiveled; the round eyes glowed in triumph. In the front Peter did not turn around. I strained to pick up the heavy book from the ground with my free hand and managed to smack George's human arm with it. He squawked and let go. I snatched my hand back and banged the hatch shut just as he slammed against the glass. I took the key around to Peter's side. Leaning over the putrid grey stomach heaving gently in and out behind the wheel, I stuck the key in the ignition. As George thrashed wildly in the back, the little doll dangling by her neck from the rearview mirror caught my eye. I ripped her down, then drew back and slammed the driver's door against Peter's bulk. "Wait here!" I ordered.

I ran in my aunt and uncle's house. In the kitchen I found a box of matches. I took them back outside and picked up the book from the ground. The old VW station wagon was rocking wildly now with the impact of George's body as it hammered the back window. Lighting a match, I held it against the pages. They refused to catch fire. Securely stitched and bound, the heavy rag stock was hard to tear but I managed to shred a few of the pages. When I held the flame under them this time, a ruff of orange circled the edges. Holding the flaming book by one corner, I cracked the hatch a few inches and tossed it in. I slammed the door shut just as the huge man-hawk head came crashing forward. It hit the glass with a satisfying thunk as the rear compartment filled with smoke.

"Start the car!" I shouted to Peter. Obediently he turned the key in the ignition. After a few tries, the engine kicked in.

I rapped smartly on the roof and stepped back. "Now *go*! Go away from here. Go to Mud Lake or hell or wherever you came from! And never come back!"

Watching the old station wagon lurch down the driveway, I felt an odd little surge of patriotism. Take your average American male poet, turn him into an alcoholic, kill him and bring him partly back to life – do all this to him and he could still manage to put a standard-transmission car into gear, make a proper left turn at the end of the driveway, and signal with the blinker light as he made for the highway. Quite a triumph for our way of life, if you thought about it.

The last thing I saw was the outsized hawk's head wreathed in black smoke against the back window. Try talking your way out of this one, I thought, and waved George goodbye. That was when I looked down and saw the grey marks branded on my wrist.

I stood there a long time – long after the headlights had vanished down the hill, until I was sure the station wagon was not coming back. Then I noticed the swimsuit doll ornament lying on the ground a few feet away. Gently I picked her up and brushed her off. I untied the string from her neck and threw it away.

Then she and I went inside for a good night's sleep.

25

It was two weeks later. Early morning mist steamed out of the ground below the bedroom window. For a disorienting moment I hung suspended between the Posturepedic and my leaf bed in the wood rat's nest in the Point Reyes forest.

I spoke to myself the words I now began each day with.

What in me is dark illumine, what is weak raise and support.

Today was Big Cup Saturday. I got up, dressed, went out the back door. The old orange Citroen Al Finch had given me as a loaner sat in the driveway. Sam lay sprawled on the hood. The black cat stretched, then jumped in a leisurely fashion to the ground as I got in the car.

These days there weren't as many dead mice in the field. The treetops were quiet at night. Sheila's

conference was over and the poets had flown away,
too, though not without one final flurry. The last day
of the conference I had come upon James Harrier
sitting on the bench outside the market engaged in
soulful chit-chat with the sixteen-year-old. I honked,
leaned out the window, and – to the merriment of all
the Bolinas burnouts loitering within earshot – yelled,
"Leave her alone, you disgusting old letch!"

As his head gave a gratifying jerk in my direction, I
added pleasantly, "And your poetry sucks!"

I sped off in a cloud of uncatalyzed exhaust.

(The teenager, by the way, grew up to become
quite a good poet herself, whether because of or in
spite of my intervention I never knew. And reader,
the man's real name in this great state of California is
Kinney. Again: that's James Kinney.)

Meanwhile I was busy absorbing the second
Dovey, and she was proving difficult to digest. One
minute I was the old me, placid, loyal and withdrawn,
remembering my family in the way I was accustomed
to; the next I was the new me, devoured by fury and
grief, all my thoughts still fixed on bloody vengeance.
I was grateful both of us were alive and well, but there
seemed to be no way of forging an amicable union. I
was either one or the other, never both at the same
time. George was right. Knowing didn't only happen
in your head; somehow it had to occupy your whole
being. This looked to be a weary effort, one I would
face every day for the rest of my life.

Evenings were difficult. I cried all the time.

The day after I sent George and Peter off, I went
back to the clearing in the grove. The bird body lying

in the dug-up pit looked very dead indeed. Gingerly I tried to pick it up. The skull with its oversized empty sockets dangled on the spine, barely attached with skeins of flesh and feathers. I filled in the hole and took the carcass to the Point Reyes Observatory. There a woman ranger my age told me it belonged to order Falconiformes, family Accipitridae.

My family too, in a manner of speaking.

She disposed of the remains at my request.

Every day after that I returned to the empty filled-in hole in the grove. Each time I came with flowers; once I even prostrated myself. Inside me the fire-blasted trees smoldered on. The next Saturday I drove through San Francisco to Colma, the southern suburb devoted to cemeteries, where my father reposed. For a long time I stood silent over the stone engraved with his name in the field full of markers. In my daypack was the can of red spray paint I had brought to deface the grave of the very big man who was such a very little man. The filthy drunk. For a long moment I clutched the can, trembling. Then I put it away.

But I couldn't stop thinking about what he did, how he must have done it, every detail of every incident before, during and after. Did he hold her under, or did he throttle her? I wanted hard evidence to back up the chatter of birds and my own elusive memories.

When I got back from Colma, I called the deputy sheriff in San Rafael. On Monday he came out and I took him to the clearing. When I told him about my mother's disappearance, he said he hadn't been on the force back then. I told him to look it up. I said I wanted the case reopened. I told him I now suspected my father, her husband, had been the perpetrator and had buried her in these woods. I told him that the hole before us was a test pit I had dug because I was looking for my mother. As, of course, it was.

The deputy looked at me. He looked at the pit. He said he would file a report.

I said I wouldn't be surprised if my former neighbor George had had something to do with the missing hiker. And by the way, had they located Peter Chook? Had they thought to make a connection between the two disappearances?

He wrote a few things down and acknowledged they were taking George a little more seriously after he'd vanished so suddenly. Maybe Old Lust's report had helped that along. He said goodbye and drove off.

I had already decided what I would do if the sheriff's office didn't follow through about my mother. Much as my aunt and uncle loathed my father, I knew they would not countenance an unseemly search. But they were childless and someday, as both of them had given me to understand, this house and this land, including the grove, would be mine. When that time came, I would hire as many workers as it took to find her. And when we did, she would get her decent burial. For now she had to wait in the ground a bit longer.

I begged her in my prayers to be patient. The important thing was, we'd made our contact and she was at peace. I had no more fear of the eucalyptus grove; it was now a hallowed site. Stored away in my aunt's laundry room I found a nice little oil painting she'd done of a sunflower. I propped it up on the desk where I could see it every day.

(Fifteen years later, the remains were excavated and identified to considerable notoriety. Who put her there was never officially determined. To the myriad tabloid and true crime shows who approached me I always refused interviews. I had the body interred in the Sunset View Cemetery on the east side of the San Francisco Bay. Sold the bungalow and never went back to West Marin again.)

In the meantime here I was, alone and uncrazy, possessed by grief, child of a killer, knowing I could kill, too. I understood that my old guilt about the Tragedy had been about more than just keeping silent about what I had seen, of course. Something in me believed I helped kill her myself. That something hadn't wanted me to go near my memories. Instead it called to George.

That wasn't all, one of the Doveys chipped in. My mother had sacrificed me to her obsession with my father. My father had committed a horrible crime. But they had loved me just the same. And I loved them. What was I to make of this tangle in them? In me? In anyone else I might encounter in my life? Looking at the grey claw marks permanently tattooed on my wrist, I couldn't begin to say.

By the time I drove past Old Lust's house and turned onto the main road, the sun shone hot and hard, burning off the dew. It was going to be a blistering day.

"Fiorella Pipit," I said aloud, looking at the amulet on my finger. True, the ring hadn't held any secret power that reared up to zap George during our last struggle. It was simply proof someone besides my mother cared about me – a better kind of power, I realized. So maybe it had helped, after all.

A few days after George's disappearance, two items appeared in the mailbox: a Pacific Gas & Electric bill addressed to Fiorella Pipit and a paperback in a brown paper bag. The book was *The Pocket Blake*, with a note on a scrap of paper that read, "Best wishes, Wm Grebe." He must have given it to Sheila to pass on. He hadn't inscribed the book itself, of course; that would have been too personal. The bill I puzzled over until this very morning, when it came to me in a flash. I was looking at Old Lust's name.

When I walked down to put it in her mailbox, a pale white hand was waving a glowing stick of incense on the other side of the tall fence. I cleared my throat and said, "Mrs. Pipit?"

The high gate opened to reveal a shriveled old crone in a faded housecoat. It took a moment to register this apparition as Old Lust without her makeup and gear. Faint amusement crossed her face as she observed my shock.

I handed over the bill. "Mail for you."

"Come in, dear. I am *purifying* the premises."

I followed her into a tiny overgrown yard with a gleaming vegetable garden in the center. A great pile of rich black dirt was heaped up near the fence. No signs of disturbance were visible now.

Sticking the envelope in a voluminous pocket, Old Lust motioned me into a redwood lawn chair so weathered it took off a piece of my skin when I sat down. She sat down across from me. It was hard to connect this wizened creature, balding under her hennaed hair, with the sex goddess I had known.

"Now that this dreadful person is gone, we will have peace again, yes?" she said in her sonorous voice.

I couldn't argue with that. "Thank you for the ring," I said, taking it off my finger.

She waved it back. "Keep it."

"Thank you." I slipped the ring back on. "It means something to me."

"And you?" Old Lust asked. "How are you?"

I blinked, startled. Nobody else had asked me that, for the simple reason that no one but me had any idea what had happened.

"Good," I said.

Old Lust looked me over with her piercing green eyes. "You are a very pretty young woman."

I bobbed my head, embarrassed. Lately people made comments like this to me all the time, as if I were suddenly visible to them for the first time. It made me feel a little naked, but mostly I liked it.

"I will give you a souvenir from my garden." She took a pair of shears from the table, clipped a thick swatch of sprigs from a lavender bush next to her chair and handed them over. "Now you must go."

I stood up. "Goodbye," I said, and Old Lust closed the gate behind me.

I never saw her again.

Aromatic lavender perfumed the Citroen's interior as I drove down Highway 1. Bolinas Lagoon was still as a mirror. A brace of sea lions sunned themselves on a sand spit. Gulls prowled the pale blue interstices of the mud flats.

In Stinson Beach I parked, unlocked the Big Cup and went in. Before I set up for business, I went through the stack of newspapers sitting by the trash for a copy of the previous week's *Point Reyes Light*. I flipped to "Sheriff's Calls":

> WOODACREW: A homeowner complained to deputies that someone had ridden a skateboard on his sheetrock and damaged it.
> INVERNESS: An elderly woman reported that she fell out of bed and needed help getting back in.
> POINT REYES STATION: Officers stood by while a man got 86'd from the Two Ball, then the Western.
> STINSON BEACH: A resident reported he had been stabbed, robbed and beaten by space aliens who kidnapped his fiancee and her children. Officers investigated, finding the man's wounds had been self-inflicted, and that his fiancee had fled when he "went berserk." The man was taken to County Mental Health for 72-hour observation.

On and on I read, about checks stolen from car dashboards, burglar alarms going off because a dog was pushing open people's front doors, coyote sightings, domestic fights, petty theft, drunken driving. Finally I found what I was looking for:

> BOLINAS: A woman complained that a neighbor was digging in her compost heap.

And right after it:

> BOLINAS: A woman reported finding a relative's missing car in a ravine on the Point Reyes

National Seashore. Rangers towed the car out of
the park.

I put the paper down. A bit understated, but it fit
right in.

It would have been out of the *Light*'s provenance
to report that a 1967 powder blue Volkswagen station
wagon, interior blackened and registered to a woman
up in Eugene recently institutionalized for severe
schizophrenia, had turned up a month later in the
Mojave Desert just off Highway 190 near Joshua Tree.
The deputy had given me this information just this
morning over the phone. They'd contacted Peter
Chook's brother in Maryland, he said, but no one
there had heard from him. He and George had flown
the coop for good, it seemed.

Meanwhile the owner of the house next door, a
middle-aged woman who lived in Santa Rosa, had
come down on the weekend to clean up the place. "It
was a mess," Al Finch told me. "He made all those
alterations to the garage without even asking her. And
both his checks bounced."

"You knew that," I said.

Al was indignant. "Knew what?"

"Knew George was doing stuff to the garage. You
stood right there and watched him."

"Well, naturally I thought he asked her
permission," Al spread his hands in outraged
innocence. Even though Al had hauled the old
Citroen out of his garage and got it in running
condition for me, what with one thing and another
my relations with the Finches had been permanently

strained. Now, I knew, they eagerly awaited the return of my uncle and aunt and the accompanying orgy of scandalized gossip. After filing all the insurance claims, I made my lie to Al good by faxing a long letter to the hotel in Venice that my aunt and uncle would reach in another week. My uncle's fabled uptightness I now regarded as nothing short of inspired prescience. Vividly anticipating a worst case scenario in all areas relating to his material possessions, he had left detailed instructions and contact information that, as it turned out, came in very handy where the Bel Air was concerned.

Once the espresso machine was on and the pastries were out of the refrigerator, I unlocked the front door for business. The AA members and a few other early risers filed in docilely, like prisoners. Even Chevy Jim, wearing a sad little smile. Joan, a bored young mother who came in every day with her three-year-old daughter, showed up a few minutes later. I always dreaded their arrival because Melissa tore through the place like a small cyclone, crawling under chairs and knocking the tops off the cookie jars. It annoyed me that Joan let her run so free, but I said nothing because Roy had told me flatly this was Stinson Beach and people did as they pleased.

"That dress looks nice with your hair," Joan said to me at the counter.

"Do you want some cake, Melissa?" I asked the little girl. Wide-eyed, holding her mother's hand, she nodded slowly.

Here is what happened next. When I looked into that child's eyes, love for her flooded me in an awkward, unexpected rush. And Melissa, unblinking, gave this huge love right back to me. We stared at each other in silent rapture. Meanwhile Melissa's mother poured herself some coffee and gave her daughter a tug. "Come on, honey." The little girl turned away and forgot me at once.

Tears filled my eyes as I polished the latte glasses. I busied myself serving and taking money, trying to quell this strange upsurge of feeling. Love had now joined the anger, grief, and other feelings that washed over me at unpredictable moments, directed toward all kinds of people and sometimes at no particular target at all. But then the old Dovey took over. In a few minutes I was able to look over in the corner at Melissa and her mother and see only a Stinson Beach working single mother and the offspring she was about to deposit at a daycare center.

After work I walked up the trail behind town to Table Rock, a flat chunk of granite partway up Mount Tamalpais so big it was clearly visible from the beach. Panting slightly, I flopped down on the hot hard surface and pulled out my black notebook. It now seemed important to have the notebook always with me. I wrote in it every day.

This was my first entry: "I believe my father murdered my mother in our house in Inverness when she came back from the beach directly below us. I believe he took her things back down to the beach so it would look like she drowned in Tomales Bay. I believe he buried her body behind his brother-in-law's house in Bolinas the next morning."

His crime that by complicity became my crime, too. And the crime, of course, had gone on secretly broadcasting itself in the way all great outrages do – in consequences. Like the invisible man in the movies who makes easy chairs sag in the middle, cigarettes smoke in midair, and footprints miraculously pop up in the sand, it had left its tracks all over my father and me and everything around us. After her disappearance, my screaming nightmares of a bogeyman suffocating the family cat. My phobic fear of him, slip-sliding under the adulation, in the weeks and months afterward. Crying out sharply if he appeared suddenly around a corner.

His grief, disintegration, and suicide.

Cause invisible, effects highly tangible. The act had left a gaping crater whose narrow perimeter – in the split-second after I looked into the back of the station wagon – I had rapidly scooted onto and proceeded to make my home.

Obviously, my notebook had to include the whole story. To skip over any of it would put me back in my zombie's exile at the crater's rim. I also wanted it to show what I had learned: that we're all angels, we're all messengers from the other state. That we have to learn to read the message we bring ourselves, read what the secret book written on our bodies says and understand it. That if we fail to do this, the foul intruder will usurp our nest.

But I wanted my notebook to do more than just cancel out George's book. I wanted it to be about the rest of my life, too – about what came after the story that would never change. My hope was to fill it with all sorts of interesting events that happened to me, some of which, I hoped, would even make me happy.

The part about George you have just read.

Far below, six or seven long swells on the great plate of ocean rolled over and over, like sausages, toward shore. I was here, I told myself, to think about my future. In the last two weeks the unexpected conviction had grown inside me that my long-awaited plans for fall no longer presented an attractive agenda. But if I did not go to graduate school, what other place in the world was there for someone like me? Bill Grebe had said that the goal of life is not to be normal but to be the one person that you are. I liked the sound of that. I knew, for example, I did not want to throw away all my books and open a gourmet cookie shop or a gardening business, the way people I knew in Berkeley always seemed to be doing. That did not seem any more like real life to me than graduate school did. But what was? Between these two unappealing poles my imagination was able to conjure up only a vague grey world of office desks. I wanted none of any of that. At the same time I was incapable of picturing what I *did* want. It was all very confusing.

It came back to telling the story. How would I ever be able to explain George? That he wasn't my own creation; that I hadn't killed Peter or the missing hiker in my sleep. That he was something real and outside me who matched something inside me, a tangle of forces pulled to me like a magnet, pushing me in and out of this world. That I called him because I had told myself a lie and had never forgiven myself. That the portal wasn't just in the eucalyptus grove, it was in me. That I had defeated him when I told myself the truth, or when I forgave myself, or –

This was what really bothered me most: exactly how I had gotten rid of my dark angel. He had said that I would have to use all of myself to get out from under him, but what had I actually used? Murderous anger and brute force, in the wake of an imaginary mother's blessing. And my own bloodlust had horrified me so deeply that I failed to kill him, finish him off for good, when I had the chance. Did that mean I was a good person or a weak person? That George had won or I had won? Either way, it didn't feel like a satisfactory resolution.

And what about that so-called other state? Was George's state the only other state? Were there more beyond it, *good* other states? Nicer messengers than George? I had to think so. Bill Grebe had said the other state was a place we all came from and went back to. Surely it had better parts than George's desert.

I took a big bite out of an apple and opened my notebook. Picked up my pen. Something was struggling to get out of me. But the glare of the sun on the white pages was too bright; I had to put it away. I lay back on the hard stone and closed my eyes.

Table Rock hung out over the world, lifting up my sweating body and plunging me into a fantastic vision of the canyon below, like the panorama I had seen on Hawk Hill but now embodied in full feeling, a kind of bright Technicolor lighting up my heart. The gulch swarmed with bees, small flowers. Tiny silver fish with bright red fins swam in the stream. Most of all, there was the great convocation of birds, hordes of white egrets nesting in the dense branches of the tall coastal redwoods – grooming, disputing, feeding their babies, sailing back and forth over the treetops like stately clippers, making such a huge noise they filled the universe. A handsome female caught my eye. Oh, her fine nest, her four chicks, her frothy white feathers arching over all of it like a splendid wedding fan!

And then Melissa came to me, my own dear daughter. Out of my heart a cloud of warm energy radiated, embracing this little girl. Yes, Melissa. How I loved her!

Suffused in sweet and dreamy feelings, I stretched peacefully and had just turned on my side when a sharp noise, a kind of crack, came from behind me. My eyes flew open. I propped myself up on an elbow and turned around. A little way up the dry slope behind Table Rock a clump of chaparral was shaking. Something was moving inside it. I waited. More rustling and quivering as the bush, agitating, shed leaves and twigs. Suddenly a round object the size of a soccer ball burst out and tumbled down the hill. Faster and faster the black and white ball spun, picking up speed, rolling across the flat surface of Table Rock until it came to rest at my feet.

George's head.

I screamed, as much from outrage as from fear.

The eyes rolled, the teeth clicked, but the head said nothing. It didn't have to. I knew why it was here. The portal was still open. In my dream I had said yes with all my heart and just as he had promised, George came back.

Clouds lumbered across the sky. Down on the beach waves broke without a sound. The head and I confronted each other. The skin around the cheekbones was scorched, I saw. Bitterness flooded me, the bottomless anger again. The grey claw marks on my wrist began to ache.

"Murderer." My rage made me stutter; I choked on the words.

The teeth clicked and chattered, but no words issued from the yellow beak-mouth under the salt-and-pepper beard.

I looked at the head. How easy to grab the hateful thing and drop-kick it over the edge of Table Rock. I pictured it plummeting into the trees that lined the narrow canyon where the trail began, then falling, bruised and battered, into the underbrush around the creek – where, my fancy continued, it would undoubtedly roll across my path again as I made my way down.

"You don't seem in such hot shape, George," I mocked him. "And whatever happened to Peter?"

Frantically the head rolled and spun in place like a wind-up toy with a popped spring. The eyes bulged, the lips mouthed words.

Pity filled me suddenly. The head was suffering. I stretched out my hand, then quickly pulled it back. Maybe pity was the wrong response. Would it make George leap up before me, powers fully restored?

I thought of that other man, the filthy drunk.

The next thought was: Enough. Punishment had been rendered. The endless silent weeping as he sat drinking in front of the television. Then Olema Bolema. His act had swept through all our lives like a wrecking ball. But in the end he had been his own judge, jury, and executioner as well as hers. Mine too, almost. But now it was over.

And, the thought came, what of that not so tiny part of me that secretly rejoiced to have him all to myself, my Oedipal rival finally disposed of? Punishment rendered there as well: to consider myself permanently unworthy of a mate.

Dusty and scratched, the head sat in the hot sun as the outrage inside me peaked and ever so slightly ebbed. George himself had not been deserving of pity, but somehow this thing was. Impulsively I reached out and pushed some of the coarsely matted black hairs off the forehead. The eyes drooped gratefully. I found myself stroking the head, tentatively at first, then slowly and easily. "Poor thing," I said. A tear streaked down the dirty cheek. I felt the head's eternal, inconsolable sadness as if it were my own. "Poor you," I said. "Poor her. Poor me. Poor all of us."

A loud exhalation issued from the head's mouth. The eyes filled with light, changed color. The face rippled and shifted. For a moment it looked just like – but no, that couldn't be. Then it changed again and it was beautiful, so beautiful I had to look away. When I looked back, the features had melted into a solid mass. Whirling like a top, the head spun out from under my hand. I watched it roll across Table Rock and vanish over the edge. I ran up and looked over. Fifty feet below me the tops of the trees poked up green and empty.

I bounded down the trail from Table Rock into the dismal little canyon. It was dank and dark in here under the redwoods. I looked high and low. Nothing was caught in the branches. Nothing lay on the ground. I peered into bushes, kicked up dead pine needles. Nothing.

The head was gone. All the overgrown canyon yielded was a large frayed feather caked with dirt, patchily iridescent, caught on a blackberry thicket bristling with thorns and flowers. Impossible to say what color this feather had once been. Some migrator, on the way south, had shed it. I left it on the bush. Summer won't last much longer, I thought.

The trail led out of the trees into a field just above the highway where a magnificent buckeye stood in full bloom. I sat down under it. You could see everything from here: mountain, ocean, the Bolinas mesa rising behind the lagoon. The sky was a deep, serious blue. Light from the blossoms reflected off my skin. I took out my notebook just as a car with an open top wound up the road. The man driving it saw me and waved. I didn't recognize him but he looked nice. I felt cheerful, lighthearted, benevolent. Just the right lines came to me –

The Angel that presided o'er my birth
Said, "Little creature, form'd of Joy and Mirth,
Go love without the help of any Thing on Earth."

– and I waved back with my marked hand even as a kind of fierceness, an uprush of energy and well-being, possessed me.

Bolinas Venus

– for Rupert Keenlyside

Pulling up in front of the Bolinas bakery, Sam had to swerve to avoid a long-haired man in a loincloth and down vest lying in the middle of the street. He sensed the Bolinas people eyeing him as he got out of the red Mercedes, so he left the car unlocked; he loved beating these types at their own game. Raising his hand in the "bless you" mode to Kevin, he climbed the bakery stairs, then came back with his coffee and fresh croissant to sit down heavily on the old wooden steps next to his son. There were no tables or chairs; that was typical Bolinas. Two feet away a mongrel nosed in the garbage cans.

Old Ford trucks and beat-up Chevelles and Monte Carlos cruised past the dilapidated Victorians on Wharf Road. The hip newcomers driving these cars sported bright-colored tight pants and pompadours; cowboy New Wave, Sam supposed you'd call it. He looked over at his stoop-shouldered son, whose floppy blonde hair hung over the embroidered collar of his Mexican shirt: out of date even with his own generation. Flecks of Danish clung to the gingery wisps of Kevin's moustache. The boy had an irritating habit of gulping his food half eaten. Sam, a methodical chewer, couldn't stand to watch. "How's Rachel?" he asked finally.

Kevin choked down the rest of his pastry. "Split to L.A.," he said in a muffled voice.

"So?"

"So what?" Kevin briefly returned his father's stare, then weakened into confession. "She met this dude passing through town. He offered her this film job down there."

"I see," said Sam. Girls were always leaving Kevin. Sam himself, on the other hand, had always been the one to do the leaving. All right, Kevin's mother had kicked him out, but nowadays Sam was careful to get involved mostly on his own terms. Kevin never asked about Sam's girls. The incumbent, Merilee, was only two years older than he was.

"Where's your glasses?"

"Lost them."

"Need any money?"

Kevin hesitated. For pocket money – it was hard for Sam to picture his gentle, nearsighted son doing this, but he did – Kevin sat shotgun on local marijuana patches. Harvest time, however, was months away. Sam reached for his wallet.

"Dad," said Kevin. "Someone wants to meet you."

Sam looked up. Two flat green eyes in a solemn moon face, very close to his, stared back. The face, cruelly scored and weatherbeaten, radiated a perverse glow of innocence. The enormous middle-aged child woman stood directly in front of Sam, blocking the sun. She was dressed in layers of sacking and tunic topped by a soiled down vest, the standard Bolinas ragpicker's gear.

"Meet Sonja, Dad."

With a wordless smile the woman stretched out her open palms. The air was cool in her shadow. Irrational fright gripped Sam. Hand still frozen on his wallet, he wondered if she wanted money, too.

"Sonja lives next to me in her bus. She remembers you from that time you came up to the mesa to look at Rachel's paintings."

Sam remembered the occasion – another money-generating scam – but certainly not this person. Had she perhaps been spying from the bushes? He turned back to the outstretched hands. Finally he got the message; he hadn't lived in the Bay Area this long for nothing. He laid both his palms ceremoniously over hers.

Sonja's smile increased by an order of magnitude. Her chapped, calloused paws quivered hotly in his.

"Sonja's a very holy person, Dad. She hardly ever says anything. Right now she's getting ready for her big trip. Every October her daughter Percy in Albuquerque sends her a Greyhound ticket and she goes down for the winter."

Sam looked up at Sonja. "How about that," he smiled. Giving her hands a dismissing squeeze, he tried to release them. But Sonja would not let go. Her insistent fingers grasped his even more tightly. With a shiver of disgust he could not quite hide, Sam shook her loose. He stood up. "Nice meeting you," he said pleasantly for the benefit of that unseen ironic observer he always played to. Secretly he felt like wiping his hands off on his pants. He passed some bills over to Kevin, who gave a little bob of his head and put them in his shirt pocket.

"So long, guys." Sam waved as if to a cheering crowd, then walked quickly to his car. Safely inside, he sneaked a look in the rear view mirror. Sonja had not moved. A great mute cow, she dwarfed the boy beside her. Silently the two watched Sam pull away from the curb.

Sam guided the old Mercedes along the twisting road around Bolinas Lagoon. He passed Audubon Canyon, then a few empty gulches bristling with coastal redwoods. The soft, steep folds of Mount Tamalpais were just now greening from early seasonal rain; a red-tailed hawk rode the thermal updrafts on the mountain.

Bolinas Lagoon, Sam recalled, was a very old place, part of a drowned valley marking the path of the San Andreas fault, where two massive plates of the Earth's crust grated against each other. During the last million years or so – Sam was a little vague on the dates – Bolinas and the whole Point Reyes peninsula, which were on the second plate and thus technically not even a part of the American continent, had migrated some three hundred miles up the California coast. And, as far as anybody knew, they were still heading north, at the rate of about an inch every thousand years.

And that's why they're so crazy over there in Bobo, Sam thought. It figured that his disappointing older son would live in a place like that. Bolinas was a time warp town; it boasted broke ex-rock stars, ex-New York poets, and its famous street people, wrinkled grey hobbits and trolls from the long-departed days of the Haight. In Bolinas you could still find All Species Preservation Festivals, communal solstice parties, that kind of thing.

Sam himself lived in Stinson Beach, only a stone's throw from Bolinas across the lagoon but seven miles by Highway 1. All these foggy little coastal towns north of the Golden Gate had their share of eccentrics and burnouts, but Stinson Beach was different. For one thing, it was a man's town, drawing rich commuter sportsmen and rough-and-ready ex-professionals, macho dropouts who were now carpenters, handymen, and the like. Stinson Beach people wore jeans and lots of plaid; the Fire Department and the bar were the town social centers. After the separation Sam's two other kids liked coming over Mount Tam to visit him there. Mark, a junior in high school, brought his surfboard and wet suit; Katrina liked to sit in Elwood's and pick up older men.

The roar of the surf was audible as he turned off the highway at Calle del Arroyo. The beach was a wide flat expanse lined with cottages that stretched three miles from cliff to point. Out at the point, where Sam lived, you could find fossil sand dollars. The ancient grey discs eroded out of thin shelvings of rubble, mimicking the live white sand dollars that littered the beach at low tide. Sam had a thing about the fossil sand dollars. Finding them or not finding them, he believed, was a psychic barometer of how your life was going. Just before school started, he had brought his nephew from Princeton out here. Before Sam was even able to tell the boy about clearing the mind of clutter to allow for the spontaneous, Stephen had found three perfect ones.

He pulled into the driveway of his redwood and glass beach house, the kind of place – he liked to say – where, when you walked in, you didn't know whether to buy a bottle of Scotch, deposit a check, or pray.

Sam himself had not found any fossil sand dollars for a good long while.

"What in the name of glory is *this*?" Sam called to Merilee next morning from the front door. On the mat lay a pile of twigs, some withered sour grass and purple lupine, bits of broken shell and colored twine arranged in a matted attempt at a circle.

"A bird's nest?" she suggested, peering from behind on tiptoe with her chin resting on his shoulder in that little-girl way he detested. A wisp of her long brown hair, damp from the shower, trailed across his face.

Irritably he shrugged her off. "Are you kidding? A giant condor, maybe."

"Look, isn't that writing?"

Sam examined the sand around the pile of refuse. "No. Somebody drew it, but it's just marks. Meaningless." He stood up and surveyed the beach.

The day was breaking sunny and hot. Indian summer weather. Sam looked down again. With one well-aimed kick he scattered the twigs and flowers all over the path.

"Awww," said Merilee.

"I'm going to get the paper." Planting his foot squarely in the middle of the mess, Sam launched himself off down the driveway. There's a lot of kid in me still, he thought. Merilee, he felt confident, would be watching until he got to the road.

This Sunday morning only one other person was on the path along the highway. That striking suntan, the Abercrombie & Fitch shirt – who could it be? The man got closer and Sam saw he was staggering. It was one of the derelicts who slept on the beach in the warmer months and hung around town during the day. The shirt, Sam realized with a start, was his own. He had put it in the Free Box outside the health food store only last week because the moths had gotten into it. Sam's skin prickled as the unkempt man reeled by, leaving a powerful animal smell in his wake. *His* shirt in that life. Winona had given it to him for Christmas ten years ago.

At the superette Sam bought the *Sunday Chronicle* and a loaf of whole grain bread for Merilee. Outside he paused to watch the motorcycle club from San Francisco, a group of middle-class, heterosexual professionals in black leather, roar through town on their weekly jaunt to Point Reyes. Frank the banker stood next to him in Levis, running shoes, and raggedy T-shirt. Over the noise he yelled in Sam's ear, "Going to the wedding?" Sam raised his eyebrows. "The wedding," Frank repeated. "Tina and Bob. Over at the Community Center." Sam laughed and shook his head. Bob was a plumber's helper and Tina was the waitress at the little breakfast place. Stinson Beach was supposed to be an egalitarian sort of town where everybody went to everybody else's social does. Sam did show up now and then, wearing his ironic smile, but he was goddamned if he was going to invite the town riffraff to his private parties and he knew more than a few others who felt the same way.

Suddenly he ducked behind the shelter of the superette veranda. "What's with you?" said Frank. Now that the motorcycles were well up the highway, his voice rang out too loudly.

"Take a look down the road and tell me what you see."

Frank looked. "Oh, my God," he laughed. "You've got to get used to that around here. It's not like you to be squeamish, Sam."

"I don't want her to see me." As soon as Sam said it, he wished he hadn't.

Frank guffawed. "What's the matter? Broken romance?" He cupped his hands and shouted. "Hey, Sonja!"

"Shut up!" Sam whispered fiercely.

But the Bolinas woman did not hear. Attended by three mangy dogs, she walked dreamily along the road. Even from this distance Sam could see the clouds of fleas swarming over the little group; that would be from the natural eucalyptus button flea collars, he thought. Sonja had shed her gypsy gear this balmy day in favor of a crocheted string bikini and ancient rubber thongs.

Unclothed, her ample body had the texture of an old leather bag with hundreds of golf balls rolling around loosely inside. The macramé had stretched impossibly to contain the sway of her long, pendulous breasts.

"What's the name of that prehistoric statue they dug up in Germany or wherever it was?" said Frank. "You know, the lumpy one without the face?"

Sam did not reply. Sonja had crossed the intersection by the gas station without looking their way. Her broad rear and the frowsy butts of the three dogs wagged purposefully toward the other end of town.

"Where could she be heading?" the banker wondered. "You hardly ever see Sonja on this side of the lagoon." But Sam barely heard him. He was gone, walking firmly home in the opposite direction.

That night at Elwood's, Sam and his cronies had gathered in their down vests and jeans to play liar's dice when Frank came up. Sam thought he had never seen such an offensive smirk.

"Hey, Sam, your girlfriend got herself arrested."

"Merilee?" said one of the others, incredulous but eager. Stinson Beachers lived on gossip.

"Sonja," said Frank. It seemed to Sam there was a small stir. "She picked a fight with the Maid of Honor at the reception. Pushed Mary right in the drainage ditch, outfit and all. They called the sheriff. Sonja's in the cooler now."

"New ladylove?" someone said. They all knew how proud Sam was of his slender young women.

An ominous red flush gathered in the wattles of Sam's neck, but he kept on shaking the box. "My throw, gentlemen." He threw.

Two days later, Sonja was out of jail and back in Stinson Beach. Reports of her, Sam knew, filtered among the townspeople. Already a few alert ears had picked up Frank's comment and ripples were coming back to Sam. Someone spotted Sonja leaving a wilted dandelion under the windshield wiper of the Mercedes when he parked it at the gas station. The town was primed to Sonja's presence and waiting to see what would happen.

Then one evening Sam met her – and not by accident, he suspected. It was early dusk on the path by the highway. Fully clothed, she blocked his way. Dogs lapped around her ankles in little waves. Locking Sam in that disturbing blank gaze of hers – drug psychosis, he wondered, or congenital retardation? – she said nothing. When he brusquely attempted to pass, Sonja stepped only slightly aside on the narrow trail, obliging Sam to brush against the edge of her filthy down vest. Then, a few paces behind, she began to follow him.

They were almost to the street light at the highway. It would be the end, Sam thought, if anybody saw them. He turned on her and stamped his foot angrily. "Go away!" The lack of control in his voice shocked him. He stamped his foot again. "Quit following me!"

"Look," he said finally, "what do you want?" Out-and-out appeasement, but for Sonja this seemed to be the password. Immediately she raised her arms in the air and swayed back and forth on the dark path. Oh, brother, Sam thought. Incantation time. I'll let her do whatever she wants and maybe she'll go away. Except go down on me, he amended quickly, I won't let her do that. No, sir. He pictured the act and shuddered.

But Sonja's intent seemed directed elsewhere. Eyes closed, she swayed and moaned, shifting from side to side with her eyes closed. Once she stepped on a dog, which let out a piercing yelp. Then she stopped dancing and began grunting. Grunt, grunt, grunt! Before Sam knew what to think, she had bent over and lifted her skirts, revealing her big bare ass. As Sam stared dumbfounded, Sonja farted in his face. Then, with a coarse, experienced laugh that held more of the barroom than the asylum, she dropped her skirts and sped off into the night.

Sam stood very still, the acrid odor lingering in his nostrils. Then, head down, he walked quickly toward town. In his mind the image of those two pale buttocks, a pair of blind fat worms, loomed mocking and triumphant.

Next morning another small pile of detritus lay on the doorstep. Sam, who had lifted his foot automatically, paused a long moment. Had last night been punishment for disturbing the first morning's offering? Lips tightening, he aimed carefully and let fly. The lupine and nasturtiums sailed through the air, some landing near the scattered remains of the previous week. He walked back into the kitchen, where his cup of coffee sat steaming on the table. When he had first gone to the front door, Sam realized, he had been checking. And had been right. Jesus.

Merilee was watching him. "What's the matter?"

"Nothing." He wished he had picked up all the little bits on the step so she wouldn't see them when she went out. Maybe there was still time if she went to the bathroom.

But Merilee was absorbed in other things. "I'm so excited, Sam," she cried, hugging herself. She had on a smart knit ensemble, rose colored, plus stockings and high heels. Today was the first day of her new job selling real estate. Sam didn't like the looks of the guy in the white Porsche who had given her the job even before she had sat for the real estate exam. Merilee was supposed to be his trainee. Trainee. Sam had never seen her out of jeans before.

"Good luck," he said casually, sipping his coffee. Sam felt he had a better chance of keeping his girls if he always seemed slightly bored.

"I'm so nervous," Merilee said. Her heels clicked as she disappeared toward the back for a last session with the mirror. Sam jumped up and ran to the front door. He brushed the remaining twigs and silver foil off the step and was back in his seat by the time Merilee reappeared. She leaned over to give him a kiss. "See you tonight." Sam smiled briefly.

The wheels of Merilee's Honda Civic crunched in the gravel outside as Sam chewed his toast thoughtfully. After his wife had left him – or rather, made him move out – Sam had evolved a definite credo about his involvements. Before, while he was married, they were informal, spontaneous, passionate. Now that he was, so to speak, unprotected, his new arrangements had become as formal as a Japanese tea ceremony, to wit:

1. No love talk, no plighting of troth.

2. No visiting of relatives (the parents of his girls were likely to be the same age or younger than Sam).

3. No questioning about the other person's outside activities (though Sam as a matter of course broke off with the girl if he found she had slept with someone else; he personally was not interested in being laughed at).

Finally, Sam's mood swings, which were frequent and severe for such a deliberate person, were to be tolerated without comment or complaint. Resistance or – God forbid – attempts at manipulation were completely unacceptable.

These requirements demanded a fairly regular switch of partners to keep up the standard, but so far, except for one regrettable experience with a French girl in which Sam had almost forgotten himself, he had no complaints about his setup, which left his heart free and clear for the real woman he would someday meet, though probably not at Elwood's – the sophisticated beauty somewhere between the ages of 28 and 35 who would see through this facade, love Sam, forgive him, and keep him up to the mark. He would take her on that special trip to Europe he had been planning over the years. When they were in Paris he would wear his suit from Wilkes Bashford and she would wear a hat with a little black veil – no, of course she wouldn't wear such a thing, that was stuff from his own prehistory, but he liked imagining it anyway.

Meanwhile the long-legged girls in jeans would do very well, the willowy ones, idealistic, with a big father thing. It was risky – they were so fickle, and often incredibly boring – but he needed those clear eyes, that fresh complexion, the unquestioning approval. Meeting the shrewd, worldly, bitter gaze of a woman of his own years and class in an intimate setting was about as enticing a prospect to Sam as an unflushed toilet.

He took another sip of coffee. This real estate situation would have to be carefully monitored; if necessary, Sam would time a suitable breakaway. There was a girl he ran into occasionally at the post office who seemed possible, but he thought he had heard someone tell him she was crazy. There were a lot of crazies in this sheltered West Marin environment. Sometimes they came across normal at first: closet crazies. He would have to do some serious checking.

Meanwhile Winona, through her lawyer who was incidentally an old friend of Sam's, had just put through a demand for $850,000 up front. Safely ensconced in the family abode in Ross, wrapped in the warm cloak of her grievances, she sent these directives over the mountain to Sam who, like some pagan god of money, was supposed to wave his wand and cause this sum to materialize in her (now separate) bank account. How had she arrived at this figure? Sam knew how. By Winona's reckoning, it would add up to about a dime per hurt. Sam was supposed to feel punished, guilty, *bad*. And pay for it. That was the whole point, blood money. Winona had money of her own. She just wanted to get him. That familiar female Gestapo ultimatum, disguised as "feelings" but just as transparent as the morning pile of doorstep crud: Love me or you're going to get it.

Well, Sam couldn't be gotten. Not that way. The angry knot inside him tightened another full twist. Sure, Winona, $850,000 – take it, you got it. Better me earning it than you or we'd have a long wait, wouldn't we?

As expected, Merilee came home full of her new job and the witty sayings of her boss Tom, a prize asshole by the sound of it. Here you had the big problem with father complexes – the mantle of godhood seemed to fit such a large number of men. To get away from the Tom-this and Tom-that and maybe explore the possibilities of the post office girl, Sam fled the house. That night and the next, he walked warily down the path to Elwood's. No one appeared to block his way; the expected trailside retribution never came. The morning offerings had also stopped. Sam felt relieved, though not without a twinge of ego. Even the crazies are fickle, he thought.

The third night Elwood's was packed. Sam had just eased himself into a chair near the Franklin stove when a group of people directly in front of him broke up, revealing a large woman sitting at the bar. Even with her back to him, Sam had no difficulty recognizing Sonja. Quickly he got up and moved to the far end of the bar.

Sonja, hunched over her drink, seemed oblivious. As nearly as one could make out, the Bolinas woman was depressed. Her tanned jowls drooped, the eyes looked more than usually glazed. Under the inevitable down vest, Sam noticed, she wore the remnants of a gauzy Indian dress. This parody of feminine attire reminded him that he had actually heard of this woman long before last week. Vague stories that she had once been married to a lawyer, had children, grown children, somewhere. Sam tried, and failed, to imagine

Sonja making their school lunches. Somewhere along the line, perhaps during the psychedelic madness, the fairies had spirited away the lawyer's wife, leaving this changeling in her place.

Sonja's drink was a fancy cocktail, a Pimm's cup or something like it – poignant echo of a bourgeois past, Sam wondered? Sonja, like all the other West Marin heavies, would undoubtedly be on medication – thorazine, stelazine, or some exotic combination thereof. She probably ought not to be drinking at all. Sam was about to mention this to the bartender but stopped himself. That would clinch it. All those watching eyes would note that Sam was taking care of "his girl." Screw it. The yellow skin, for all its cellulite slackness, looked tough and battle scarred. Sonja had already survived, if not very well, some fifty-odd years without his assistance.

Sam fell into conversation with the man next to him, a retired naval officer who was now a chimney sweep in Point Reyes Station. When he glanced over in Sonja's direction again, the stool was empty, the Pimm's cup with its soggy lemon a melted ruin on the bar. Sam cast a nervous look over his shoulder. She was nowhere in the room.

Later, walking home under the frosty stars, he felt his shoulders braced protectively – against the cold? But he reached his dark house unmolested.

Crawling into bed Sam fell determinedly on Merilee's thin gangly body – licked it, devoured it, then gave it a thorough what-for. Except for an occasional moan Merilee said nothing the whole time and rolled over on her back at precisely the same moment Sam rolled over on his. A split-second later, catapulted into dreamland, he found himself wandering through a barren landscape. Not wandering, searching. He was on some kind of mission, in this desert of rolling hills that were not exactly sand dunes. The object of his quest was unclear, but the frustration attached to it was not. He had been thwarted for lifetimes. Eternities. Failure had become an enduring condition he had built his life around. But now there was a sense of hidden excitement. Something momentous was about to happen. He stood on the edge of a deep pit, looking down. There was something in the bottom of the pit, curled up like a snail. Then this object was moving rapidly toward Sam – or was Sam himself plummeting into the pit? Panic mounted, but he could do nothing to prevent the converging of himself with she who could not be named, this enormous, grossly naked woman in flexed position, flesh smeared with red ochre, looking more like a giant lizard than a human, eyes closed but oh, God! if they should open –

Sam's own eyes flew wide apart. He lay on the designer sheets next to Merilee, heart pounding furiously. Still half in the dream, his mind pored over its details. The dusky red of her skin. The objects arranged around her body – black, shiny, sinister. And Sam was supposed to be doing something. He was supposed to be – *not* touching those objects. Definitely not. He shivered at the thought. And the eye, the one visible eye. If it had winked open – and it had been just about to, Sam knew for certain – then what would have happened?

Sam jumped out of bed and put on his robe against the chill. He walked into the dark kitchen and sat down at the table. A crescent moon shone in the window. On the beach, over the crashing waves, a dog howled. Sam sat in darkness for a long time. How long he didn't know. When he finally glanced over at the luminous dial of the stove clock, it was half past four. He had not been thinking about anything much; it had been, he supposed, a kind of trance. Sam got up. He went back into the bedroom and climbed in next to Merilee, bolt awake, awaiting sunrise.

In the next few weeks Sam's life took a turn for the worse. For starters, he couldn't perform. At first Merilee had smothered him in sticky understanding. When nothing changed, she subsided into puzzled hurt and now, Sam fancied, a certain childlike indifference, though she still came home promptly after work and cooked dinner like a good girl. Night after night he tried. No luck. Once Merilee gravely suggested counseling. "*Ther*-apee," he mocked, then brought her off with his mouth. But who was he kidding?

Smells haunted him. Odors of fish, rotten leaves, dead animals filled his nostrils, even when he was safe in his office in the City. He thought about translucent membranes, blue veins, dogs smacking their chops as they ate the placenta of their pups, thin watery menstrual fluid.

After one more night of disaster, Sam got up early and trudged down the beach. He could hear the salmon boats right outside the shorebreak but couldn't see them; the sun lay inside a giant fogbank like a heavy, moist pearl. Transparent jellyfish the size of dinner plates were scattered on the beach. There were tangles of kelp, orange rinds, Clorox bottles, the matted feathers of dead seagulls. A flock of reptilian-looking pelicans cruised low overhead.

Sam walked and walked. At the end of the beach he sat down on a rotten piece of timber. The ocean lapped listlessly against the ugly grey sand; a bad tidal smell rose off the lagoon. Directly across the channel the frame houses of Bolinas floated ghostlike over the river of fog.

Sam tapped his foot rhythmically – like a horny teenager, he realized, and stopped. But not before his toe had struck something hard in the sand. He scratched around and there it was, waiting for him. Elated, he cupped the fossil sand dollar in his palm.

A sensation overwhelmingly cold and impersonal rose from the petrified shell with its shirred five-pointed star pattern. Sam pocketed the fossil and got to his feet. Feeling better than he had in a long time, he strode briskly back down the beach, skin tingling from the prickly dampness of the fog. He whistled as he slammed the front door and lifted his eyebrows to Merilee in ironic greeting. Why strain to prove a point? Tonight he would show her.

By mid-morning his elation had faded. Merilee had gone to work, then phoned back an hour later to say she wouldn't be home for dinner. The fog congealed into rain. Sam paced impatiently, tapping the sand dollar in his pocket through the heavy fabric of his pants. His energy was back, the luck (he hoped) was back, too. What to do with it? Stuck in this godforsaken boring little town, shacked up with a girl barely out of her teens in a beach house with sinking foundations. Sam slammed out the door and jumped into the Mercedes. The back tire whirled monotonously in a patch of mud, then skidded free. He was off.

The rain had slackened when he pulled up at the superette. Two or three of the regulars lounging outside the entrance exchanged glances as Sam got out of his car. He ignored them. When he came back out with his *Chronicle*, Timmy, a burly wastrel and son of his lawyer friend Roger, beckoned him over. Noting the open Coors in Timmy's hand, Sam glanced at his watch – ten thirty in the morning. His unspoken judgment did not faze Timmy, who grinned broadly. "You made the headlines, Sam!" he shouted. The others sniggered.

Sam started, looking down at his paper. "Not there," Timmy said. "Here." He pointed up at the side of the superette, where an enormous heart ten feet high had been crudely spray-painted in indelible red:

Sam gaped. Then, realizing he was being watched, he quickly swallowed and tried again. "Which of you jokers is responsible for this?" That was not what he had intended to say. The menace in his voice made them laugh even harder. "Assholes," he muttered. Spinning on his heel, he jumped into his car – exactly the wrong, uncool reaction, the tireless observer inside him noted. As he roared off, Sam just had time to hear one of the fellows reciting the old jumprope rhyme: "First comes love, then comes marriage, then comes Sam and Sonja with a baby carr. . ."

Sam did the lagoon road at something faster than his usual pace. He took the unmarked turnoff to Bolinas on two wheels and gunned through town without slowing down. When he got to the Day-Glo painted mailbox on the mesa road, he turned onto the bumpy dirt driveway that led to Kevin's and pulled up beside the converted barn with a squeal of brakes.

His son sat on the rusted carcass of a wheelbarrow, deeply engrossed in a task Sam could not quite make out. Surprise showed on Kevin's face as he looked up. "Dad," he said simply.

"Hi," Sam returned curtly through the car window. Now that he was here, he could think of no plausible reason for his visit. Kevin, he now saw, was whittling a long wooden dowel blank. Out of habit Sam needled him. "I thought you didn't believe in killing God's creatures."

"The deer eat all our vegetables. We hunt them to save our crops and because their natural predators are gone." It sounded like a speech Kevin had made a lot.

"Very commendable," said Sam.

By that curious second sight of sons Kevin seemed
to sense his father's confusion. "Why don't you get out
of the car?" he said reasonably and Sam, to his own
astonishment, obeyed. He walked over and sat down
on a redwood burl. Kevin picked up a formidable bow,
hand carved, and bent it between his legs. The effort
made the tendons leap out in his narrow arms. "This
is the way I string the bow," he said patiently, as if he
were talking to a child, and Sam nodded. He watched
Kevin's hands move over the bow and realized with
a sense of wonder that there were a few areas of life
– terribly limited ones, of course – in which his son
had managed to achieve a kind of competence. They
sat pleasantly side by side while Kevin worked. It was
Kevin, however, who broke the silence. "When did
you take it?"

Sam was puzzled. "Take what?"

His son shot him a shrewd look. "What you're
high on."

"I'm not high on anything." Sam felt impatient.
The mood was spoiled; he was starting to become his
old self again and Kevin had turned back into a fool.

But this time Kevin did not respond to the
unconscious cue. His shoulders did not hunch over
protectively, his eyes did not drop to the ground. He
kept at his work without the slightest sign of concern.
Sam realized with alarm that his son had not believed
him. His hand shot into his pocket and fingered the
sand dollar for reassurance. Fat lot of good it's done
me so far, he thought.

Kevin indicated a narrow goat track that ran
behind the barn. "Sonja lives up there."

Sam started. "Now hold on."

Whittling again, Kevin did not look up.

"Did you hear what I said?" Sam paused. "I said, hold on. I want to know why you said that. Do you hear me?"

"Said what?" said Kevin.

Sam made an exasperated noise. "You know what. Don't play dumb with me. *Why* did you say it? That's what I want to know."

Kevin's attention was absorbed in the exquisite point he was putting on his dowel blank. Flick, flick! went the knife. Fighting the impulse to kick him across the barnyard, Sam took a deep breath. "What have people been saying to you, Kevin? Please tell me that, please."

Kevin looked up. He was genuinely puzzled, Sam saw. "I don't know what you mean, Dad. What are people supposed to be saying?"

"I want to know what made you bring up this woman Sonja. What made you mention her out of left field like that."

Kevin's mother's small blue eyes shone up guilelessly at Sam. "Well, because you met her the other week when we were at the bakery, that's why. I don't know why I said it. It just seemed like something to say."

Sam let out his breath. "All right. Never mind." He got up and paced around the yard. Kevin was watching him closely, he realized. Speculating, as he rested the arrow on his forearm and sighted it in Sam's direction. Well, screw him. Kevin might think he was getting one up on his old Dad at last but Sam could take up the reins any time he wanted, no problem. It was just that right now –

Kevin dropped the arrow and rushed over to him. "Dad, what's the matter?" His curried breath, that crap his food cooperative ate for breakfast, brought Sam back from wherever he had just gone. Shaken, he got to his feet, brushing off Kevin's attempts to help him. He had fallen to the ground in a kind of faint, it seemed. There was mud all over the seat of his new blue jeans and the creeping dampness had already hit his buttocks. "No, no, no," Sam said to every query of Kevin's as he strode to the car and jumped in. He started the engine and let out the clutch; Kevin had to leap back to get his foot out from under the rolling wheels as Sam took off.

A new downpour of rain began as he reached the intersection of the driveway and the mesa road. Water gushed from the sky; the wipers could barely clear the windshield. Hands shaking slightly on the wheel, Sam crept along the road. The concentration took his mind off what had just happened, though he wasn't exactly sure what *had* happened. Gaining confidence, he picked up speed. Around a steep bend a large uprooted tree blocked the road. He slammed on the brakes. The car spun straight across the glassy surface of the road like a shot bolt. There was a tremendous impact; Sam felt a sudden suffocation.

When he came to again – was it minutes or hours later? – he was not slumped over the steering wheel but in motion, walking purposefully up the road. Where am I headed? Sam asked his goal-oriented body. The Day-Glo mailbox, it answered. Kevin. Sam gave in without a murmur – it seemed like a good idea and besides, his head ached horribly – but a few minutes later he was forced to admit that he had either overshot the mailbox or was headed in the wrong direction. He stopped, feeling dizzy and strange. If only a car would come by. Resisting the impulse to sit down in the middle of the road, he walked over to the shoulder. Here was a side road of sorts – not Kevin's road, but still a road. Surely someone lived at the end, even though the rutted dirt track did not look as if it had been recently used. Sam hesitated, then started up it. I'll give this a hundred yards, he decided sensibly.

The track wound through one of those messy eucalyptus groves that molted leaves and bark all year round. Mist straggled through the treetops; water dripped through the bare branches onto Sam's head. The underbrush was alive with scurryings, unexplained clicking noises. A dismal place, he thought, keeping his eyes on the track.

Still looking down at his feet, Sam rounded a bend and walked straight into the back of an enormous vehicle. Stunned, he reeled to one side. It was an ancient yellow school bus heeled slightly over in the earth like a sailboat catching the wind. Painted in black on one side were the letters TAMALPAIS UNION HIGH SCHOOL. All four enormous tires were flat, their rusty rims deeply settled in the earth. Next to the bus lay the dead remains of a campfire; around it sprawled a pack of dogs too enervated to challenge Sam. A persistent sound of croaking came from a nearby mud pond covered with lily pads. An occasional pad popped up like a tea kettle lid. Tiny eyes regarded Sam.

I shouldn't be here, he thought suddenly, feeling an overwhelming impulse to run. Too late. A strong hand clamped onto his shoulder. "Oh no," Sam groaned aloud. Slowly he turned back around to face those implacable eyes.

Sonja did not look at all surprised to see him. She raised her hand casually to the scruff of his neck. Sam's knees buckled as she hauled him onto the bus like a wayward puppy.

Force-marched down the narrow aisle, Sam felt his gorge rise at the rich assortment of smells – damp rot, incense, cat piss, the musk of a female animal's den. Sonja laid him out on a filthy piece of bare foam – her bed, he realized – and dragged a stained sleeping bag over him. Sam submitted without a struggle. The will to resist had deserted him. He was cold and tired and needed to rest. Who cared if the sleeping bag stank a little? He could handle this. Let her take care of him, let him catch his breath. Soon he'd slip away and no one would be the wiser about this accidental tête-a-tête. A fleeting worry about the Mercedes scudded through his brain. Where was it, in what kind of shape? Wrapped around a madrone tree, some part of him replied. People would start searching for him, but not for a while; the car was still registered to Winona's address.

Sonja lit a Primus stove in the driver's seat. Heating some water for him, Sam guessed. The old training died hard. This thought produced a strained chuckle. Pieces of corrugated cardboard and tattered bits of fabric were draped over the cloudy, fly-specked windows. Half the seats were torn out; the other half were stacked with cardboard boxes full of junk, rusted-out car batteries, pieces of rubber tubing, stacks of yellowed newspapers. As far as Sam could see, there was no source of heat in the bus other than the portable stove she was now pumping. He shivered under the ruined sleeping bag. Jesus, the woman was hardy.

Soon a cracked mug of steaming liquid appeared under his nose. Herbal tea, Ovaltine of the hip. He propped himself up awkwardly on one elbow. Now that he had stopped moving, every bone in his body ached. Avoiding her eyes, he took the mug from Sonja. Broken springs creaked as she sat down in the seat opposite his pallet. She was, he sensed, staring down at him. Like a great patient cow. Beneath his shock and fatigue Sam felt irritation rising. If there was one thing that bugged him, it was people – women – hovering around. With an angry motion he waved her away.

The next moment tea was all over Sam's jacket and his face burned from a stinging crack of the hand. It took him a moment to put it together. Sonja had *hit* him. His nose was bleeding from the blow. He looked at her in amazement. Back in her seat across from him, placid as ever, Sonja did not seem upset. Sam began struggling to his feet. This would not do, it would simply not do. He was going to have to leave a little sooner than he was ready to, it seemed. Immediately Sonja rose and pushed him flat on his back, knocking the breath out of him.

As he lay gasping, a *National Enquirer*-type headline flashed across Sam's brain: "Madwoman's Sex Prisoner Held Hostage in Bus." Then a subhead: "Middle-

Aged Broker Forced to Perform Unspeakable Acts."
Then a smudgy wire press photo: a weeping Sam,
shielding his face with his hands, led away by police
for sex abuse counseling, a handcuffed Sonja flashing a
triumphant grin to the popping of flashbulbs. Hadn't
there been a movie like this once? Only a girl victim,
of course. In a basement or something.

Sam decided to speak. "I thought you *liked* me."

Looking down at him, Sonja appeared to consider
this statement. In the dark schoolbus her impassive
face was cast in shadow. But even in broad daylight,
Sam felt, he could not have read her expression. He
watched the movement of her enormous chest in and
out, in and out, under the bulky layers of Free Box
clothing. Sonja's body odor alone, dense and rank,
made him forget he had ever smelled anything pleasant
or fresh. Something clawed at his foot. Sam screamed.
An ancient black and white tomcat, one eye milky and
blind, the other half hidden under a drooping eyelid,
with a neck muscular as a prizefighter's, was creeping
up Sam's body to join his mistress. Sonja's free hand
reached down absently to pet it. The hideous creature
let out a loud ragged noise like a diesel engine, full of
sputtering and misfires.

Helpless, staring up at her and the cat, Sam felt
the full force of Sonja's silent attention. Just as he had
feared, once he started looking into those green eyes
he could not look away; like a fly struggling on the
surface of a pool, he did not want to be drawn under.
But he was fascinated, too. That deeply etched female
face seemed to open up something wonderful and sad
inside Sam. The hand pushing down on his chest kept

him mired in this muck, this terrible pain and joy. Sam wanted no part of it, good or bad; he wanted to be free. He struggled again, horrified at how weak he had grown. Sonja's arm was pinning him to the earth; the massive trunk seemed to grow straight out of his heart. But there was something even stranger: though her face was as weatherbeaten as the redwood siding on Sam's house, the skin on the inside of Sonja's arms was not. It was soft, unmarked. Luminous, even. More than anything in the world he wanted to touch it.

Sonja did not stop his tentative hand as it brushed against the wondrous skin. Or his cheek as he slowly raised up and laid his head against her arm. Waves of dancing light zigzagged through him, lifting him up. He felt like a bubble of champagne rising to the top of the glass.

With a jolt Sam came to his senses, thinking: I'm crouched inside a squalid schoolbus nuzzling this stinking bag of fat. He made a convulsive movement toward the door. Sonja pushed him down again. This time a new feeling possessed Sam. He was dying. A heart attack, shock, exposure from the accident – whatever the cause, he was "passing on." On Bolinas mesa. In a derelict's bed. "No, no, no," he whispered. Sonja's face now seemed fixed in the firmament a million miles above him. Desperately Sam looked up at her for some sign of pity. But there was nothing in those merciless sky-eyes watching his pathetic struggles way down here. Sam was plunged into despair. Nothing seemed left to do except the thing he now did. "Kevin," he called softly, without hope. "Kevin, help me."

As soon as he said this, some constricted thing within Sam released itself. Rapidly a series of changes unfolded inside him; it was as if his very cells were mutating. Under Sonja's hand his body rippled and heaved through a roller-coaster metamorphosis. And the new, emerging Sam wanted something. What did he want?

Sonja.

Abruptly the shaking stopped. All was still. From her impossible height Sonja lowered herself to Sam, who shut his eyes in terror and joy. He knew the moment of consummation – his death – had come. There was a pause, a hiccup of silence. Then two human lips pressed softly against his in a delicate kiss.

A rich sensation of pleasure flooded Sam's breast. Slowly he opened his eyes. "That's all?" he said incredulously. "Just a kiss?"

Sonja's face was close to his. Now her eyes were warm and green, filled with a joyous love light. Sam basked in it. Though her arm was off his chest, he still felt pierced through and through.

"Sam loves Sonja," she said. It was not a question.

Sam rose humbly from the bed. Awkwardly, because the aisle was so narrow and full of junk, he dropped to one knee and kissed the splayed dirty foot before him. "Sam loves Sonja," he said, eyes full of tears. It was the noblest moment of his life.

Outside the schoolbus night had fallen. Feeling silly and wonderful, clothes torn and dirty but soul feather light, Sam loped down the darkening path, vaulting logs like a graceful buck. Sonja had set him free, the free-est he had ever known, but it was the oddest sensation: he felt he had the strength of four legs, not two.

When he came out of the eucalyptus grove, Sam was not on the mesa road, as he had expected to be. Instead he stood on a small rise overlooking an enormous red roof. With a shock he realized he had come out behind Kevin's barn. Surefooted Sam galloped down the twisting dirt path but hesitated, suddenly shy, outside the front door. Prowling around the side of the barn, he came to an unshaded window and peeked in. In the twilit room Kevin lay asleep on a bare mattress, dirty sheets twisted under him. The strung bow lay at the foot of the bed next to a sheaf of homemade arrows. But Kevin was not altogether Kevin. Inhabiting his son Sam saw a powerful spirit, the mingled essence of Winona and himself, a radiant winged being whose luminous exhalations filled the shabby room with light. Kevin had been conceived in love. Sam had forgotten that simple fact – if, indeed, he had ever realized it at all.

Removing his clothes, he sank to his knees in the heavy undergrowth. He knelt outside the shining room a long time. Then he got up and began to walk, very fast, down the driveway to the mesa road. He had to get home, had to get back to Stinson Beach. Then he thought of Merilee and stopped dead in his tracks. What was he to do about Merilee? He tried to picture her face, but all he could see in his mind's eye was her slender body, which seemed wrong. Then he watched the body turn from very young to very old. The creature "Merilee" became a skeletal hag. He could see the bones under the skin, the once-firm flesh withered into sinews. In a moment he would raise his eyes to the skull –

Sam was shaking his head to dispel the vision as a set of headlights swung around the next curve. He waved frantically. The old Volkswagen stopped a little past him, exhaust chugging, taillights glowing ruby red in the dusk. He ran up to the driver's side and said it.

"Sam loves Sonja!"

The young couple inside regarded him. Without speaking, they rolled up their windows in unison and pushed down the door locks. The car rumbled off.

Choking in the exhaust, Sam thought: they must be from Stinson Beach. A saying popped into his head. Love laughs at locksmiths. He laughed, too. Around the next bend the wreckage of the red Mercedes appeared. Yes, it had been a madrone. Sam passed by without a second glance. He had to hurry, hurry, set things right while he could still see it all so clearly. Just wait till I tell them at Elwood's, he exulted.

It was dark now, dark as only a country road can be. Overhead the torrent of stars flowed like a river. The brightest star lit up the cloud tops over Duxbury Reef, spilling light onto the Bolinas cliffs, the shaggy treetops, even the cracked pavement of the road. Sam stopped in wonder. The evening star had risen to guide his ignorant feet through the darkness; she would lead Sam safely home. Poised trustfully, he drew a breath. Then he rushed eagerly down her glittering, crooked path.

Agony brought him awake – the excruciating sensation of being flayed and burned alive, of millions of tiny ants biting his body. The pain grew past bearability. He bellowed in anguish and woke himself up.

At the first rush of sights and sounds – too-bright sunlight, seashell-patterned sheets, the muffled roar of crashing waves – he thought: what well-lit corner of hell have they put me in? Then someone touched him. Sam screamed.

"Calm down," a girl's unsympathetic voice said. "I have to put some more Calomel lotion on you."

Merilee? Sam jerked his head around. To his relief she looked the same as always, though incredibly young: that light brown hair, the unlined child's face. What had he been expecting? A new wave of torment swept his body. He looked down and saw to his horror that it was he, not Merilee, who had been transformed. Sam now wore some unholy creature's bright red bumpy skin, covered with a disgusting milky crust that broke and ran in spots. "What happened?" he moaned.

Gently but impatiently Merilee was rubbing a thick liquid into his arm. Her lips pursed in disapproval. "You rolled around in some poison oak, I guess."

"Oh, Jesus." Though it hurt incredibly, he turned to look at her again. Why was she so mad? His memory was blank – or rather, it was a whirl of disturbing images that seemed to have very little to do with his present position in time and space. He remembered the schoolbus – oh, yes – but little else. "How did I get here?"

"You showed up naked at Elwood's. They called me to come take you home."

Sam digested this information. In a calm voice he asked, "What else did I do?"

"What else, you jerk? What do you mean, what else? Oh, you wrecked your car, too. They were all out searching for you."

Even in anger Merilee's face was childlike – though she had sounded there, for a moment, alarmingly like Winona. Sam stared at her, fascinated. She was – she hasn't even been *born* yet, he thought. Like I have. For some reason it made him think of how Katrina's hair stood straight up when she was a baby, as if she had seen a ghost.

But Merilee had just called him a "jerk." That had been uncommonly bold of her. Now she was saying, "You want to know what else you did? You –"

"Please give me the phone," Sam croaked. The itching had abated enough for him to realize he had a severe head cold. Wordlessly Merilee handed him the receiver. Sam punched the buttons with his monster's fingers. Buzz, buzz, then a voice. "Kevin," Sam said.

"Dad, Dad, what happened to you? The car –"

"I'm all right. Don't worry. Listen, son, I've got to tell you two things. Number one, I love you. Number two, can you get a message to Sonja?"

There was a short silence on the other end. Then Kevin said, "Sonja's gone to her daughter's. She hitchhiked out early this morning."

"I see," said Sam. "Well, you take it easy, son. Goodbye." He put down the receiver. Merilee looked at him without curiosity and said, "As soon as I get another layer of this gunk all over you, I've got to go. Tom and I are showing houses today."

A cushioned pang, like a bell tolling underwater, rang through Sam's ravaged body. Of course the fellow was now Merilee's lover. Amazing how unmistakably he could sense it. He could also see the broken bits of plaster where his own image had fallen and shattered in her good but unformed heart. The young animal in this one was stronger than the tender feelings. This one, in fact, did not really love him and so perhaps – perhaps – he had not been so disgraceful to her after all. But some of the others, one or two he had sent away – he could summon those faces easily now and see that precious light shining –

Tears sprang to his eyes. Looking uncomfortable, Merilee let go his hand and got up. She thought Sam was upset about her, he saw. "See you later," she said, clicking out the door. High heels again. Ah, the exhilaration of being the winner, the one in amatory control – how well Sam knew it. He almost smiled to see how cocky, how energetic, the prospect made her. Her new friend Tom would notice that special aura and he, too, would be ensnared. A few heartbeats later, Sam heard the Honda roll jauntily out of the driveway, spitting gravel.

Alone now, he struggled out of bed. Barely able to keep from falling to the floor in a frenzy of scratching, he managed to wrap a towel loosely around his swollen body. He shuffled to the patio door and let himself out onto the beach. Waves pounded brightly on the bare sand. Sand dollars – live ones – lay everywhere; the ocean had brought them up overnight. Up the coast, beyond the end of the spit, Bolinas shimmered in the salt spray mist. Sam stared a long time at those white cliffs, the ones that, four hundred years ago, had reminded Sir Francis Drake of Dover and caused him to dub this land Nova Albion, the ones that still lit up like mirrors every afternoon from the rays of the sinking sun.

Sam believed in cutting your losses. His skin would heal. The Mercedes would get a new front end. That big red – *design* on the superette wall would fade in a couple of years – though he would still have to leave town, of course. But the great event itself was settling into place at the center of his heart with the same disturbing permanence as that elusive presence just now peeking over the mesa – the evening star that was also the morning star, palely receded, yet undeniably present, in the greater luminosity of the daytime sky. Sam loved Sonja. With pounding heart, one puffy hand clutching his bath towel, he watched her start to rise.

Author's Note

When I was young, I was in the habit of moving house. A lot. Not a physical house, just a big pile of book boxes and an old trunk with my name stenciled on the front. On one of those many restless, nomadic relocations I lit down, in 1976, in Stinson Beach, a tiny seaside enclave of the humble retired and the stinking rich sheltered in the shadow of Mount Tamalpais just north of San Francisco. After more forthing and backing – to the Hawaiian Islands, back to California – I touched down there again for a few more years early in the next decade.

Across a heavily silted lagoon from Stinson, heading north, sits its sister town, Bolinas. In those days these two West Marin County hamlets – one populated with macho sporty outdoor types in jeans and down vests who drove jeeps and SUVs, the other a New Age dream of floaty fabric, incense, yurts, and utopian hopes – made a perfect yin and yang in my imagination. They fused into a powerful fictional territory, my own personal Yawknapatawpha, in which the two tales in this volume were birthed: the story *Bolinas Venus* first, followed a few years later by *Neighbor George*. Unlike Faulkner's county, however, mine is a place where the rules of the natural world get upended, where nonmaterial forces suppressed and denied elsewhere find human vessels. Bad screeching energies circle the ocean cliffs for prey. More benign forces enact gentle erotic reeducation inside an abandoned school bus.

The real-life poets who had made Bolinas their home in the 1960s were mostly long gone by the time I began writing these tales, so I made up a brand new set – notably all male, reflecting the flavor of the time, or at least of my mindset at the time. I also drew on a favorite poet from my own Berkeley undergrad days, Geoffrey Chaucer, for a frame. Though William Blake and Robert Duncan occupy pride of place, readers with sharp ears may (or may not) pick out faint echoes of the *Wife of Bath's Tale* and the *Parliament of Fowls*.

There is maybe a Rosebud-type story around the name George. It was what my brother Jerry Nelson, who died many years ago, called both his imaginary companion and his teddy bear when he was very little. I still have that raggedy bear of his. It is very unlike the companion I gave Dovey.

Bolinas Venus first surfaced in an elegant letterpress edition titled "Queen of Hearts" designed and printed by the late San Francisco master printer Jack Werner Stauffacher. Later it popped up in my story collection

Wild California, issued by Five Leaves Press in Nottingham, England. *Neighbor George* debuts in this edition. When it and then a second novel failed to find publishers back when I first wrote them, I made a promise to myself: If I couldn't find a place in fiction to depict the special zone I was obsessed with – that interface between what's inside us and what's outside, between the psychological and the metaphysical, the material and the immaterial – then I would find other ways to put it out in the world. That quest resulted in the nonfiction works *The Secret Life of Puppets*, where interested readers will find quite a lot of scholarly lore about the language of the birds and other esoteric topics, and its sister volume *Gothicka*.

Now here I am again, all these years later, standing at the Palomarin trailhead on the mesa above Bolinas, just reopened after the twin threats of raging wildfires and the coronavirus epidemic shut down the Golden Gate National Recreation Area for months. Getting here, I cruised past the stately but despised eucalyptus trees bordering the northern edge of Bolinas lagoon, taking in the stillness of the lagoon: snowy egrets poking in the shallows, hawks and turkey vultures sailing overhead, the deep shadowed folds of Mount Tamalpais looming behind, a bright slice of ocean ahead. Then, like surfing the tube of a cresting wave, I shot up the steep little road overarched by more ancient eucalyptuses to the mesa. Past the fire station, the cattle farm, the defunct remains of the old Marconi radio station, to the end of the dusty gravel road.

And here I am. Above the parking lot I look for the clearing in the trees where George tells Dovey a house once stood. That is a piece of information I remember gleaning from some historical source or other. There's no sign of this clearing now, here or farther up the trail. Is it overgrown, or did I make it up?

Past the woods the open trail is hot and dusty. No wind. The sun blazes down. I wear a covid mask, so do the people who pass me. Wild scat litters the bare ground – bobcat, fox, raccoon. A few horse turds, too. A green lizard freezes next to a blackberry bush. The ocean crashes soundlessly against the base of the steep cliffs far below. Ahead lie the Alamere beach waterfall and three little swimming lakes.

I remember the last time I swam in those lakes.

But that was then and this is now.

And George and Dovey tread this trail in a different frequency altogether.

– *Victoria Nelson*

Palomarin, West Marin County
California, USA
October 23, 2020

Strange Attractor Press
2021